The Labyrinth Home

Scott A. Musick

Acknowledgements

I would like to thank my first and continuing teacher, Mom, whose love and encouragement have always been unwavering. To my fourth grade teacher, Mrs. Rena Allen, who ignited the writing spark. A special thank you to Carol Hannigan at Sacred Journeys for her patient Shamanic Training in both the Basic Class and the Advanced Class; through her classes, I was able to find my own healing and spiritual home. Ron Donaghe and the staff at Two Brothers Press, I am eternally grateful for your editing work, words of encouragement, and mentorship. Finally, to the staff and instructors at the University of Metaphysical Sciences where I have not only earned degrees but also gained enlightenment.

Disclaimer

All characters appearing in this work are fictitious. Any resemblance to real persons, living or dead, is purely coincidental.

About the Author

Scott Musick is a Licensed Massage Therapist, Reiki Master, and Ordained Minister. He has an A.A.S., a B.S., a B.MSc., and an M.Div. Scott is currently completing a PhD. in Transpersonal Counseling. He is an adjunct instructor for a college in southeast Ohio where he lives with his partner, his son, and their animals on a small farm.

The Labyrinth Home

Chapter 1

With the cool autumn breeze blowing around her, Helena sat on the ground near the pond listening to the trickling spring that fed it. A shudder went through her eighty-year-old frame and her long white hair danced in the wind. Her thin hands grasped the fleece jacket she wore and pulled it close. The full moon reflected brightly on the water and her grey eyes followed a ripple from a poplar leaf falling into the glassy pool.

Although she was chilled, a fire burned deep inside her spirit. "She's on her way now," she whispered as the wind howled into the valley where the pond rested. Her eyes closed and her arthritic hand clasped onto the staff that she always had with her on any journey outside of her 150-year-old farmhouse. The staff had been hand carved by her father with a face of a cherubic angel near the top. It was the last thing he had carved and just before he passed over, he handed it to her and called her his beloved angel for the final time. As Helena held onto the staff, she felt her heart emboldened by the power of her father's love.

"Oh, Daddy," Helena whispered, "this is going to be a tough night. Are you with me?"

The trees around the pond bent with the weight of the wind and more leaves streamed around her. She slowly opened her eyes. Across the acre pond her vision caught sight of a stream of light. A half smile spread across her face.

"Yes, Daddy, I see you," she said as she started her familiar rocking with staff in hand. "I'm going to need your help." The light drifted across the water towards her. When it was within three feet, it stopped and hovered just above the grass, wet with dew. The energy emanating from it warmed Helena's face and the half-smile became full.

The sound of a vehicle coming up Helena's graveled drive broke the autumn night's sounds. Still facing the pond, she slowly pulled herself to a standing position with the aid of her staff. The beams of light from the vehicle cast a shadow in front of her, making her look larger than her five-foot frame. The Hummer stopped at the edge of the gravel with high-beams cascading down the gentle slope towards the pond where Helena stood.

The hovering light was washed by the Hummer's headlights and Helena muttered, "Looks like it's show-time, Daddy."

"Helena!" a woman's voice shrieked from the Hummer as the door of the SUV slammed shut. Helena turned to face the lights and stamped her staff on the ground to steady herself. A gust of wind blasted her and she winced, causing the lines of life to fill her face. Her vision was blurred with the sudden intrusion of the headlights, but she could see the outline of a woman rushing towards her as if on a march to war with a book in her hand.

"Helena!" the voice squawked again.

"Deborah? Is that you?" Helena called out, trying to sound surprised.

"Don't act like you didn't know it was me!" the voice replied tersely.

"Why, it's been thirty years since you've paid me a visit, but I had an idy you might be coming by tonight." Helena spoke with her somewhat exaggerated Appalachian twang, but made no move towards the voice.

With a tone both accusatory and demanding Deborah moved into plain sight of Helena's vision and asked, "Where is he?" Helena looked her over from head to toe. She took notice of the perfectly colored blonde hair cut conservatively short but with a classy flair. Although Deborah's voice sounded angry and defiant, the only sign on her face was in her beautiful blue eyes, cold as ice, created by the contacts she wore. Helena wondered if it was plastic surgery or injections that hid the emotions of the sixty-year-old woman confronting her. "That's a very nice pants suit you have on, Deborah."

Disarmed by the remark, she replied, "Thank you. It's an Anne Taylor cashmere wool blend." Helena's eyes traveled to Deborah's feet and noticed the beautiful, lacey, round toe pumps that matched perfectly with the brown crocodile belt. Helena could not help but chuckle softly at the sight of the distinguished woman standing in a well-kept field of grass in the middle of Hocking Hills Ohio with her heels sinking into the soft earth. Deborah's ire returned at the sound of Helena's chortle. "Where is he?" she demanded again.

Brushing off the question as if she hadn't heard it Helena said, "What's a get-up like that cost—a few hundred dollars?"

The women were now face to face about a foot apart. Although the women's builds were similar, Deborah was five inches taller without the aid of the Anne Taylor pumps. This caused Helena to cock her head sideways and up, to look her in the face.

"I didn't come here to discuss the cost of my wardrobe, Helena. I want to know where he is!" Her voice climaxed again to a near shriek while she pressed the book with both arms firmly against her well-rounded bosom.

Helena could not resist one more question at the sight of her well-formed breasts. As she held onto the staff with her right hand, she slowly raised and pointed her left directly at Deborah's chest as she asked, "And… how much for those girls?"

"Have you lost your mind, old woman?" Deborah questioned. "This is exactly why I have come to get him! Your influence on him will only continue to degenerate his soul."

"Lost my mind?" Helena asked rhetorically in a sing-song voice. "I surely hope so. I've been giving up my ego and its addictions for a good fifty years. Ki is just starting on his journey and awakening to his purpose. You should be happy for him. Serenity is the perfect place for him right now. Here, there are no pressures from family, community, or religious dogma to hinder his growth. These hills have been here longer than all of humanity and have much to teach an open spirit. Ki is in the right place at the right time for his special nature."

"His name is *Kyle* and his nature is being coerced and brain-washed by a false prophetess—you!" Deborah's fury took on a life of its own. She stepped closer to the older woman and leaned into her face. "You are the cause of his misdirection! You are a heathen teaching a pagan religion. You will be judged for the blood on your own hands and for leading so many sheep to the slaughter! You will be condemned to an eternity in hell where there is weeping and gnashing of teeth. I feel sorry for you, old woman. If you don't get your life right with God, eternal damnation will be your reward!"

Helena pounded the staff into the ground between the two women and a soft snicker slipped from her lips. "He prefers to be called Ki now. A young man in his thirties is quite capable of making up his own mind about matters of spirit and his purpose in life."

A bolt of lightening tore through the night sky, followed by a crack of thunder. Helena closed her eyes. Strength surged in her spirit and her bent body straightened to its full height.

With eyes still closed, she spoke in a low voice, as if in a trance, "Ki is a Japanese word, and translated means life-force energy. Deborah is a Hebrew name and means bee. In Biblical times, she was the fourth judge of Israel before the monarchy, a prophetess, and the only female judge. She had a fiery spirit that helped conquer Sisera and the Canaanite army. After this defeat, there was peace for forty years. You, my bee, are searching for a new flower. There is no nectar left in the flowers from which you have supped. You are tired and worn from the constant flight to the same flower, devoid of nutrition. Your honey is like vinegar to a parched mouth, rancid and sour. Instead of finding restoration and life in a new field, you try to cover the old with designer fragrances, clothes, and surgery. Yet in the end, you find your soul withering as your hive empties. Although the queen may still wear her crown, she has no loyal subjects."

"Stop that pagan channeling, in the name of Jesus!" Deborah commanded in her evangelistic voice, fine-tuned with over twenty years of charismatic preaching from her and her husband's mega-church in Columbus, Ohio. She shivered from the chill of the October night, the approaching storm, and her own inadequacies. Another bolt of lightening created a schism in the sky as the wind and thunder shook the poplar and pine trees around them.

She tried to regain her vigor by speaking again, "No weapon formed against me will prosper! And I command you Satan, in the name of the Lord to pick up your weapons and flee." She reached her right hand towards Helena's forehead and was about to grasp her arm when a gust of air almost knocked both women off their feet. Helena opened her eyes and steadied herself with the staff. Deborah tilted to the right as her left hand, tightly grasping her book, flew out to for balance. The book fell from her hand and hit the ground with a thud.

"My sword! My sword!" Deborah cried as she knelt to pick up her book.

"I'm going inside now, Deborah. There's a storm coming and it's best you get back on the road."

Deborah sprang to her feet with her book in her right hand. She shoved it in Helena's face and spoke with an icy tone, "Do you know what this is? Can you remember what the sword of the spirit is? It is the Word of God as written in the Holy Bible!"

"Oh, yes. I know what that is." Helena smiled and then started quoting, "When I was an infant at my mother's breast, I gurgled and cooed like any infant. When I grew up, I left those infant ways for good[1]." Helena paused and took in a deep breath. "There's so much more to it than your literal eyes can see. I know you have spirit eyes that just need to be opened. Listen to the voice that speaks truth and not to the dogma of your husband."

Shaking the Bible at Helena, Deborah accused, "You are possessed! A demon has a hold of you and you just need to be loosed from its grip!"

"Possessed?" Helena nodded. "Possessed am I. But not from some supposed demon. I am possessed by an extravagant love—a love that you have yet to learn." Once again, her voice lowered as she began to recite, *"If I speak with human eloquence and angelic ecstasy but don't love, I'm nothing but the creaking of a rusty gate. If I speak God's Word with power, revealing all his mysteries and making everything plain as day, and if I have faith that says to a mountain, 'Jump,' and it jumps, but I don't love, I'm nothing. If I give everything I own to the poor and even go to the stake to be burned as a martyr, but I don't love, I've gotten nowhere. So, no matter what I say, what I believe, and what I do, I'm bankrupt without love.*

Love never gives up.

Love cares more for others than for self.

Love doesn't want what it doesn't have.

Love doesn't strut,

Doesn't have a swelled head,

Doesn't force itself on others,

Isn't always "me first,"

Doesn't fly off the handle,

Doesn't keep score of the sins of others,

Doesn't revel when others grovel,

Takes pleasure in the flowering of truth,

Puts up with anything,

Trusts God always,

Always looks for the best,

Never looks back,

But keeps going to the end.

"Love never dies. Inspired speech will be over some day; praying in tongues will end; understanding will reach its limit. We know only a portion of the truth, and what we say about God is always incomplete. But when the Complete arrives, our incompletes will be canceled[2]."

"You speak in riddles which make no sense, old woman! You pervert the Word of God for your own gain. The Bible speaks clearly against witchcraft and you are a witch!" Deborah screamed, struggling for breath.

Helena started to move up the gentle slope towards her house. "I believe..." Helena turned back towards Deborah as she paused for effect, "...that you are reflecting your own persona onto me. It's you who's gaining from the multitudes of the spiritless that give to your church. It is *you*, my bee, with your expensive cars, expensive clothes, and expensive surgeries. *You* try to hide the darkness of your spirit with all these fine things. Your prosperity is material only. While your body may be adorned like royalty, your soul suffers and has grown as bankrupt as the most impoverished people of this Appalachian community. Witchcraft you say? A witch am *I*? No, not me—not in the sense that you think. A tribal Shaman...maybe. An earthy pagan...perhaps. A wise crone...I hope so." Helena's eyes looked sad as she searched the ground in front of her for any final thoughts to share with Deborah. "I sense I have told you everything I am supposed to tonight. Good night, Deborah." With the aid of her staff, Helena turned back towards her house and started moving up the slope.

Deborah came up behind her in a swift motion, grabbed her shoulder, and whirled the older woman around. "I am not leaving until you tell me where Kyle is!" Deborah grabbed Helena's shoulders and shook her with enough force to disorient her. "Let me see Kyle now! Where is he?"

"Take your hands off of me, Deborah! Ki is not here. He's on a journey and I don't know when he'll return." Helena grabbed the staff with both hands to keep her balance as she leaned into it.

Deborah, enraged by Helena's answer, let out a scream of exasperation, "Damn you! Damn you to hell!" She released her grip on Helena and kicked her staff with the round-toed pumps. The staff easily slipped along the wet grass. Helena lost her balance and fell to the ground. As she hit the dew-soaked slope, her body slid with the momentum of the impact and careened down the hill until it came to rest with a thump against an old pine. Deborah was half-way to her Hummer when another bolt of lightening ripped through the dark sky. The crack of thunder that followed so startled Deborah that she seemed to leap the remaining fifty feet to her vehicle and was safely inside as a second bolt struck. From the sound it made, Deborah knew that it had hit something. "Maybe God sent that one for you, old woman," she muttered as she started the Hummer, turned it around, and then headed down the drive back towards Columbus.

Rain started falling in a torrent, unusual for late October in the Hocking Hills. The place where Helena's body rested after the slide down the slope was now covered with a large limb from the pine tree that had been hit by the last bolt of lightening. Through the pine needles, the only sign of her motionless body was her silky-white hair, stark against the green of the needles. That, and the red of her blood as the October rain washed over the severed limb of the great pine.

Chapter 2

Ten year old Kyle's head twisted on the pillow as he slept in his twin bed. His yellow-blond hair was disheveled from his rocking, and the sweat that beaded along his brow. Lips moved as if speaking, but made no sound. A single tear fell from his right eye and moistened the pillow. His heart raced, both in his natural state and within the dream state that had engulfed him.

In his nightmare, he saw nothing but darkness, but there was a presence in the blackness. He could sense it. Hot air seemed to come from the dark figure, suffocating his very breath. The odor of sulfur permeated his entire being and his lungs yearned for fresh air. Kyle's mind raced, trying to discover what this entity was. Whatever it was, it was not something he wanted to confront.

Kyle rarely experienced the response of "fight," but he was very familiar with the one of "flight." So it was in this dream. He decided to run. The line between dream and reality was breached. Kyle shot out of bed to escape the terror, but he knew the presence was following him. As he reached the door to his room, he screamed in terror. He raced down the short hallway, ran into the bathroom, slammed the door, and with his body held it closed against the intruder.

His scream had awakened his mother. She ran to the bathroom just outside her bedroom and pushed on the door. It pushed back.

Kyle, still in his dream and believing that the creature was trying to push through the door, screamed, "NO! Go away!" Kyle's mother leaned her weight into the door. Kyle propped his legs between the lavatory cabinet, and his back against the door.

"Please!" he begged with tears in his eyes, "just go away. I'll be a good boy. I promise."

"Kyle!" his mother exclaimed. "Kyle Leroy! Open up this door. Mommy is here. No one is going to hurt you." She was well acquainted with the night terrors that seemed to find Kyle about once a week. It was early Monday morning and she remembered that the same scene had played out last Monday morning at about two.

Kyle began to separate from his dream upon hearing his mother's voice and his body relaxed. As he did, she opened the door and turned on the light, flooding the small bathroom with illumination. On the floor sat Kyle in his Winnie-the-Pooh pajamas with no-slide feet. *No wonder the door wouldn't open,* she thought. She bent down and grabbed his hand. "Honey, it was just a dream. Why don't you let me take you back to your bed?"

"I'm scared," he said. "I don't want the boogey man to get me."

"Oh, Kyle, you just need to tell that mean old devil to flee," she answered somewhat groggily. "You know you have angels 'round about you to protect you. You just have to call on the name of Jesus and Satan will have no power over you!" Deborah let go of his hand and twisted her long, brown hair between her fingers, loosened for sleep from its usual bun. "Let's get back in bed before your father wakes up. You know how tired he is after preaching late."

"I'm *scared*, Mommy!" he reiterated with tears in his blue eyes. "I don't want to go back to my bed."

Deborah's face became stern, "Now, Kyle Leroy, don't talk to me with that tone. I won't have you waking up the entire house just because you don't have the will power to overcome the devil! Trust me, if you don't take control of yourself and your father wakes up, *he* will take control with his belt."

Grudgingly, Kyle stood. He knew better than to be on the receiving end of his father's belt, no matter how terrifying his dream. Slowly, he made his back to his room while his mother stood at the end of the hall. "Can I have a light on?" he inquired sheepishly.

"Kyle," she whispered with an emphatic tone, "you have the light of Jesus inside of you and that should be enough to brighten your night!"

He turned back towards his room and ran to the bed. Jumping in, he grabbed his Winnie-the-Pooh bear and quickly pulled the covers over his head. "Dear Jesus, please don't let the devil get me. Please!" he whimpered.

As Kyle drifted off to sleep, he found himself dreaming again. This time, fear was replaced with peace. A woman stood before him—a woman that looked like his mother, but shorter, and with grey hair. She had a sweet spirit about her and smiled when their eyes met. Her lips didn't move, but he felt her talking to him in his mind. *Come here, Baby Bee.* She held her arms wide open and bent towards him. Without hesitation, he ran to her. As they embraced, he felt a soothing rocking back and forth. All fears from the previous dream quickly faded in the arms of this woman. He heard her humming a tune and thought he recognized it as one of the hymns sung in church, but couldn't be sure. When she reached the chorus, he heard her alto voice with a typical Appalachian twang singing the words and he realized it was a hymn sung during an alter call at church,

> "*Come home, come home,*
> *Ye who are weary, come home;*
> *Earnestly, tenderly Jesus is calling,*
> *Calling, O Kyle, come home[3]."*

For the rest of the night, Kyle spelt peacefully with visions of the kindly lady, rocking him in her arms.

Kyle sat with his sister, Ruth, on the bus ride home from school the next day. Ruth was two years older than him and this was the last year that they would ride together before she moved to the Junior High School in the small village of South Point, Ohio. Their stop was one of the last on their route, out on Solida Road. While many of the other students lived on dirt roads cut out of the hollows of the hills, Kyle and Ruth lived on a black-topped cul-de-sac in a neighborhood known as Woodview Acres. The neighborhood was filled with young families, so there were many kids at the stop. Most of the boys were older and intimidated Kyle. This is why he sat with Ruth for the bus ride back and forth to school.

When the bus arrived at their stop, a group of kids eagerly exited the bus and started walking up the street towards their homes. One of the older boys started verbally harassing Kyle. Kyle put his head down to hide the tears that he couldn't contain, no matter how hard he tried. Ruth, always the protector, attacked the boy—first to his shin with her black and white saddle oxfords and then with punches to his arm. "Leave my brother alone!" she yelled.

"You're brother is a queer!" the chubby boy retorted, but not before he got another fist from Ruth.

"He is not!" Ruth added another swift kick to his shin. Kyle had no idea what a queer was, but he knew by the seething way the word was uttered that it wasn't a nice thing to be. The second kick was enough to send the young bully wincing in pain to his own house. Ruth wrapped her left arm around Kyle as they continued walking to their home, "You have to stop crying, Kyle, every time one of those bullies says something mean. That's why they keep picking on you. I know you're not a queer, but crying don't help."

Kyle looked at his all-knowing sister and asked, "What is a queer, anyways?"

"Oh, it's just his way of calling you a sissy. And, if you don't stop crying," she continued, "you'll always be picked on."

Even as she spoke the words, she knew that her brother could not change his sensitive nature. It was probably her favorite thing about him. He always knew what she was thinking and was ready to comfort her when she was down.

"Next year," she continued, "I won't be around to punch the bullies down. You're gonna have to try to fit in better." They had arrived at the front door and about to open it, when they heard their parents' voices through one of the opened windows.

"Deborah, it's an opportunity of a lifetime," their father sounded both excited and irritated. Ruth put her index finger to her lips and motioned for Kyle to sit on the stoop of the front porch. The deep baritone sounds of their father moved in the sing-song style that he had perfected as an evangelist. "I've put in my time at these hillbilly, backwoods churches up and down the river long enough. I can barely make ends meet with what I collect in the love offerings. God has a greater vision for us than even I had! This will be a great move."

"Eli, I will follow whatever you feel is right and the calling of God." Deborah paused and bit her lower lip before continuing, "I'm just concerned about moving the kids. Kyle's nightmares are coming more often, and he has such a hard time making friends."

"Kyle needs to toughen up," Eli retorted bitterly. "He's way too soft for a boy of ten. I don't know what's wrong with him. When I was ten, there wasn't a kid who I wouldn't stand up to. I may have gotten my tail-end whipped, but I sure was going down with a fight. I think he spends too much time hanging out with the girls in the neighborhood anyway. Maybe a move would force him to make friends with other boys. And another thing, if I see him playing with one of Ruth's dolls again, I'm gonna tan his hide!"

"Let me talk to him, Hon," Deborah replied. She could sense that he was building to one of his tougher-than-nails moods and wanted to head him off.

"You coddle him, Deb! He's never going to become a man with you hovering, and Ruthie protecting him all the time."

Deborah looked at the clock hanging above the kitchen sink and grew restless. "I know you're right, Eli. The kids will be home soon. Tell me more about this pastor position you've been offered so that I can pray about it too."

Outside, Kyle looked nervously at Ruth. He started to open his mouth but she quickly put her hand to his lips. Then she leaned over to his ear and whispered, "Don't say a word. If they hear us outside, they'll quit talking and we won't find out about moving until the moving truck is packed."

Kyle wasn't as concerned about the move as he was in the sound of disappointment in his father's voice when he talked about him. *I'll never be the son Daddy wants,* he thought.

As the kids listened, they learned that their father had been offered a position as the full-time pastor with a new church outside Columbus. Apparently, one of the members had been a faithful follower of Eli's evangelistic preaching for several years. He had heard him at several of the local churches in the Tri-State area and thought he was a forward-thinking Pentecostal that their new congregation needed. They had formed a home

Bible study after their previous church went through a split over one of the women cutting her hair and wearing make-up.

They heard their father's voice beam with pride, "They think I have great charisma and want me to build the church from ground up. They're calling themselves Earth Reaping Church. They want to show the world that it's not how you dress that gets you to Heaven, but what's in your heart. I think it's about time things changed, and I really believe God is calling me into this next move."

"So, you'd be okay if I wanted to cut my hair and wear make-up?" Deborah was intrigued with the idea of actually putting some color on her face. In fact, the thought felt so good she wondered if it was Satan tempting her to agree with the move.

"Well, Debbie, the truth is…" he paused as if speaking from the pulpit to get a crowd's attention, "…you ain't gettin' any younger. When a wall starts looking gray, it's time for a fresh coat of paint." He chuckled at himself for being so quick-witted and then winked at his wife.

Deborah didn't know whether to be hurt or laugh with him. She made a mental note to look a little closer in the mirror before going to bed to see if there were lines appearing on her face. Forty was just a few months away for her and she wasn't looking forward to it. She felt her youth slipping away and desperately needed more than being a housewife to feel fulfilled. *Maybe being a pastor's wife in a new church is just what I need,* she thought.

Instead of replying to his comment she said, "I wonder where the kids are? They should be home by now."

Ruth jumped off the porch step and waved at Kyle to follow her into the house. As she opened the door, she saw their parents through the living room window, sitting at the kitchen table.

"We're here!" she announced with a playful tone. "You should have seen Kyle on the walk up the street. That bully Chuckie started picking on him and Kyle just punched him in the gut. He went running to his house crying like a baby. I don't think he'll mess with Kyle again." Always the protector and intercessor, Ruth did her best to take the heat off Kyle.

"Oh, my!" their mother exclaimed.

"That's my boy," their father chimed, his face beaming with pride. "Way to go, Hoss. Now that's what I call laying on hands!"

"Oh, Eli! Encouragement is one thing, but don't be sacrilegious," Deborah lectured. "Kids, go get your homework done and I'll get supper ready. And when we say grace this evening, we'll say a prayer that Jesus will save Chuckie and change his ways."

Ruth and Kyle started down the hallway toward their rooms. When they reached Kyle's bedroom door, he said, "Thanks, Ruthie. I wish I could take on Chuckie like you do. Maybe Daddy would be more proud of me then...maybe it would make him like me."

"Daddy likes you, Kyle. He just doesn't know how to deal with someone soft-hearted like you. Besides, God made you and *She* loves you!" The reference to God as a woman made Kyle laugh. It was one of the things Ruth did when they weren't in ear-shot of their parents. She then said with a grin, "Piss on Chuckie anyways!" This caused Kyle to really break out into a full-throttle giggle before heading into his room. Her work done, Ruth made her way to her room to start homework.

Chapter 3

It was a typical Sunday evening service for the "holy roller" church in Flatwoods, Kentucky, no more than a thirty-minute drive from their home in Ohio. It had been two months since Kyle and Ruth had first learned of the move to Columbus. This would be the final service with the congregation that they had called home when their father was not on an evangelistic crusade. Eli was speaking tonight for the last time. The entire family sat in the front pew dressed in matching outfits sewn by Deborah with the exception of Eli who wore his best Sear's suit.

The song service was in full swing with "I'll Fly Away" found on page 333 of the Hymnal. Southern Gospel music enlivened the small church as voices joined together with clapping hands and tapping feet that echoed off the hardwood floors and wooden pews. The pianist, a woman in her seventies, plunked away in a rhythm not unlike a popular "rock-a-billy" tune. The organist, a rather chubby woman who jiggled as she played, slid along her keys, giving voice to the instrument reminiscent of a 1960's rock song. A saxophonist squealed with heavenly jubilation. The drummer kept time along with tambourines and maracas, urging the musicians, choir, and congregants forward.

The air was thick with the mixture of women's perfume, men's aftershave, and human musk. Once perfect "up-dos" were beginning to wilt with the rise of fervor and humidity in the modest sanctuary. Some attendees sat, but most stood on their feet with hands either in motion keeping time or uplifted, trying to touch the face of God. Kyle and Ruth sat in their pew with Fun Pads and pencils in hand while their parents stood singing. Eli would bellow out, "I believe it!" and raise his well-worn black leather King James Version Bible in the air at the end of each chorus.

Two pews behind the family the sound of tap dancing suddenly reverberated off the hardwood floors as one of the women of the church started dancing and whooping with ecstatic joy, or as the church called it, "shouting." Startled by the scream, Kyle jerked his head quickly and turned to look at his mother to see if she had noticed. Deborah's eyes lifted towards heaven while her arms reached out, seeming to paint an invisible canvass. Kyle looked to his other side at Ruth, smiling and giggling quietly as she pointed towards the pulpit of the church. Kyle looked first at the choir and then to the pulpit where he saw the pastor of the church, Brother Hall, eyes closed, tambourine in hand, lifting each knee in turn to his chest..

"There goes the Indian dance," Ruth whispered with sarcasm in Kyle's ear. "Guess we're gonna get some rain."

Kyle looked at his sister and then said through a chuckle, "Don't make me laugh or I'll get in trouble."

At that moment, another woman came running from the back of the church and fell to her knees in the space between the front pew and the altar. She lowered her head to the floor with her arms stretched behind her and started shaking her head and upper body back and forth like a voodoo dance. Kyle's eyes grew big at the sight of the woman's bobby-pins desperately trying to keep hold of the hairpieces on top of her real hair.

Ruth leaned over again to Kyle and wryly said, "She should really be more careful. It's all fun and games until someone gets an eye poked out!" Kyle's laugh burst out of him without warning and his head flung back hitting the wooden pew. Dazed by the impact, he came back to reality when his mother grabbed him by the hand. As she tugged him up the aisle towards the church door, he realized the mistake he'd made.

The fresh air outside was a welcome relief from the stale air inside, but the sound of his mother's voice was not so comforting.

"How many times have I told you not to kid around in church?" Deborah's voice was controlled yet raised as she pulled young Kyle behind her, towards their copper-colored Ford Gran Torino. "What you were doing in there is next to blasphemy! Of all nights! This is the last time we'll be here and your father is preaching." She yanked open the passenger side door and reached into the glove box.

Kyle started crying and begging, "No, Mommy! Please don't!"

Deborah pulled a hard plastic Avon hairbrush out of the glove box. She moved within inches of Kyle's face and he saw the steel cold wrath in her eyes.

"No more coddling from me! Do you hear me? Do you?" she demanded. All Kyle could do was cry. "Spare the rod and spoil the child," Deborah quoted to him. "You will not be spoiled because me!"

Then she flipped him around and started beating his bottom with the hairbrush. One…two…three whacks with the brush. Kyle couldn't stand it anymore and tried to run. With his mother holding his left arm, he was limited to running circles around her and leapt with each new blow. He tried to put his right hand between the brush and his buttocks, but felt the stinging sear of pain against his hand. "Stop fighting me!" she ordered, thwacking him with each word. "The Bible says to honor your father and mother!"

"Stop it!" a woman's voice commanded from behind Kyle and Deborah.

Kyle thought it was the voice of an angel, but Deborah recognized it with disdain. "The boy has had more than enough!"

Though frozen by the sudden intrusion, Deborah raised the brush once more. Ready to deliver another blow to Kyle, the voice persisted, "Honor whom?"

"Get in the car, Kyle!" Deborah said icily. As he leapt inside the vehicle for sanctuary, she slammed the door behind him. She tried to gather herself before turning to face the familiar voice. Kyle, now safe from additional punishment, quickly looked through the window to see the woman who had commanded his mother to stop. Deborah turned and looked directly at her. Kyle's eyes grew large with wonder at the sight of the woman. He slowly regarded her from head to toe and then looked back at her face. She was dressed in a loose-fitting purple dress that seemed to dance in the light spring air. In her hand was a walking stick almost as tall as she was.

"You're my angel," he said from inside the car as he looked directly at the woman who came to him in his dreams. Though she could not hear him through the closed window, she smiled at him and shook her head. Kyle could almost feel a sense of warmth and love sweep over his entire being as their eyes locked. *You hang in there, little bee.* Kyle felt the phrase resonate within his spirit

"Stop looking at him, Helena!" Deborah exclaimed. "I told you years ago that you were not welcome in my life or in my family's."

"He's growing like a weed…" Helena trailed off and then seemed to return to her thoughts. "I really don't understand how calling me by first name is practicing what you preach to *your* son. Do you allow him to call you Deborah?" Helena paused and looked her directly in the face, trying to find some reaction of love from her, but all she sensed was the thump of the music coming from inside the building.

"I'm quite a bit older than Kyle and very capable of making my own decisions about how to honor someone who isn't happy about the man I chose to marry. Besides, Eli is who I submit to now, and I'm not required to honor the harlot who raised me without a father."

Helena let the dig tumble harmlessly off her spirit. "Oh, child…you *had* a wonderful father in your Papaw Buck," Helena said, looking at her staff with sad eyes.

"What are you doing here? And how did you know we were here?" Deborah implored.

"I *always* know where you are. You know that. The boy is like a beacon from a lighthouse," Helena pointed to Kyle inside the car as she spoke. "You know... *I* know."

"I've never understood you! And you've never understood me. So, please leave...now!"

"Deborah, please! Stop your buzzing and readying for attack." Helena paused, looked at her staff again, and then continued, "I've come with sad news. Your Papaw Buck went home to the Great Spirit yesterday. I thought you would like to know...personally." Helena noticed a slight shift in Deborah's energy with the news of her grandfather's death. "I thought you might come for the funeral on Wednesday," she said sweetly in her Appalachian twang.

Deborah's shoulders heaved with a sigh and her gaze went towards the ground as her head hung low. "I'm sorry to hear that Papaw Buck has died." She started searching the black-top parking lot for anything to focus her attention on so that she wouldn't break into tears.

Helena reached out her hand and touched Deborah's cheek. "My, Bee, I am here for you. It's time to come home and honor his passing. Daddy would be very proud to know that you made it back for his service." Helena's hand warmed as it rested on her daughter's face.

Startled by the sudden heat on her face, Deborah pulled her shoulders back and her face upright. Helena's hand dropped to her side as Deborah asked, "Did Papaw Buck find the Lord before he passed?"

Helena sighed with disappointment and slowly blinked her eyes before answering. "Deborah, Daddy knew his Maker very intimately. His passing was very peaceful and—"

"So it won't be a Christian funeral?" Deborah said, cutting her off before she could complete the thought.

"The service will be just as he would have wanted it. Honoring his Cherokee heritage and spirituality he taught us throughout his life."

Seeing her excuse for not attending the funeral, Deborah announced abruptly, "Well, then we won't be able to make it. I won't have the children around such heathen practices. Thank you for letting me know, and I'll pray that you find Jesus before you pass so that you won't have to spend eternity in Hell with Papaw Buck. Good-bye, now."

Neither woman moved from her position but stood facing the other for what seemed, to Deborah, like an eternity.. Helena tapped the parking lot with her staff and then said, "Let me give Kyle a hug and kiss."

"Absolutely not, *Mother*!" It was the first time Helena had heard the word mother in over a decade. And even though Deborah said it with malevolence, it felt good to hear it again.

"Until you get right with God, I won't have you in our lives. I do *not* want the children to know that their grandmother is a half-breed heathen!"

"Then just let me say hello to him. I won't tell him who I am. I won't make a move to hug him. I just want to hear his voice."

Deborah thought for a moment and decided that if push came to shove she could be standing out in the parking lot until church was out and then have to explain Helena to not only her husband, but all the congregants as well. "Okay, *Helena*," Deborah over em-phasized her name. "Just a quick hello and you'll be on your way?"

"Just a quick hello and I'll be gone."

Deborah searched the parking lot trying to under-stand how Helena had made the three-hour trip when she spotted a white Lincoln that she had never seen be-fore with a woman about her age sitting in the driver's seat. Noticing Deborah looking at the Lincoln, Helena spoke.

"That's my friend D.J. She helps at Serenity with cooking and cleaning. I couldn't have asked for a better employee or friend." Helena chuckled slightly before adding, "In case you're wondering, I left the broom at home in the closet. The older I get the harder it is to ride."

Deborah was not amused with her mother's wicked sense of humor and changed her mind about allowing a quick hello with Kyle.

"Oh, Child...have you lost your sense of humor? I apologize. I'll just say hello and then be on my way."

Reluctantly, Deborah opened the car door. Kyle bounded out of the vehicle and ran straight into the arms of Helena like a puppy, happy to see his master after being gone all day.

"Well, hello to you, too!" Helena cooed.

Heat instantly arose in her hands as she looked the boy in the eyes. She placed her hands over each ear. Kyle felt a tingling sensation move from his ears to the middle of his head and then cascade throughout his body. The pain and numbness from the beating vanished and a sense of peace enveloped him.

She gently pulled away from him, and taking his hand she said, "It was nice meeting you, Little Bee. Maybe we will meet again."

Then she smiled the warmest smile that Kyle had ever seen.

Without a moment's hesitation, he replied in what sounded like sarcasm to Deborah, "Yeah, in my dreams!" Deborah felt like she had just won a little victory with her son being disrespectful to Helena.

"Maybe so…maybe so," Helena echoed as she walked towards the Lincoln.

Deborah followed the woman with her eyes to ensure that she kept her word and left. As she watched the white Lincoln drive off, Kyle quickly hid a piece of the purple material that Helena had given him from her dress, in his pocket

"Who was that woman, Mommy?"

"Just some strange old woman, Kyle. Let's not mention this to your father." Deborah looked down at her son questioningly, "Have you straightened up now? Are you ready to behave in church?"

"Yes, Mommy. I'm sorry for being disrespectful in the Lord's house."

"That's better, son. Now let's get back in there and hear what Daddy has to say for his last sermon in this church."

Together, they walked back inside. The music and singing continued, but Eli was now at the pulpit with microphone in hand.

"Woo!" Eli exclaimed in his classic Pentecostal preacher voice. "The Holy Ghost is in this place tonight, huh!"

Deborah and Kyle quickly moved down the side aisle of the church and sat next to Ruth on the pew. Ruth shot a glance at Kyle as if to say *I'm sorry,* and he returned her smile warmly so that she would know that he was doing all right.

"If you need a healin' in your body…in your mind… in your spirit, then make your way to this sacred altar so that I can lay hands on you tonight. This is the last time that I will speak from this pulpit for a while, as my family and I are moving to Columbus to start a new church."

Eli wiped his sweat-covered brow with his signature white handkerchief. Moisture formed around his lips from saliva as he recited, "…for verily I say unto you, If ye have faith as a grain of mustard seed, ye shall say unto this mountain, Remove hence to yonder place; and it shall remove; and nothing shall be impossible unto you[4]." Slowly the front of the church started filling with people from the congregation. Eli approached one of the women standing before him. "And what is your affliction, Sister?"

"Oh," she wailed, "it's my husband. He's been out a runnin' with women and a drinkin'. I just want to stand in the gap for him."

"Did you hear that folks?" Eli asked into the microphone. "This precious woman is here as a living testa-

ment to Christian matrimony in spite of her husband's
ways. She fully understands the scripture which states:
'Wives, submit yourselves unto your own husbands, as
it is fit in the Lord[5].'" He placed his hand on her forehead and shouted, "Oh, Hallelujah!" The woman started shaking her head violently back and forth as Eli's
grasp held firm. "Yes, Lord...yes, Lord. Let the Holy
Ghost fill her to overflowing!"

Before he could finish the sentence, she dropped
to the floor laying face-up, muttering in an indistin-
guishable language, the hem of her dress pulled up to
her waist and her slip barely covering her thighs. Eli
couldn't help but notice her beauty, sprawled on the
floor in front of him. He unconsciously wiped his
mouth with the white handkerchief and quickly moved
to a gentleman leaning on a cane close to her to avoid
the snare of the devil lying on the floor.

"Oh, Brother Eli," the pitifully dressed man whined,
"I've been a havin' leg troubles and can barely git
'round."

"Do you have faith of a grain of mustard seed, Brother?"
Eli cajoled. The old man nodded his head. "And do
you believe...do you believe the Holy Ghost is here tonight to perform a miracle for you?"

"Yes, siree! I do. I sure enough do!"

Eli placed one hand in the small of the man's back and
the other on his stomach as the elders of the church laid
hands on the man's back, "Then in the name of Je-he-sus
I command this devil of affliction to leave your body!"

Eli's grip tightened and the man jerked back and
forth. The old man closed his eyes and tilted his head

towards heaven. Tears streamed down his face and he let go of his cane. Suddenly he started leaping up and down with his arms straight down his side and hands gripping in fists.

Eli stepped back and commanded the elders, "Loose him and let him go!"

The elders backed away as the little old man leaped back and forth across the front of the church. The music built to a climax and the congregation broke into a fury of revelry. Eli spun in a circle and squealed with joy, managing to avoid entanglement with the microphone cord. Deborah jumped to her feet, dancing her own jig to the rhythm of the night with hands held in the air. The choir bellowed, "There's Power in the Blood" and the whole building shook from the thunderous stomping of feet and clapping of hands.

Kyle slid closer to Ruth for protection from their mother's ecstatic dance. Normally, Ruth would have whispered something derogatory about the happenings around them, but was afraid of getting Kyle in trouble again. Suddenly they heard their mother's voice ringing out above the fray of exoticism, prophesying in a language that sounded like Native American to the children. The music immediately stopped and the crowd grew quite. This always shook Kyle to his core. It made him uneasy to hear someone "speaking in tongues", but when there was a "prophecy in tongues" it really frightened him.

The silence in the room was eerie and death-like—except for the sound of Deborah's unknown tongue. She rattled off in her language for several minutes before quieting. Kyle felt a stirring in his stomach area that frightened him.   *Oh, thank God, she's stopped,* he thought.

Five seconds after Deborah quieted, Sister Hall started interpreting the message in a loud clear voice.   "For now is the beginning—a new beginning…a new day. I will raise up a new leader and my blessing shall be upon him. He shall confound those in power over him. Do not ask, 'Is this of God? As the Father hath loved me, so have I loved you: continue ye in my love[6]. If the world hate you, ye know that it hated me before it hated you. If ye were of the world, the world would love his own: but because ye are not of the world, but I have chosen you out of the world, therefore the world hateth you[7]." There was a short pause before Sister Hall's voice lowered and wearily said, "Thus saith the Lord."

Brother Hall made his way from behind Eli and tapped him on the shoulder. He motioned for the microphone and Eli handed it to him. "Brothers and Sisters, we have heard the Word of God through the gift of prophecy. The Holy Ghost just spoke to me and told me that the prophecy tonight is for Brother Eli and his family as they plant a new congregation in Columbus, Ohio. God has also told me that I should anoint Brother Eli with oil and by the laying on of hands as a sign of our commitment to his ministry and God's blessing on it."

Sister Hall took the cue from her husband, gathered the anointing oil from under her pew, and made her way up the two steps to the pulpit.

"Sister Deborah, would you join your husband here as we anoint and commission him?" Brother Hall asked as he looked towards her.

Deborah moved forward to stand behind Eli as they faced Brother and Sister Hall. Sister Hall handed her husband the oil. Eli knelt before them on his knees with arms outstretched at his sides while Deborah laid her hands on his shoulders. Brother Hall poured some oil in his left hand and placed it on Eli's forehead while Sister Hall rested her right hand on her husbands back.

"In the name of Je-he-sus, I anoint you by the Power of the Holy Ghost and send you forth to fulfill the divine calling on you life. May the prophecy you witnessed tonight be your guiding light as you follow the path of eternal life. Amen...and...amen."

After finishing his prayer, Brother Hall removed his hand from Eli. He handed the microphone back to Eli and the women returned to their pews. Members of the church shouted hallelujahs while others with tears in their eyes clasped hands together as if in prayer.

Eli wiped the moisture from his face and spoke into the microphone in a soft voice befitting the moment, "Surely the Holy Ghost has spoken to us tonight. I am just a man and cannot offer any other words of wisdom to the move of God at this time. I am humbled by God's blessing and Brother Hall's obedience." His voice cracked and tears streamed down his face. "Let us bow our heads. Saints, please be in prayer at this time. If there be anyone here tonight that is not assured of where they will spend eternity come to this altar right now and get your life right with God."

The pianist started playing the hymn *Softly and Tenderly Jesus is Calling* and soon the choir joined in with humming. "Young people, if you're sitting in your pew trying to decide if the trip to the altar is worth it, I want to share a story with you," Eli began as tears continued to flow down his cheeks and his voice cracked with emotion. "I was at a church last month preaching and the high school quarterback was sitting in the congregation during an altar call much like this one. He had everything going for him—good looks, good grades, senior year of high school, the cheerleader girlfriend who sat next to him in the service, a new sports car that his daddy had given him—the hero of the community. He heard me ask the same question about where he was going to spend eternity. The piano was playing and the choir was singing, 'Come home...Come home.'" Eli wiped the tears from his cheek with the handkerchief before continuing. "'Ye who are weary...Come home'...His beautiful cheerleader girlfriend felt the pull of the Holy Ghost on her heart and ran to the altar. But he just sat there...arms crossed...looking defiant. What did he need to be saved from? He had everything going for him. He was young and had his whole life ahead of him. Besides, he could make a deathbed confession and accept Jesus into his heart then. *Right?* Well, the good news is his girlfriend got saved at the altar of that church that night. The bad news is that while I was praying with her, the quarterback left the service and got in his shiny new sports car. And not a mile from the church..." Eli's voice raised as he built to the climax of his story, "...CRASH!" He yelled into the microphone causing everyone's heart to skip a beat including Kyle's.

Eli's voice lowered and wailed as he sat on the step down from the pulpit to the altar, "The quarterback was killed instantly when a drunk driver ran a stop sign and hit him head on. Instantly, he went from being on top of the world to spending an eternity in Hell. Now... I ask you again...if you were to die tonight, do you know where you would spend eternity?"

Eli stood and faced the choir, motioning with his arms for them to raise their voices from the soft humming to full signing. The pianist stroked the keys harder. Weeping people slowly made their way down the aisles and knelt at the altar. Eli beamed with pride as watched the altar fill from his persuasive message of eternal damnation. *What a service for my final one in this hick town,* he thought.

Chapter 4

Generally, after the wild happenings of the Pentecostal ritual, Kyle would have had nightmares, but this night was different. Instead of screaming and flailing, he slept peacefully. Instead of the terror that usually haunted him during slumber, he had thoughts of warmth and serenity, despite the drama of the night and the impending move.

In his dream world, he stood in a beautiful pasture near a large pond of water, surrounded by low sweeping hills. Normally, he would have been afraid at being alone in an unfamiliar place, but this place seemed sacred.

Kyle looked around the serene landscape and noticed the woman from his dreams walking in his direction. She seemed to float across the green grass with a staff in her right hand. A light spring wind caused her long white hair to trail behind her as she moved closer towards him. As he watched her make her way down the gentle slope, he felt a warm breath on his neck. Startled, he looked over his shoulder to find a horse nuzzling him from behind. His eyes widened as he quickly turned around to face the chestnut animal with a white blaze down the middle of its face. The horse looked at him tenderly and seemed to nod as if to say hello.

"Oh, my! He's beautiful," the lady's familiar voice said, as she moved into earshot of Kyle.

Kyle noticing that his gentle angel lady was standing next to him and asked, "What's his name?"

"I'm not sure. It's the first time I've seen him here. I think you brought him with you. Why don't you ask him his name?" she replied. Kyle looked at her questioningly and quietly thought that talking to an animal was silly. "Oh, don't think that talking to an animal is crazy," she said as if she had read his mind.

He turned to look at the horse again before inquiring, "Who are you?"

The horse neighed and bowed before him. With his head held close to the ground and one leg pointing towards Kyle as the other was bent beneath him, the horse responded in poetic form,

"Horse am I—

Chestnut all over

With a blaze of white on my face

And a splash of white on my left rear leg.

Masculinity and femininity

Are perfectly balanced within me.

Strength and grace

Are the stabilities I offer.

Whether running full speed

As muscles ripple across my body

Or delicately trotting

To dance with the sprites,

I bring Spirit into equilibrium

As both Mother and Father.

I protect vigorously

By rising on my rear legs

With front hoofs pummeling the air.

I nurture tenderly

By nuzzling my head

Into my master's breast.

Freedom and discipline

Are the lessons I illustrate.

Peaceful power

Is my soul's exclamation."

Kyle stood in awe before the beautiful beast. He felt a deep connection to this wonderful horse, but didn't know what to do next. After a moment of silence, Kyle exclaimed in a joyous tone, "Did you just talk?"

The chestnut horse rose back to standing position before answering with a question back to Kyle, "Did you just talk to me?"

"Of course I did," Kyle answered defiantly, "I'm a boy and we do talk!"

"And I am a horse," the chestnut replied with a hurt tone. "Which is sillier, a boy talking to a horse or a horse talking to a boy? I would suggest that you feel honored that I am communicating with you."

Kyle felt his face flush, sensing that he had hurt the horse's feelings. "I'm sorry, horse. I've never talked with an animal before. Do you have a name?"

The horse snorted as if insulted, but his reply was gentle despite his indignation, "You humans are so fixated on names. I suppose if you want to call me a name it would be okay if you called me Skye."

"Skye!" Kyle exclaimed. "Why would a horse be called Skye?"

The lady beside Kyle put her hand on his shoulder and whispered, "Now, don't be rude, Kyle. I think it's a perfectly wonderful name." She turned her head, looked at Skye, and said, "Now, Horse, why don't you show Kyle why your name is Skye."

Before she could finish, Skye turned, galloped away and leapt into the air, and although he had no wings, began to fly. He soared into the blue and penetrated a fluffy white cloud, disappearing from sight of the two earth-bound humans.

Kyle's eyes widened and his mouth popped open. "Wow! Wow! Wow!" he exclaimed. Suddenly, Skye reappeared through the clouds and gently landed in front of them. He shook his black mane and whisked his tail as if readjusting to the pull of gravity.

Kyle's angel looked at him and then at the horse. "Well, Kyle, what do you think now? Is Skye an appropriate name for this great horse?"

"Yes, yes, yes!" Kyle cried with glee as he jumped up and down. "Can I ride him?" he begged.

"That would be Skye's decision," the woman replied gingerly.

Sky shook his head and whinnied before speaking. "I think we'll wait until another time before you ride upon my back. I sense that you need a little maturity before you're ready to fly the skies with me."

Kyle's face turned down. "Aw, shucks!" he said with dismay.

"Besides," Skye continued, "this kind Spirit would like to visit with you for a while," and he nodded towards the lady. "I'm just here to introduce myself and let you know that I'm here for you when you're ready to get better acquainted."

The lady smiled at Skye. "As always, Skye, you're such a gentleman. Thank you for stopping by...and you're right. Kyle and I do need to spend some time together. Our time grows short, since the beautiful innocence of childhood is lost to adolescence."

"I know," Sky replied with a nod and a sad look in his eyes. "Kyle, remember my strength and my grace as you move through life. What I am, so are you. I *am* here for you."

As Skye finished his sentenced, he turned towards the pond and slowly started walking into the water until he was completely submerged. The only trace of him was a small circle of ripples dancing across the glassy pond.

Kyle turned to the woman. With a concerned look on his face, he asked, "Will he be alright under water?"

"Oh, yes, he'll be fine. He can fly and stay under water. Isn't that a wonder, Kyle?"

Kyle wasn't sure whether to say anything or not about the mysterious horse. Instead he looked at the woman and said, "Okay...so I've met a flying horse that swims and his name is Skye, but I don't know your name. What do I call you?"

Leaning on her staff, the woman knelt. "What would you like to call me?" she asked.

Kyle regarded her and then looked down at the grass. His small hands started picking at the blades as he thought about what to say. In his heart, he felt a comfort about this lady as if she were a wool blanket on a cold winter night. "Well, Child, who do you say I am?"

Without thought, Kyle answered excitedly, "Grandmother! I think you're my grandmother."

"Blessed are you, Kyle, for this was not revealed to you by anyone, but by Creator in heaven. It is an honor to hear you call me Grandmother." Her smile broadened as a solitary tear rolled down the right side of her face.

"Mommy looks like you—except younger," Kyle mused. "But Mommy told me that her parents died. Are you a ghost?"

"Oh no, Kyle. I am very much alive. Remember? I was in the parking lot of the church this evening when she was spanking you." Kyle nodded. "I am *dead* to your mother because we had an argument many years ago—before you and Ruthie were born. It's hard to explain to someone as young as you are, but you'll learn more as you grow older. Right now, things are very simple to you and trying to explain the relationship between your mother and I would only make them seem more complicated. You have enough on you right now and I believe that your open spirit is about to close for a time. Our time is short."

"What do you mean my open spirit is about to close?" Kyle asked.

"Sweetie, most children loose their connection with Spirit as they approach the teen years. For some, it's because of the indoctrination of religion. For others, it's because of the indoctrination of human-ism or the combination of both. Right now, you see things and dream things that most adults ignore, or pass off as a trick of the eyes or mind. Adolescence is a shocking time for the spirit just like it is for the body. As the body forgets what it's like to be a child, so does the spirit. You will be moving to a new place in the next couple of days and it will only sever our connection. This move will only accelerate the clos-ing of your spirit."

Kyle looked pensive for a moment before speaking. "Are you saying that you won't come to me anymore?"

"Oh, I'll try. I'm just not sure you'll be open to it."

"But, I *want* you to come around," Kyle's eyes filled with tears. "Mommy is afraid of Daddy, so she's hard on me. Daddy doesn't like me 'cause I'm not tough

enough and I play with girls more than boys. But, you…
you're different!"

"Give your mother some time. It may take a while,
but I *know* that she'll come into her own sometime. As
for your father…well…he's just afraid of you because
you're different." She paused for a moment as she
thought about how to encourage the young boy. "Your
father doesn't understand you. He prefers to see things
in black and white or right and wrong. He knows that
you're gifted spiritually and that he pales in comparison,
so he does his best to deny your gift. Unfortunately,
this is the way of most adults. If they notice someone
brighter than they are, they try to subdue or conquer
the more enlightened person. It has been so throughout history."

Kyle interjected, "But, I'll never be the son he
wants."

"That is his dilemma to face, Kyle. He may not
want you, but you are the son he *needs*. The Native
Peoples would have been honored to have a Two-Spirited boy in their tribe—*I* am honored to have you as my
grandson."

"What do you mean Two-Spirited?"

"Well, just as Skye explained to you in his greeting, your spirit is perfectly balanced. You possess both
strength and grace. It really is the closest a human can
be with Creator. My people have always seen it this
way." She pulled herself to a standing position with her
staff and then reached for Kyle's hand. "Walk with me
to the spring that feeds the pond and bring the blade

of grass you've been playing with. I want to show you something."

Kyle grabbed her hand and they moved together towards the babbling spring. As they drew close, the flow and force of the water caught his attention. Without any provocation from his grandmother, he let loose of her hand and dipped the blade of grass into the current. He felt the tug of energy pulse through the long blade as it struggled between the water and his firm grasp. Reluctantly, he released it and watched as it first went limp and then joined the flow of water. He continued to gaze as the grass floated away, moving in an unseen current of water.

Grandmother smiled at him as he looked up to her. "Kyle, I want you to listen to me very closely. I have three lessons for you tonight and each of them will help you along your journey to your spiritual home. The grass and spring is the first lesson." She paused momentarily before continuing.

"How like the blade of grass we are! We go about our lives doing what seems natural to us, yet knowing there is a greater source and power than our own. All are drawn to the source. Maybe, like the blade of grass, we choose to accept the nourishment provided for us trickled through the ground or saturated by a heavy rain. The only problem with this for us is that the source is muddied by others' opinions, dogma, or meaningless tradition.

"Yet, the source remains crystal clear in its clarion summons of spirit. 'Pluck yourself from stagnation!' Source urges. So we make our journey forward to find the well. We approach, slightly guarded, and carefully examine the force of its flow. As we get closer to the source, we are intimidated by its power. Like the blade of grass, we wrestle against the power of our Source clinging to human nature that is so natural and comfortable for us, but once we surrender and the refining surge cleanses, we find ourselves renewed and gently floating with the ebbs of Spirit.

"The creative Source will tenderly guide us with light nudges as we glide across life's pond. There is no need to grapple for the familiar murky dew we once lived for. The spring supplies all that is required for an abundant life. Open your eyes a little more. Journey to Source. Dive into the flow. Move as you are channeled."

As his grandmother finished, Kyle looked in wonderment at the blade of grass still moving with the pulses of the water. He giggled slightly before saying, "You're very smart. I hope I can be as smart as you some day!"

Grandmother reached out and ruffled his wavy hair. "Oh, you will be much wiser than me some day. Now, look into the pond. I want to show you something." Kyle bent towards the pond with his hands on his knees as he obediently peered into the water. Grandmother reached her staff towards the water and almost imperceptibly tapped it. Bubbles rose to the top, first gently and then like a pan of boiling water. Gently the bubbles spun on the surface of the water before becoming a steady whirlpool. In the center of the whirlpool, a scene emerged that looked like a movie to Kyle. Kyle instantly recognized the vision as the scene from the church service earlier in the evening when his mother was prophesying in tongues.

"Oh, I really don't want to watch this," Kyle nervously told his Grandmother. "Daddy got the word for him and all that speaking in tongues scares me."

"It's okay, sweetie," she soothed. "I want you to see *and* listen to the interpretation. We won't watch the tongues part. The insight was meant for you...*not* your father." Kyle reluctantly watched as Sister Hall started her recitation. "Now, listen, Kyle," his grandmother spoke. When the scene had finished playing before them, the water bubbled again and the picture faded.

"Did you have ears to hear, Kyle?" Grandmother asked. Kyle looked confused but nodded anyway. "Let me help you with it. Sister Hall said that your parents' generation was being judged and that a new one would rise up. You are part of the next generation and you will be the leader of a new view of God—a spiritual awakening. Those in the previous generation will not understand why you will be used by the Divine since they will judge you as unholy. When she talked about the vine and branches, she was saying that you need to stay connected to your source to continue to grow spiritually. The whole world won't hate you, but *your* world will crumble around you when you realize your calling and acknowledge Creator's love for all. This is your second lesson tonight: Know that you are called to greatness, stay connected to Source, and practice Divine Love in all things."

Kyle stared in wonderment at his grandmother. It was almost too much for him to understand. Sensing his confusion, Grandmother smiled at him and said, "I know it's a lot for you to understand at this age, but one day it will all make sense."

"It sounds a little scary, Grandmother. *Me* a leader of a new view of God? I've heard Daddy preach about the Antichrist and it sounds like that's what I may become. I'll never serve Satan or lead people away from Jesus!"

"Oh, Sweetie, I so wish you didn't have all this dogma in your life," she responded sadly. She looked around the pond and then said, "The very fact that you worry about becoming the Antichrist is proof positive that you aren't him. It's people who *think* they know everything about God's mind that are the Antichrists. They profess to have all the answers and point others to their church or their view of God and say it's the only way to get to heaven. They have become the very thing that Jesus preached against—religious zealots creating an exclusive club filled with members who follow them blindly. Trust me; you will understand this in time."

Kyle seemed comforted by her answer and said, "Hey! Didn't you say I had three lessons to learn?"

"Yes, I did. And this one will be used immediately," she said with urgency. Once again she tapped her staff to the water of the pond. The water bubbled, then whirled. Another movie appeared in the middle of the whirlpool. This time the scene was not one Kyle had seen before. When he looked, he saw his sister, Ruth, crying in bed. Her hair was matted with sweat and her face was white, except for the red blush of fever on both cheeks. Her lips were drawn and chapped. Their mother bent and placed a cool washcloth on her forehead.

The water in the pond bubbled again and the picture melted in the swirls.

"Ruthie's sick!" Kyle exclaimed.

"Yes, Dear, she is. When you awake, I want you to go to her and place your hands next to her ears. Just lightly touch her until you *feel* you should stop."

Kyle looked at his grandmother questioningly. "Should I take the piece of your dress that you gave me tonight when I see Ruthie?"

"You can if you want to, but I only wanted you to have a piece of me with you wherever you go. The important thing in this lesson is that you learn that healing someone's energy also heals their body. You *are* a healer, Kyle. Don't ever forget it."

"A healer? You mean like when Daddy lays hands on people in church?"

Grandmother's face scowled at Kyle's comparison between himself and his father, but she decided it was best to answer him with tenderness. "Yes, Kyle. Do you remember the warmth you felt when I touched your ears in the church parking lot? That is the same thing you will do for Ruthie. Now it's time for you to wake up and take care of your sister." She looked at the boy one more time and a wave of love emanated from her towards him. "You're a special spirit, Kyle."

"I love you, Grandmother...I love you."

Kyle's body started stirring in the twin bed of his bedroom. He slowly pulled himself out of the dream and the sleep that had engulfed him. He opened his eyes and stared at the swirls on the ceiling, made years before with a drywaller's brush. When he was accustomed to his physical surroundings, he gently slipped out of bed. He bent towards the floor, feeling with both hands for the pants he had discarded before putting on his pajamas. Once he found the plaid dress pants, he searched the pockets for the piece of material Grandmother had given him when they met in the parking lot of the church. "There you are," Kyle whispered. With the remnant in hand, he silently crept through the hall, passed his parents' bedroom, and then entered his sister's room.

Ruth was in bed on her back just as he had seen her in his dream. She murmured intelligible words in a fevered dream. Kyle tiptoed to her bed and gently laid the piece of material from his grandmother's dress on Ruth's chest. Then he placed a hand on each side of her head. He could feel the dampness of her scalp even though his hands were barely touching her hair. His eyes closed and he felt a warm tingly sensation in the palms of his hands. The heat was soothing to him and Ruth stopped muttering. He slowly opened his eyes and saw a faint violet aura around his hands that appeared to grow with the heat As he watched the violet color, it turned blue. His hands and forearms seemed consumed with the glow. A stream of steady white light emanated towards Ruth from the center of his palms, followed by the purple and blue energy.

Ruth opened her eyes with a jolt. Her eyes searched Kyle's as if searching for an unseen object before rolling upwards and closing her lids. The fevered red that had dotted Ruth's pallor diminished and her natural pink tones returned. Kyle noticed that the heat in his hands seemed to be fading and the beautiful blues and purples started to diminish.

"Kyle Leroy, what on earth are you doing?" Kyle jumped at the sound of his mother's accusatory whisper from behind him. His hands quickly dropped to his sides and he turned to face her. Deborah walked over to the Ruth's bedside before he could answer and placed the back of her hand on the girl's forehead. "Looks like the fever broke," she whispered. Kyle slowly backed out of the room hoping to return to his own bed before his mother questioned him further.

"And what is this?" Deborah asked as she picked up the piece of cloth off of Ruth's chest and held it in Kyle's direction.

"I dunno," was all he could muster.

"Kyle Leroy, how many times have I told you not to lie to me?" Although she was whispering, he heard the anger flaring in her tone. "Where did you get this?"

"I just found it." He desperately wanted to yank it from his mother's hand, but didn't dare move.

"I want you to go to your room right now, young man, and I'll be there in a moment!"

Kyle glumly walked back to his bedroom as tears filled his eyes. His mind raced frantically, trying to find a story about the purple remnant so that he could get it back. The sound of his heart beat rapidly in his ears. *"Stop crying, Kyle,"* he told himself. *"You have to come up with something or else you'll never get the piece of Grandmother's dress back!"*

His mother walked into his room and turned on the over-head light, nearly closing the door behind her.

"Are you going to tell me where this came from?" she asked as she flashed the piece of cloth in front of Kyle's face.

"Uh...I..." Kyle stammered.

"If you tell me another lie, you are going to get a spanking. I want to know where you got this and what you were doing in Ruth's room!" Deborah grabbed Kyle by the shoulders and started shaking him. "Do you hear me? Tell me now!"

When she stopped shaking him, Kyle answered between heaving breaths, "The...the lady...at...the...the...church...gave...it...to...me."

"What lady? The one in the parking lot?" Kyle nodded. "And what were you doing in Ruth's room, boy?"

"I was *just* praying for her 'cause she's sick," he squeaked. "Grandmother said..." but before he could get another word out he felt a stinging blow of his mother's hand across his face.

"*That* woman is *not* your grandmother. Don't ever let me hear you say that again!" *Slap!* "Do you understand me? Do you?"

Kyle could barely keep his thoughts together from the hits to his face, but managed to say "Yes, Ma'am," through the tears. His stomach ached from the pain of the blows as well as his mother's venomous hatred of his grandmother.

"I knew I shouldn't have let her speak to you. I knew it would only bring a devil in this house!" She crumpled the remnant in her right hand in front of Kyle's face. "This is *just* an old rag and that woman is *just* an old hag! Never...and I mean never, speak of her again. If your father *ever* found out that you had any contact with her, and I let you…" with a worried look on her face, her voice trailed off.

Feeling bold despite the onslaught from his mother, Kyle asked, "Can I at least keep the material?"

Deborah's eyes turned ice cold. "You will *never* see this rag again!" She grabbed Kyle's arm and shoved him towards his bed. The momentum from his mother's thrust sent him flying and he banged his shin on the metal side rail. A yelp escaped him as he scurried under the sheets.

"Now, go back to sleep and I don't want to hear another word about any of this!"

Out in the hall, Ruth, who was now feeling like she had never been ill, had watched the entire explosion through the cracked door. Sensing that her mother would be exiting Kyle's room, she stealthily made her way back to her own bed and crawled quickly beneath the sheets. She watched her mother leave her brother's room and move through the hallway to Ruth's. As her mother approached, Ruth closed her eyes and pretended to be asleep. She felt her mother touch her forehead again and heard a soft sigh before Deborah said quietly, "Well, at least the fever is gone." Ruth opened one eye just enough to see her mother's hands near her face as she sat on the edge of her bed. In her left hand, she twisted a piece of purple cloth between her fingers.

Deborah left Ruth's bed and walked towards the sheer, covered window just three feet from the end of the twin bed. Ruth followed her with one eye as Deborah held the piece of material in the moonlight cascading through the opaque curtains. "Why can't you just leave us alone, Mother?" She spoke to the cloth in a tearful voice as if it could hear her. "You are not welcome in my life or my children's lives. Stay away from us! Do you hear me? Stay away!" She turned towards Ruth's door and walked out.

Ruth, still in her bed, started thinking about what she had just witnessed over the last several minutes. She remembered Kyle coming into her room and touching the sides of her head. She remembered a gentle pulse of energy filling her body. She recalled that within moments of his touch the fever had broken. She also felt like she felt she had never been sick. What she could not understand was what had happened between her mother and Kyle. And the possibility that they had a grandmother that they did not know, set her rebellious nature on fire. *"Why would Mommy tell us that her parents were dead if Grandmother is still living?"* she wondered just before she fell back into a deep sleep.

Chapter 5

Thirty-three year old Kyle reached out of the window of his silver Volkswagen Passat to punch in the key code to the iron gate that was the start of the driveway to his parents' twenty-acre compound just southeast of Columbus. Waiting for the large gates to swing open, he caught his reflection in the rear-view mirror. The blonde hair of childhood had been replaced with the adolescent, hormone-induced light brown color. It was moderately long and would have reached his shoulders if not for the natural curls and soft ringlets that framed his head. His cool blue eyes were surrounded by dark rings and he noticed the furrowed look of his brow. He turned his face side to side and silently wished that his face were more chiseled than the appearance his slightly puffy cheeks gave him.

He heard the familiar clang of the gate as it fully opened and drove through. The house sat in the middle of the compound with a blacktop drive that ran past the house to stables in the far right corner of the property. Directly in front of the house was a circular drive paved with brick. As he approached the house, he noticed the silver pine colored Toyota Prius parked in the circular drive. A faint smile spread across his face as he recognized Ruth's car and the bumper sticker that read "*W.W.B.D.*" in large letters and underneath "*What Would Buddha Do?*" Kyle pulled onto the brick drive and parked directly behind the Prius. He briefly regarded the

7,500 square-foot, million-dollar home as he emerged from his vehicle with a plastic grocery bag in his hand. He felt the warm April day enliven his spirits in spite of the recent bout of depression. He had not been looking forward to stopping by his parents' house, but now felt a sense of relief knowing that Ruth was there. He moved his six-foot athletic frame towards the front door and without knocking, entered the home. He looked around the entry way and into the great room where he saw his mother's back, reclined on the coach with her eyes closed. Quietly, he walked past her and into the kitchen which was an extension of the great room. He pulled two bottles of white grape juice out of the grocery bag and placed them in the refrigerator.

Ruth entered with a wool blanket in her hand and a serious look on her face, which melted into a warm smile upon seeing Kyle. Her five-foot petite build looked especially small as she held the over-sized wool blanket. "Hey, brother! Let me cover Mom up with this blanket and I'll give you a hug," she said enthusiastically, walking towards the couch. Kyle followed her as Ruth covered their mother as she slept. "Doesn't Mom look perky?" she oozed with a sarcastic grin on her face.

Kyle giggled as he had when he was a little boy, when Ruth alluded to their mother's breast augmentation, before asking, "Can she hear you?"

"Hell, I hope so. But I think she's sleeping with Mr. Vicodin right now and probably can't hear a thing." Ruth looked directly at her mother and said, "Isn't that right, Mom?" Deborah didn't move and her breathing remained steady. "Dear gawd, I hope those new twins lower after a few days. It looks like her chin is resting on her boobs, doesn't it, Kyle?"

Kyle walked over and hugged his sister. "I'm so glad you're here, Sis. I don't know what I would do without you and your sarcasm. Did you take a personal day to come check on Mom?"

"No. I wouldn't dare leave my Kindergarteners for Mom's Boob job. We're on spring break this week, so I thought I'd try to be a good daughter and check on her. Mark and Naomi needed some quality father-daughter time together so I left them to fend for themselves."

Mark and Ruth had been married for twelve years and Naomi was their six-year-old daughter. The two had met in college and bonded instantly when they discovered that they had attended South Point Elementary School together. When they graduated from Ohio University, both took teaching positions back in the children's rural, southeastern Ohio hometown and married shortly thereafter.

"I see you brought Mom her white grape juice. Doesn't she know that a little wine works better?" Without waiting for Kyle to answer, she added, "I think even the Bible says something about a little wine for what ails you. I know...I know...alcohol is sinful, but...Vicodin is another story. *That's* okay because it's prescribed by a doctor. Unfortunately, I think Mom is just as acquainted with her doctor as a drunk is with his bartender!"

"Have I told you how much I love your independent spirit?" He chuckled again.

"Well, I don't have a clue as to where that comes from," Deborah groggily said with her eyes half-open.

"I can't believe that my children have turned out the way they have. Why couldn't you have turned into a church musician like I wanted, Ruth?"

"Uh-oh," Ruth said wryly, "sounds like Mr. Vicodin is a truth serum. We're going to get it now."

Deborah managed to open her eyes through the fog of the painkiller. Her short, blonde hair was matted to the sides of her head. She tried to fluff with her hands as she continued, "You were so well-behaved until your brother arrived, Ruth. God knows I did my best with you kids, and this is how you repay me, by tormenting me after surgery?"

"I'm sorry, Mom," Ruth answered flatly. "I suppose we should be more considerate after your *elective* cosmetic surgery. After all, it's not like every woman of sixty-three has the endurance to get a new pair of boobs just because she wants them."

"Please, stop it, Ruth!" Deborah snapped. "Honestly, I don't know where you get that sarcastic tone."

"Maybe it comes from your side of the family, Mom." Ruth's tone was flippant and Kyle sensed that she was trying to contain her anger.

Deborah ignored the comment and asked sweetly, "Did you pick up my grape juice, Kyle?"

"Yes, Mom. It's in the fridge."

"Would it be too much trouble for one of you to get me a small glass of juice?"

Ruth welcomed the reprieve and said, "I'll get it." She quickly walked over to the kitchen and opened the cherry cabinets in search of a juice glass.

Deborah looked at Kyle and scowled. "You look *re-ally* tired, son. Are you still having trouble sleeping?" Without allowing Kyle to answer, she continued, "You know, if you hadn't divorced Laurel and let her run off with the kids to Hilton Head, you'd be sleeping just fine. How on earth you messed up a marriage to such a beautiful woman I'll never understand. One of these days, you'll realize your mistake and wish you could get her back!"

Kyle felt the blows of his mother's words pummel his spirit. His light demeanor wilted with the oppression of letting down his parents and children. It had not been quite a year since his marriage had ended and just three months since his ex-wife, Laurel, had moved abruptly with their ten year old twins, Caleb and Olivia. Kyle desperately missed the children and hated the distance between them.

Ruth heard her mother's comments as she brought her glass of juice. "Here's your juice, Mom." She almost shoved it in her face trying to keep her from talking. "Hey, Kyle, would you walk with me to the stables? I need some air. Mom has her juice, she'll be fine for a few minutes alone." She looked sternly at her mother daring her to object.

"Sure. I could use some fresh air," Kyle answered.

They quickly left the house through the front door. Kyle looked at Ruth's car and said, "I love your bumper sticker."

"Yeah, well I love irritating Mom and Dad. Can you tell, Brother?"

The smile returned to Kyle's face. "Oh, yes...I can tell. I just wish I had your spunk to stand up to them like you do."

They started walking up the blacktop drive towards the stables. "Well, I can understand holding your tongue with them since they're also your employers, but, what Mom was doing in there about your divorce is just wrong. You shouldn't have to put up with that shit!"

"That's just it, Ruthie. I'm so entwined with them. I see them at work Tuesday through Friday in the church offices. I attend church with them on Wednesday and Sunday. They take Monday's off, but I'm there at the church office doing work. Saturday is the only day I get to myself. Now that Laurel has moved away with the kids, Saturday's are just miserable. And honestly, I am not feeling right about church, let alone being employed as their personal assistant." He paused for a moment and wondered if he was spilling too much to his sister.

Ruth encouraged him to continue. "It's alright Kyle. You can tell me anything."

"Ruth..." he stuttered, "I...I...I'm just not happy with any of it. Dad is working on his twentieth book now. I basically do all the writing for him. I mean, he gives me an outline filled with grammatical errors and then I write the entire thing for him. If that isn't bad enough, I don't think I believe his message anymore—it's become pure dogma. He and Mom have become master manipulators and I'm just a part of the show! I'm afraid to say anything to them for fear of losing my job. I've seen too many other employees let go because they dare to question Dad's authority…or *anointing* as he calls it. Have you seen him on television lately?"

Ruth answered tersely, "I have *never* watched any of his extravaganzas. I wouldn't even know what channel to pick him up on."

"I don't know how you could miss him. Just ask him which one he's on in your area. I'm sure he could tell which of the 1,500 stations or cable affiliates play his daily show in the Tri-State."

"I'll pass on that one, Kyle. I haven't had any desire to be exposed to any of that psychological manipulation since I was eighteen and left for Athens. I just wish you weren't so entrenched with it."

"I don't know what I would do for a job if I left. Oh, and get this…Dad just bought a $500,000 jet."

Ruth grimaced. "It's so nice to see them practicing the real essence of Christ's teachings isn't it? I'm pretty sure I remember reading in the Bible where Jesus lived in a million-dollar mansion, had a half-a-million dollar jet, a five-thousand-seat church, a bible college, and a private Christian school. I wonder how much he charged to attend one of his conferences? Do you think Jesus would have let Mary Magdalene get a boob job?" Kyle chuckled at his sister's cynicism. "I can't even imagine what the operating budget must be for their little enterprise."

"Try close to 40 million a year," Kyle offered. "The church and school properties combined total more than $27 million."

"Are you kidding me?"

"No, I'm serious."

"And how much do they pay themselves?"

"That's a very good question, Sis. I have no idea... and I probably don't want to know."

"I'm sure it would shock the socks off me. But, Kyle...you don't have to stay with them. I'm sure you could find a job here in Columbus making what you make now, if not more." Having said that, Ruth decided not to press the issue, and changed the subject. "Have you heard from the kids lately?"

"I just talked to them last weekend. They say they miss Ohio, but are very guarded about what they say on the phone. I hope I did the right thing with the divorce...I had hoped that I would have more contact with them." Kyle felt uneasy talking about his divorce for fear of revealing too much.

Ruth sensed his anxiety and said, "Kyle, I think you did the right thing." A long pause ensued as Ruth wrestled with her own intuition. "You know you can tell me *anything*, right? Nothing would change the way I feel about you, Little Brother...nothing." She fought her urge to question him outright about her suspicions.

"I know, Sis...I know." Kyle longed to open up to her, but his self-condemnation stifled his true feelings. "You know...last Sunday in church as I was sitting there before the service started, I realized that I go to church for a different reason than most of the other people."

"What do you mean?"

"Everyone else is there for the social interaction and Dad's show. They want to hear jubilant music, see Dad work up a sweat as he acts likes God's chief cheerleader, and let everyone see how holy they are because they're one of Reaper's 13,000 members. If they get their faces in the camera, it's an even bigger bonus for them because they can say they were on television." Kyle paused before he stated his reason for going to church. "I go to find a connection with *God*, not with other people."

"That's good, but you can't discount the fact that you have to go because Mom and Dad expect it," Ruth pointed out.

"Maybe that's part of it. Maybe that's why I feel disillusioned with the whole thing. When I hear Dad preach, I feel like he's pointing a finger at me and telling me that I'll never see heaven. You remember how he uses scripture to condemn people and get them to run to the altar? It doesn't work for me anymore. The truth is, I am who I am no matter how many times I go to the altar."

Ruth ventured a guess, "Would you be referring to 1 Corinthians 6:9-10?" Kyle's body tensed with Ruth's question. Visibly shaken, he placed his right hand over his mouth as if to keep his lips silent. Ruth noticed the tremors and regretted asking the question. Tears formed in his eyes and he looked away from his sister. She lowered her voice and put a hand on his back, "Kyle, I just want you to know that if you need time away for a couple of days, Mark and I would be happy to let you stay with us. You'll always be welcome in our home...no matter what."

Kyle took comfort in her words and composed himself. "Ah, Sis, this divorce has just been tougher than I thought. I'll be okay." Looking for a way to change the subject he asked, "Hey, did Mom ask you to come to her Mother's Day service at church next month?"

Ruth rolled her eyes and was happy to see a more relaxed Kyle. "Oh, yes. She said it would be wonderful to have three generations of Basil women on the stage during the opening of the service."

"And what did you say?"

"I told her I'd think about it. I just can't imagine what Naomi would do in one of those wild, charismatic services. It'd probably scare the hell right out of her!" she added with a laugh.

Kyle joined in with his own giggle, "Yeah, Dad loves calling you Presbyterians the Frozen Chosen. In fact, he's even used the phrase of scaring the hell out of people—of course, from his perspective, that's a good thing. I'm sure Naomi would think that she was at a rock concert in Dad's stadium-sized church."

Ruth put her hands in the back pockets of her jeans as she always did, and felt a remnant of material. She remembered why she had wanted to talk to Kyle outside. "Hey, Kyle not to change the subject, but I found something that I thought you might want…especially with all that you've been going through with the divorce and everything." From her right rear pocket, she pulled a piece of purple material and held it out to her brother. "When Mom asked me to get her blanket out of the cedar chest at the foot of her bed, I found this in the bottom. I thought you might want it."

Kyle stared at the ragged remnant and twenty-three years melted away. He reached for it and barely had it in his right hand before asking, "How did you know that

I would want this?" As he touched the cloth, the light returned to his eyes and the dark circles underneath them disappeared.

"I know we never talked about it, but I clearly remember the night that you came into my room when I was burning up with a fever and laid that piece of material on my chest. The warmth from your hands was soothing to my head and I immediately felt better. I was outside your door when Mom was tearing into you about that rag and Grandmother."

"Oh, my god!" Kyle whispered. "You know about Grandmother? Is she still living? Do you know where she is?"

"I don't know, Kyle. If she's still alive, she must be close to ninety by now. Wouldn't it be neat if she were?"

"Well, I'm going to go ask Mom right now!" Kyle turned for the house. Ruth had to run to catch up with the brother who was a foot taller than she was.

"Kyle, not now." He stopped moving in the direction of the house. "I know this going to sound shocking coming from me, but give Mom a break. In her mental state, she probably couldn't give you a straight answer. I'll see what I can find out. If you start asking questions, she might clam up since she told you never to mention Grandmother again—I certainly remember how she reacted years ago. We don't need another replay of that today. Give me some time and I might be able to work something out of her."

"Okay, Sis. You're probably right...and I want to hang on to this old rag this time." He put the piece of material in his front pocket. "Thank you." Then he hugged her.

As they turned, they saw their father's silver Mercedes-Benz coming up the drive. Eli waited for them at the front door. The two men were about the same height, but Eli outweighed him by thirty pounds, carried mostly in his stomach. He still had a full head of unnatural-looking reddish-brown hair, colored from a good dose of Just For Men, slicked back with too much hair product. "How's my frozen chosen daughter doing?" he said with a smile.

"Oh, I'm hotter than you think, Dad," Ruth replied. "Just ask my husband."

Eli's smile twisted into a look of righteous indignation. Kyle, like a ten year old again, could hardly contain his laughter. "Will you never tire of trying to shock me?" Eli inquired.

Never at a loss for words, Ruth answered, "Only if you tire of reminding me how on-fire you are, Dad."

Eli rolled his eyes and shook his head. "How's you mother doing?"

"She's fine, Dad," Kyle answered.

"Well, I need to get back on the road," Ruth said. "I'll just grab my purse from inside and tell Mom good-bye." She went through the front door to retrieve her purse. Kyle started to follow her when he felt his father's hand grab his arm.

"I need to get going, too, Dad. I have an appointment."

"That's what I wanted to ask you about. Do you feel like you're making progress with the support group, son?"

Kyle's answer was vague, "It's certainly opening my eyes."

"Good. Good. I'm glad to hear that. You know my stance on this issue is the same with any other sin: hate the sin and love the sinner. You haven't told your sister have you?"

"No, Dad. Only you and I know about this, unless you've talked with Mom about it."

"No. No. I won't tell her. It would kill her, especially in her current state with the surgery and all." He looked Kyle directly in the eyes and placed both hands on Kyle's shoulders, "You're doing the right thing. I'm sure that pretty soon you'll be feeling much better. And who knows? Maybe you and Laurel will be able to reconcile. Wouldn't that be great to have the family back together again? God is in the restoration business!"

Kyle stared into his father's manipulating gaze and gave a compliant nod. Just then the front door opened and Ruth interrupted, "Dad, Mom needs to see you. She wants her laptop and a Bible or something to work on a sermon."

"Okay kids…I'd better get in there and help my little lady. I'll tell her that you'll see her tomorrow, Kyle, after you leave work." Kyle recognized the recommendation was really an order, and nodded.

When Eli closed the door behind him, Ruth narrowed her eyes and asked, "What was that all about? I'm telling you, Kyle, you need to find another job and get away from them for a while."

"I know, Sis…I know."

"Kyle, I'm serious," she lectured. "This is no different than when we were kids and you let the bullies run all over you. You have to stand up for yourself. I can't keep kicking Mom and Dad in the shins for you. Go get yourself a pair of saddle oxfords and kick 'em yourself!" She smiled at her brother.

He chuckled. "I hear you. I hear you. I'll stop at the mall and see if I can find a pair of men's size twelve oxfords on my way home."

"You do that, Little Brother!" She hugged him, "I love you, Kyle."

"I love you." With their good-byes said, they returned to their cars and drove off the Basil compound.

Kyle sat in his car in the parking lot of the old stone church where the support group met. There were no other cars were in the parking lot except for the one he recognized as the facilitator's. He decided to wait a few minutes before entering. Reaching behind the driver's seat, he pulled out a journal. Kyle had started keeping a diary when he was ten, after the family had moved to Columbus. He now had several volumes of poems, stories, essays, and prayers compiled in his journals. Each was titled on the inside cover.

As he opened this journal, he looked at the title: *The Turbulent Maze.* He had started this journal just after his divorce and was still filling its pages. Thirty minutes remained before the start of the support group. He began to write.

Dark Fowl

I feel its smothering grip

As it sinks its teethe to sip.

My joy quickly seeps away

And Darkness sweeps through my day.

I thrash against its bold lies

While the pain forces my cries:

Why? Why must you torment me?

Why won't you take flight and flee?

Its wings pound to quiet my voice

Keeping me from my good choice.

It's claws tear at my weak soul—

I know that I am not whole.

It mocks me with furies zeal

Allowing no time to heal.

The wounds: left open, bleeding.

The fowl: still picking, feeding.

I fight to loose its tight grasp.

Is that light I see at last?

The struggle continues on—

Hope is not completely gone!

—Kyle

When he was done, he looked at the time and saw that it was getting late. He had better hurry to the basement meeting room if he wanted to make it by start time. He quickly entered the church and walked down the stairs to one of the Sunday school classrooms. The room had a circle of chairs for the participants, but the only other person in the room was the facilitator, Blake. He smiled at Kyle, pulled his hand out of his khaki pants, and extended it to him. "Good evening, Kyle." Kyle shook his clammy hand.

"Hello, Blake." Kyle's deep baritone voice contrasted starkly to Blake's softer, slightly wispy tones.

"Looks like you're the only to make it tonight. Why don't we go to my office instead of this musty classroom?" Before Kyle could answer, Blake walked out of the room. Kyle followed him down the poorly lit hallway, around a corner, and up a flight of steps with a sign that read: "Staff Only." The stairway led to a newer addition of the church which held several offices. They walked towards an open door. Kyle assumed was Blake's office.

"Make yourself comfortable, Kyle," Blake said, motioning towards a modern-looking futon sitting against a wall across from an old metal desk.

Kyle picked up the accent pillow, sat down, and held the pillow in his lap. Blake sat on the opposite end of the couch and leaned forward with his elbows resting on his knees. Although Blake was in good physical condition, Kyle noticed his thinning gray hair and guessed that he must be in his early fifties. He knew that Blake was an avid runner, because he had talked about the importance of prayer in previous meetings and that he found the best time for him to talk with God was during his runs.

"How was this week, Kyle?"

Kyle was uncomfortable with the change from the classroom to the office. He brushed it off as a reaction to a change in routine, something which he never adjusted to very well.

"It's been okay. Nothing unusual."

"Any temptations?"

"Just the usual occasional passing thoughts."

Blake moved a little closer to Kyle before continuing, "Kyle, you've been participating in the group for several months now. Do you feel like it's helping you?"

"Honestly?" Kyle looked at Blake before continuing. "I have to tell you that nothing has really changed for me. I've spent most of my adult life trying to keep myself busy with marriage, family, and church—always trying to do the right thing so that my mind wouldn't wander. I've tried denying the flesh. I've tried to put off the old man and put on the new man as the Bible teaches. I confess my sins to God. I have Dad lay his hands on me and cast out devils. I've prayed for deliverance in my private prayer time. I opened up to my wife when I was married about my struggle so that I would have some accountability. Then the divorce came because of my honesty with her. At this point, I'm still not sure that divorce was the wrong thing. Dad believes the divorce was wrong. I assume you think it was wrong. I've really been participating wholeheartedly in this support group, yet, nothing has changed for me. I have to tell you...I'm just tired—physically, mentally, emotionally, and spiritually. If I could turn a switch and make the feelings go away, I would have done it years ago. The truth is...the switch doesn't exist and I think I just need to accept it."

"You sound like you're throwing in the towel. You *do* have power over this."

"So I've been told. For years. Which makes me a failure, right?"

Blake moved his leg close enough to Kyle's so that their knees were lightly touching. "Not a failure, Kyle. It's just like any other sin. There's always temptation. And, sometimes we fail, but God's grace is sufficient for us and He forgives us. Same gender attraction is no different." Blake's hand patted Kyle's thigh. "I'm a living testimony. You've heard my story...and I've never been happier than I am now with my wife. I'm living proof that you can overcome an unnatural attraction to men!"

Kyle was uneasy now that his personal space was violated, but this man was an authority and he rarely questioned those in positions over him. "So, I'll always have these feelings?"

"I still struggle with temptation at times. The devil does his best to get under our skin so that we'll fall from grace. The truth is, when I see a man I'm attracted to, occasionally I do feel a longing. And I would never say this in the group, but I *have* stumbled occasionally. It's just part of the process of overcoming. When you stumble, you just get back on track again and allow God's grace to forgive you." Blake's hand moved a little farther up Kyle's thigh and slipped beneath the pillow he had across his lap.

Kyle suddenly realized what Blake was saying when he felt the tips of the man's fingers brush the zipper of his pants. Kyle pushed the pillow aside and leaped from the futon to a standing position. Blake stood, too.

"I have to go," Kyle said nervously as he started backing stepping.

Blake moved towards Kyle who stood with his back against the wall of the small office.

Although Kyle was five inches taller, Blake looked longingly up into Kyle's face and said, "It's okay, Kyle. I know you feel the attraction, too. No one else is in the building. It's just you and me. I won't tell anyone. Your father will never know. If we give in now, we can be assured that God will forgive us." Blake's hands grabbed Kyle's waist and he pressed himself against Kyle. "Oh, god, you feel fantastic, Kyle."

For the first time in his life, Kyle felt a burning rage inside of him, ready to explode. He grabbed Blake by his arms and shoved him backwards. The force propelled the facilitator over his desk. The computer monitor crashed to the floor as Blake's body thrashed about before sliding to the floor head first near the chair behind the desk. He quickly recovered and got to his feet only to see Kyle leaning over the desk, grabbing the front of his shirt. Kyle drew his fist back threateningly and started yelling through his tears, "You're a liar, Blake. You hide behind this therapy shit only to hit on your clients. How many more have you done this to? Huh? I bet I'm not the first, am I? You're just as queer as I am except you hide behind the church and a wife!" Kyle dropped his fist and let go of the trembling man.

"I'm so sorry, Kyle. I don't know what came over me. The devil was tempting me." His voice sounded even more effeminate than before. Kyle turned to leave when he heard Blake add, "I do hope this will stay between you and me."

Kyle spun and yanked Blake around the desk by the front of his shirt, shoving him against the wall with two loud thuds. "You lying son of a bitch! Don't you worry your two-faced head about a thing. We won't see each other ever again. I won't be back to another Deliverance International meeting. The *only* thing you've been delivered from is reality. I certainly don't fit the poster boy image of this organization! Nor do I want to." Kyle released the man and left the building.

When he got inside his car and reached inside his pocket for his keys, Kyle felt the piece of purple material. He pulled it out along with his keys, unlocked the door, and sat down. He held the material in front of his face and started sobbing. He tried to put his key in the ignition, but couldn't, he was trembling so badly. "Oh, my god. Oh, my god. What did I just do? If Dad finds out I left the support group, he'll kill me." Kyle finally managed to start the car. He headed slowly towards his apartment.

Chapter 6

It was after midnight. Kyle couldn't sleep. His mind roiled. Sitting at his desk in a pair of fitted boxer trunks, he wrote in his journal:

What can I say? There's so much to write; yet, it's difficult to function when there's no one to confide in. I'm in a strange state of being—someone on foreign soil, a stranger in a new land. What to do? Time moves so slowly, but too swiftly. I'm filled with contradictions and paradoxes. I want to make everyone happy. I wanted to be perfect: son, brother, husband, father…in my quest for perfection, I've become very unhappy—very "out of touch" with who I am. I really thought that time, routine, and familiarity would eventually change me. It has not. I am who I am.

I miss my kids. I hurt so badly. I long to see them smile at me…to hear them laugh…to watch them run. Oh, God! I just want to hold them in my arms…hug them…kiss them…and say "I love you, Caleb! I love you, Olivia!" Oh, God, I hurt. I mourn.

I've never had to fight so hard in all my life as I am fighting now. What is so difficult is that I seem to fight against myself the most. It's so difficult to do something for yourself when you've spent a lifetime of doing for others. I have felt self-worth by making everyone else happy. How do I make decisions on my own? How do I decide if something is right or wrong? For years, I based my decisions on what would make someone else happy. I am afraid and unsure.

I think that facing your own lies is probably one of the toughest things in the world to do. Over the last few weeks, I've examined my life and my lies.

I don't like what I have seen.

What have I seen?

A lot of deception.

A lot of hiding.

A lot of fear.

Deceiving those I love.

Hiding my identity.

Fearful of being exposed.

I've come to a point in my life where I can no longer lie to make everyone else happy. While I have made so many happy, I've been tormenting myself into a deep sense of self-loathing.

I've struggled for years to gain acceptance from Mom and Dad while being someone I'm not. I thought if I just did the right things (had a family, a house, a degree) I could earn their pride...their love...their acceptance. But, I can no longer play the game—I never have enjoyed games because only one person wins and the other loses.

No more games.

It's time to retire.

Kyle placed the pen down and shut his journal. Still wide awake, he reached for the computer mouse. After moving it back and forth a few times, the screen popped back on. He logged into his instant messenger and hoped to find his one buddy online. He looked through his contacts list, but didn't see anyone on line. About to log out of messenger, an instant message box popped on the screen.

1pianoman: "hey writer"

Writer1: "hi, pman"

1pianoman: "can't sleep again?"

Writer1: "no…was hoping to find you on"

1pianoman: "nice…so you been to bed and back up?"

Writer1: "yeah"

1pianoman: "I just got out of bed, too…one moment"

Writer1: "ok"

Kyle stared at the screen while he waited for his friend to return. They had met through a personals website and had chatted for over a month. *1pianoman* never gave his real name. Although Kyle had reservations about chatting with *1pianoman* because he was married, he was his one contact who completely understood his religious background and his struggle with his orientation.

1pianoman: "I'm back…thought I heard my wife moving around…better safe than to get busted"

Writer1: "I understand…would be the same way for me if I was still married"

1pianoman: "had a tough day today…feel really bad about what I did"

Writer1: "really…what?"

1pianoman: "you know I work out at the gym every day"

Writer1: "yeah"

1pianoman: "after my workout I was in the sauna and this really hot muscle dude was in there with me…"

Writer1: "go on"

1pianoman: "he just sat there staring at me…you know the look…I started praying, asking God to protect me, but my carnal nature took over…we ended up fooling around in the sauna"

Writer1: "wow…so that's why you feel down now?"

1pianoman: "absolutely…I feel like I let my wife down again...God down…my church…my family"

Writer1: "I know exactly how you feel…sometimes I wonder if I'm just struggling against what God created, though"

1pianoman: "yeah, but we both know what the Bible says about us…besides, I'd loose my job at my church as music minister if anything like this got out"

Kyle always felt uncomfortable when they started talking about jobs. He had told 1pianoman that he was a writer, but not that he was the personal assistant and son of the largest church in Columbus. Kyle knew from previous chats that 1pianoman was employed by a church in the Columbus area as a minister of music, but didn't know which one. That was their connection. Each had to hide their orientations because their livelihoods depended on it.

Writer1: "I know…I know"

1pianoman: "It would be great if we could meet for a cup of coffee sometime…some place in public so that there wouldn't be any temptation for us"

Writer1: "yeah…but since neither one of us knows what the other looks like it would be hard to find each other…lol"

1pianoman: "well, I know you've told me before that you're about 6 ft…170 lbs...athletic, blue eyes, brown hair...I'm sure I'd be able to pick a hot guy like you out of the crowd...lol"

Writer1: "I don't know about the hot part but the rest of the description is right"

1pianoman: "the only thing I wouldn't know is what you'd be wearing...maybe you should start with what you're wearing now"

Writer1: "I told you, I just got out of bed"

1pianoman: "so...what do you sleep in?"

Writer1: "my underwear"

1pianoman: "what kind...boxers, briefs, boxer briefs, bikinis..."

Writer1: "is someone horny?"

1pianoman: "always...so what you wearing?"

Writer1: "a pair of Cin2 camo-green boxer trunks"

1pianoman: "I bet you look hot!!!!!"

Writer1: "now I'm blushing"

1pianoman: "would luv to see you blush in your trunks"

Writer1: "back to coffee...would you like to meet tomorrow?"

1pianoman: "ok...back to coffee...besides I don't need to tent out my boxers...I could take a long lunch and meet you at the German Village Starbucks at noon...work for you?"

Writer1: "I think that would work for me...but how do we find each other?"

1pianoman: "here I'll send you a pic...do you have one?"

Writer1: "yeah...give me a minute or two to find it... I'm not the quickest with chat stuff"

Kyle started looking for a picture of himself that he had saved on his computer. He heard the beep of the chat program letting him know that 1pianoman had sent his picture. He stopped looking for his picture and opened 1pianoman's file. When the picture appeared, Kyle's face went ashen. He instantly recognized the picture as Earth Reaper's minister of music, Dan White. His heart started racing and quickly typed a message back.

Writer1: "I just realized I have a doctor's appointment tomorrow at 11:30...no way I can make it for coffee"

1pianoman: "too bad...how about later in the day?"

Writer1: "I don't think so...busy all day"

1pianoman: "you don't like the pic I sent...not hot enough for you?"

Writer1: "no...it's not that...you're a very good looking man...I just don't feel right about meeting...I don't think it's fair to your wife"

1pianoman: "that's why I said to meet at Starbucks... that way there's no temptation"

Kyle was struggling with what to type next. The truth was he had always found Dan attractive. Too many times during the praise and worship service, Kyle found himself forgetting the words to the songs and focusing on the song minister. He had always felt that Dan was very engaging during their conversations in the church offices. Dan rarely broke eye contact when they talked and there had been times when all Kyle could think about during a discussion was kissing the thirty-year-old minister.

Writer1: "what would happen if someone close to you found out about your struggle?"

1pianoman: "how close?"

Writer1: "someone in your church"

1pianoman: "OMG...we know each other don't we!"

Writer1: "it's okay, Dan...I won't tell a soul"

1pianoman: "OMG...you do know me! What are you going to do?"

Writer1: "Dan, calm down...I'm not going to tell anyone...I have just as much to loose as you do...maybe more"

1pianoman: "Who are you????? Tell me!!!!"

Writer1: "you're better off not knowing, that way you won't feel uncomfortable around me"

1pianoman: "great! so now I'll be paranoid around everyone in the church...this is great...I knew I shouldn't have sent the pic...I suppose you're going to hold this over my head"

Writer1: "please, Dan...I don't want to 'out' you... I don't want to blackmail you"

1pianoman: "then why don't you tell me who you are?????"

Writer1: "well, I don't want anyone else to know"

1pianoman: "great! So you know about me...and I'll just have to guess between the 15,000 members about you...I trusted you too easily...I gotta go, I feel sick to my stomach"

Writer1: "Dan...wait...you still there?"

1pianoman: "WHAT?????"

Writer1: "It's Kyle...okay...I'm Kyle...you know...the pastor's son"

Kyle stared at the screen. It seemed like an eternity before Dan responded.

1pianoman: "really...you mean it...you're Kyle Basil?"

Writer1: "yep"

1pianoman: "holy shit...I'm sorry...really sorry... I had no idea that I was chatting with you...I mean I had always secretly hoped...and after your divorce I thought maybe it might have been the reason...but I really thought it was just wishful thinking on my part"

Writer1: "no...it's really me"

1pianoman: "so Pastor Basil has you in the reparative therapy group...I mean, you told me that your father was paying for counseling, but I had no idea that the guy I was chatting with was referring to my boss"

Writer1: "my boss, too...don't forget...and I'm not participating in the group anymore"

1pianoman: "really...do you feel healed?"

Writer1: "not healed, but I feel like I am getting better"

1pianoman: "so the therapy works?"

Writer1: "not the way my father intended"

1pianoman: "what do you mean?"

Writer1: "Dan, if you want to talk about this maybe we could do lunch together tomorrow...but really I'm concerned about being alone together...I know your wife, and I don't want us to do anything to hurt either one of you"

1pianoman: "I agree...let's do lunch"

Writer1: "see you at the office tomorrow?"

1pianoman: "sure...see you then...night"

Writer1: "good-night"

Kyle looked at the clock on the computer screen and saw that it was shortly after one. He ran his left hand through his hair and then rubbed the back of his neck before stretching with both arms above his head. As he reached for the ceiling, he felt his skin tighten across his six-pack abs. "I gotta get some sleep." He walked back to his bedroom and started to climb back into the bed when he thought about the piece of purple cloth. He went to the dresser and fumbled in the dark until the soft material grazed his fingertips. He picked it up and crawled under the sheets on his side. Kyle placed his hands under his pillow with the remnant between them.

Soon he dreaming, sitting at the edge of a familiar pond. The water was clear and smooth but for the occasional bluegill darting beneath the surface.

"Well, if it isn't my two-spirited grandson!" A voice said. Kyle turned. To his right, sitting on a large stone, was his grandmother. She wore the purple prairie-dress he remembered from his one encounter with her as a child. In her left hand, she held a staff. Her smile radiated towards him and he responded with one of his own. "It's certainly been a while, hasn't it?"

"I'll say," Kyle replied. "Am I in trouble for being away so long?"

"Oh, heavens no! Love never gives up. I knew it would be a while before we spoke again. I know you have many questions for me."

Kyle regarded her, not sure what to ask first. As he hesitated, she began. "The answer to your first question is yes. I'm still living. The answer to your next question is you will find me in the fullness of time. You will have to find your way through the winding labyrinth by yourself. Serenity is found by looking inward, not by following another's path."

"That hardly seems fair," Kyle responded. "So, when is the fullness of time?"

"You will know—just like you knew to reconnect with me now."

"I think the piece of your dress helped with that." Kyle paused before continuing. "Okay. Help me understand this term "two-spirited.""

Grandmother leaned forward on her staff while still seated and squinted her eyes. "What do *you* think it means?"

"I think it has something to do with me being gay."

"I'm not too fond of the term gay because it focuses primarily on sexuality, when in reality two-spiritedness has more to do primarily with your spirituality and uniqueness. The secondary aspect of your sexuality simply follows your spirit."

Kyle interrupted his grandmother's explanation, "I'm not sure Dad and the rest of the charismatic community would see my orientation anything other than demon possession at worst or plain old sin at best."

Helena stamped her staff on the ground. "I told you years ago that he is threatened by your giftedness—him and the rest of those in power." Her voice became gentler as she continued. "Let me help you understand just how special you are from a Native American perspective. Nearly all the tribes in the Americas recognized and honored two-spirits. Because two-spirited people have both male and female spirits combined in one body, it's believed that they can see all perspectives of an issue. In the current culture, being gay, as you put it, is a categorization of physical attraction to a member of the same sex. But, in the tradition of my people, they held was a much-honored place in the community. Two-spirited people are the direct messengers of Divine and the seers of all things unseen. As such, they are the shamans, healers, and spiritual leaders in the tribe. This is *your* heritage, Kyle. This is *your* gift."

"I just don't know..." Kyle hesitated. "I mean the Bible says..."

His grandmother stamped the ground again with her staff, "Misinterpreted nonsense when it comes to *homosexuality*! The ways of Spirit never change! You have been subdued and brainwashed for more than thirty years, my precious child. And, why? Why? Because you radiate energy on a level above the typical human. Why do you think you are pulled or attracted to other two-spirited men? I know in some circles they call it 'gaydar', but the reality is that the energy frequency of two same-spirited individuals draws the attention. Your father knows that he will never have the connection to Spirit like you do. People like him usurp your energy for the sake of power alone. Your father's love is not for Spirit, but for power." She paused and looked at her young student. "Kyle, you have struggled for years, not only because you didn't fit into the mold of what boys or men were supposed to do or be, but because you know deep inside yourself that your connection to God is very different than the 15, 000 people who attend your father's church. Am I right?"

Kyle chuckled, "I was just telling Ruth that today."

"So...stop resisting the natural flow of life. Be the blade of grass in a fresh spring of water, as I showed you years ago. Remember those lessons? You have been rooted in bad soil. You aren't like anyone else. You can't *be* like others. It is unnatural for you. You have tried every path, but your own. In a traditional community of my people, you would have been identified at an early age with your giftedness. The signs of you playing with dolls and having only girls for friends as a young boy would have been evidence enough for my people to have taught you at an early age about your gift. The special secrets and traditions would have been given to you. It is sad that this is not the case in our current culture. As religious as this nation is, it is one of the most spiritually deprived because it subdues the true teachers."

"But, Grandmother, I'll loose everything if I do what I feel is right...my job, my family, my friends..."

"I know, Kyle. I know. And this was foretold." Helena closed her eyes and recited, "If the world hate you, ye know that it hated me before it hated you. If ye were of the world, the world would love his own: but because ye are not of the world, but I have chosen you out of the world, therefore the world hateth you[8]." She opened her eyes and looked directly at her grandson. "Do you remember that? Remember that your world will crumble around you?"

Kyle nodded his head. "What do I do now?"

"Your spirit will guide you to serenity. Listen to the still, small voice that is always speaking to you and you will find your path."

Suddenly, a blaring beeping noise shattered the air around them. Kyle's body jolted awake and he reached to turn off the alarm clock. Pulling the piece of purple material from under his pillow, he held it in front of his face. "Well, Grandmother, I guess I have some searching to do."

Kyle sat at his computer in his office at the church, editing the final draft of his father's latest book entitled *A Holy War on Secular America's Political and Media Elite.* In Eli's latest book, he was taking aim at the "liberal left media and political machinery that is degenerating the country". His call to arms included asking readers to donate to his latest not-for-profit organization, The Foundation for Biblical Ethics, which would help infuse Christian values back into mainstream America. Kyle's body involuntarily shuddered as he read the excerpt he was editing:

You can not call yourself a Christian and vote for anyone who supports abortion or the gay agenda. Here's what the Word of God says in 1 Corinthians 6:9-10 (King James Version):

Do you not know that the wicked will not inherit the kingdom of God? Do not be deceived: Neither the sexually immoral nor

*idolaters nor adulterers nor male prostitutes nor homosexual of-
fenders nor thieves nor the greedy nor drunkards nor slanderers
nor swindlers will inherit the kingdom of God.'*

*It is understood by most followers of Christ not to partici-
pate in sexually immoral activity; however, when it comes to
our elected officials, we have thrown the commands of God out
with the trash. The very act of voting for a politician that
supports these immoral causes is the same as participating in
the act itself! The blood on the abortionist's hands is the same
blood you have on your own if you voted for an official that
supports the killing of a child. If you voted for a candidate that
supports gay marriage and gay rights, you might as well lie in
bed with someone of the same sex. You will stand before God
on Judgment Day and give an account of your voting record!
Your inheritance will not be in the Kingdom of God, but in the
eternal fires of Hell.*

*It is time to wake up, Church! Shake the slumber from your
head and speak with clarity to your elected officials. While we
were able to amend the state constitution in Ohio to never accept gay marriage, the battle still rages in other states. And,
don't think for a moment that the war is over! All it takes is an
activist judge to overturn a law and state that it is unconsti-
tutional. It is time to quit allowing a small minority to dictate
their agenda to the overwhelming history of the true definition
of holy matrimony.*

Kyle stared blankly at the computer screen and
wished he could just walk away from editing his father's
book and never see it again. He thought about the explanation of two-spirits from his grandmother and wondered if they were allowed to marry in their tribes. *That
would be a slightly different perspective on Dad's 'overwhelming*

history' Kyle thought.. A knock at his office door broke his train of thought and he quickly said, "Come in."

Dan White opened the door, stepped inside the office, and closed the door behind him. He was dressed in his usual fitted khaki pants and polo. Kyle looked at him and smiled while trying not to notice how well the pants and polo hugged Dan's fit build. "Um, Kyle," Dan began tentatively, "are we still on for lunch today? I just finished putting the score together for Pastor Deborah's Mother's Day Service, so I can break any time."

"Wow! The Mother's Day service is a month away and you already have the music for it? You're on top of things."

"You know how your mother likes a good plan. She asked me to have it ready before this weekend so that she can hear it while she's recuperating from her biopsy since she won't be able to attend services Sunday." Kyle chuckled quietly inside of himself at the word biopsy. That was another of his mother's plans. Instead of telling the congregation that she was having breast augmentation, it was "leaked" that she was having a breast biopsy. "How is your mother, anyway?"

Kyle thought of Ruth's comment the day before and said, "Oh, she's feeling rather perky." He thought it best to change the subject and decided to answer Dan's question. "I forgot and packed a lunch today, but I could still go with you."

"That's cool. I packed mine, too. Since it's such a nice day, maybe we could just eat at the outside pavilion together." Dan was referring to the recreation park on a section of the church's property.

"Yeah, that works for me. I can break away now, if you like."

"I'll just grab my lunch out of my office and we can go," Dan answered a bit nervously.

Kyle gathered his lunch and met Dan outside of his office. They walked in an uneasy silence to the pavilion. The scent of spring was in the air and a gentle breeze urged them towards a picnic table. They sat across from one another, and dug into their lunches, both waiting for the other to speak. Finally, Dan could not take the stillness anymore. "What are we going to do about this?"

Kyle took another bite of his turkey breast sandwich before answering. "Dan, I don't know what you're going to do and I'm not sure what I'm going to do. I know that I'm *not* going to say a word to anyone about you, so I don't want you to worry about that."

"Thanks, Kyle. I can't believe I was stupid enough to send you a picture." Dan laughed nervously. "I've just struggled with this all my life."

"So have I, Dan, and quite honestly I'm tired of struggling. The truth is, I'm gay, and there's nothing I can do to change it."

"Oh, come on, Kyle. You're not a fag. You've been married and have kids—just like me. All you need to do is get remarried and everything will work out."

"Really? Do you *really* believe that, Dan? Surely you don't! I use to believe it, but not now."

"You're not gay, man!" Dan's voice was emphatic.

"Are you trying to convince me or yourself? I don't know about you, but I've always been attracted to men.

There's just this drive in me to be held and loved by another man. It's not just sexual. There is so much more to it. Surely you understand."

"So, you're just going to throw in the towel on finding deliverance?"

"Dan, I don't believe anymore that there is deliverance. For over thirty years, I've condemned myself for finding men like you attractive. Even when I was married, I was sure that I wouldn't make it to heaven because of my pull to other men."

"But you have children, Kyle. That proves something doesn't it?"

"Yeah, it proves I have a vivid imagination and was able to father children. It doesn't prove that I was cured or healed or whatever term you want to use. I'm tired of the self-loathing, Dan. I can't tell you what the right choice is for you, but I really think that I just need to be honest with myself and everyone else."

"Whoa, Kyle! It sounds like you're going to do something totally irrational. You can't just come out and say you're gay. You have a family, even if you *are* divorced. You have a responsibility to your parents and this church. My God, you're on the payroll here! Your father depends on you to edit his books and the website. I'm sure he plans on leaving the church to you when he dies. This huge enterprise could all be yours! Are you even thinking about what you're saying?"

"Yeah, I've thought about it all. I haven't made any firm decisions, yet. I'm just saying that I'm tired. I realize that I would be loosing out on a lot if I were to admit to being gay, but I feel as if I'm dying a slow death now."

Dan looked around to make sure no one was near. When he confirmed that they were alone, he said, "Kyle, there is another option."

"What do you mean?"

"Look…we both have a lot to loose if anything got out about either one of us. It would be a perfect situation for both of us to comfort each other."

"What?" Kyle wasn't sure what he was hearing.

"You know…we each have needs that we could meet for the other. We have the perfect cover since we work together. No one would suspect a thing. I mean, I've always found you attractive and I'd be lying if I said I'd never daydreamed about you and wondered what you look like out of your clothes."

Kyle sat in silence. His left hand trembled as it held his uneaten sandwich. He looked across the picnic table at the handsome, blond-haired man. . Dan's dark brown eyes searched Kyle's face longingly as his left hand rested across the table within inches of Kyle's right. Kyle felt an electrical pull on his fingers towards Dan's hand. He wanted to run from Dan's seductive stare, but at the same time couldn't pull himself away. He felt dizzy as the blood drained from his head and filled his lower body.

"You feel it, too, don't you, Kyle? Why fight it? It's perfect for us both."

The urging in Dan's voice and in Kyle's own body were too much. "Dan, I need some time alone." Dan looked confused. "I'm not turning you down, Dan. I just need to think about it for a while. I'll see you back in the office later?"

Dan felt confident that Kyle would come around and answered, "Absolutely. Thanks for hearing me out. Let me know what you think, man." Dan stood up from the table and leaned onto it with palms down towards Kyle. "You don't have a clue how handsome you are…do you, Kyle?"

Kyle's face flushed red. No one had ever told that him before. "I guess not, Dan. Thanks." Kyle followed Dan with his eyes as he made his way back towards the church. His stomach was jittery and his hands trembled. *What am I thinking? Stop it! He's a married man.* Kyle grabbed his lunch box and shoved the empty plastic bag into it before getting up from the table and returning to the church.

Chapter 7

Kyle was in his office when his father walked in. Enthusiastically, he said, "Son, this is hot. I need you to write a script for me to tape tomorrow in the studio. We're going to start offering a prepaid debit card to covenant members of the church." Kyle was dumbfounded by his father's request. "Are you in there, boy? Did you hear what I said?"

"Yeah, Dad. I heard you. I'm just not sure what you're talking about."

"I'm talking about a prepaid debit card that people can use to make purchases anywhere they'd be able to use a credit card."

"Okay," Kyle responded hesitantly.

Eli was visibly irritated by his son's lack of enthusiasm. "This is important. I need to start airing the piece immediately, so, get to it! Write something for me. Are you taking notes?" Kyle grabbed a notepad and pen and nodded. "Okay, I want to say something about supporting the ministry work of Earth Reaping Church with every purchase—but save that part for the end. It's a one-minute spot, did I mention that? The focus should be on witnessing, since the debit card will have the Earth Reaping emblem on the front. Say something about a portion of every purchase helping the effort in bringing the country back to its Godly heritage and Biblical morals."

Kyle asked, "What? Do you mean to say that the church will profit from this debit card?"

"Just get the script together for me. I need it right away!" Eli's tone that told Kyle not to ask questions. "I'll have it before the end of the day?"

"Yes, Dad."

"Good. Oh, almost forgot...I have to make a pastoral visitation call so I'll be leaving in a few minutes. Just email the script to me and I'll get it in the morning when I come in."

Kyle fought to conceal his expression of exasperation and quickly answered, "It'll be there. I won't leave until it's finished."

"See you in the morning, Kyle."

"See you, Dad." Eli left Kyle's office. Kyle looked at his notepad and shook his head. "Boy, Dad, you sure know how to make money don't you?" Kyle whispered. He wasn't sure whether to jump into writing the script or finish reformatting the church bylaws file that his father had sent him after lunch. He reread the paragraph he was working on:

"The government of the Church is in the hands of the Pastor, who has ultimate authority under Christ; as such, the church must function as a theocracy with the Pastor as the sole authority in church affairs. It is our belief that a democracy is not God's way, and the purpose of the Church is not to do the will of the majority, but the will of God. Thus, all final decisions regarding the church in every aspect are in the hands of the Pastor as appointed by Christ."

Kyle shook his head again and rubbed his eyes. "Sounds like a dictatorship to me," he mumbled to himself. He saved the file and opened a new one to begin work on the script his father had requested. Although Kyle didn't believe or necessarily like everything about his father's style of ministry, he did enjoy writing and could loose himself for hours working and re-working words—even if they were someone else's. When he heard a rapping at his office door, he looked at the clock on his desktop and realized it was after six.

"Yes...the door's open." Kyle answered.

Pastor Dan walked into Kyle's office and closed the door behind him. "I was hoping you were still here. What are you working on?"

Kyle rubbed his eyes, leaned back in his chair and stretched. "Dad needs a script by tomorrow for the church's new debit card. I was just polishing it off and getting ready to go. What are you still doing here?"

Dan smiled at him and said, "Looks like we're working on the same thing. Pastor Eli wanted a moving piece of music for the introduction of the script. I was writing something inspirational for the ad."

Dan stood in front of Kyle's desk and stretched his arms towards the ceiling. When he did, his polo lifted upwards and Kyle couldn't help but notice the thin trail of hair that started at Dan's belly button and then disappeared into the waistband of his pants. Dan plopped down in the chair in front of Kyle's desk and reclined back with his legs stretched out wide in front of him. He placed his hands on the inside of his thighs. Kyle's glanced at Dan's fly. Dan noticed the fleeting look and smiled at Kyle. "What are you thinking, Stud?"

Kyle felt his face flush with blood and stammered, "I was thinking that your dinner is probably going to be cold if you don't get home to your wife and kids."

"It's no problem. I called and told her I'd be late tonight because of the ad." Dan grinned and rocked his legs back and forth. "I think we're the only staff left here. It looks like all the other offices were locked up for the day."

"Well, I should get out of here, too." Kyle stood up and started collecting his briefcase and lunchbox.

Dan jumped up and walked around to stand next to Kyle. "Is there anything I can help you with?" Dan's hand gently grabbed Kyle's arm. Kyle turned and looked at the minister of music and felt his body quiver. Dan noticed and grabbed Kyle's other arm with his free hand. "Its okay, Kyle. No one is here but you and me. I'll lock the door if you want." Dan's brown eyes beckoned. Their faces moved close. Kyle could feel Dan's warm breath on his lips and the racing of his heart. Their lips touched. The energy of passion pulsed through the two men. Dan pulled Kyle close and surrounded him with his firm arms. Kyle felt the warmth of Dan's body and wanted to surrender to the sweet ecstasy of the moment.

Kyle pulled back and placed both hands on Dan's chest. "Dan," he started with labored breath, "I...I can't do this."

Dan placed both of his hands on the sides of Kyle's face, "Its okay. We're not going to hurt anyone. It's just two friends showing their love for each other."

Every part of Kyle's body was urging him to satisfy its longing, but his mind was taking control. "No, Dan. I just can't. God knows I want to…"

"So do I, Kyle. And I know you want to, also. I can feel how much you want to." Dan's grip on Kyle's waist tightened as he pulled their bodies together.

Kyle felt the physical intensity growing between them and yearned to submit to the passion of the moment, yet, his mind overruled his desire. "I'm sorry, Dan. Really I am. We can't do this. You're married. If you weren't married, I don't think I would hesitate—except for the fact that we're in my father's church." Kyle chuckled nervously as he pulled away.

Dan released him. "Okay, Kyle. I can't say that I'm not disappointed. I guess you could feel how badly I want you." Dan backed away and smiled at him with a cocky assurance. "God, you're a heck of a kisser! Those thick lips of yours are pure heaven. Maybe some other time, Kyle?"

"Maybe, Dan. Maybe." Kyle regained his breath and composure in spite of his body's desire to resume what they had started. As Dan left the office, he turned looked at Kyle one last time before closing the door.

Kyle sat and placed his head in his hands as he rested his elbows on the desk. After several moments of deep breathing and shaking his head, Kyle shut down his computer. He was just getting ready to leave his office when his cell phone rang. He looked at the caller ID and recognized his parents' home number. "Hello."

"Kyle, it's Mom. Are you still at the church?"

"Yeah, I'm still here."

"Is your father still there?"

"No. He left several hours ago. He's not home?"

"No. I haven't seen or heard from him."

"Well, Dad was going to do some visitation the last I talked to him. Maybe he's still calling on someone."

Deborah let out a sigh. "Well, it would be nice if he would check on me. I *did* just have surgery."

Kyle rolled his eyes, thankful that they were on the phone, rather than in person for her to see his disrespect. "I'm sure he'll be home soon, Mom. You know Dad's never late for supper."

"Oh, there he is now, Kyle. I'll talk to you later. Bye."

"Bye, Mom."

Eli walked into the kitchen where Deborah was just hanging up the phone and looked around the room. "What's for supper, Deb?"

"Hi, honey. I'm home. How are you doing with your recovery?" Deborah sarcastically intoned.

"Ah, come on, Debbie. There's no need to be that way with me. I'm just a little hungry. I've had a really tough day"

Deborah's anger boiled over. "And, I'm just a little sore from the surgery. I would've thought that you'd be a little more concerned about *me*, instead of your stomach! After all, I did this for *you*," Deborah stood up straight and pushed out her new accessories with one arm propped on the counter.

"I'm sorry, Hon. How are you feeling today?"

"Better," she said, softening. "Where were you? I tried calling your cell phone but you didn't answer."

"I'm sorry about that. I had to stop at the hospital after I left the office to visit one of the members. I left the phone in the car so that it wouldn't ring while I was praying with Mrs. Perry. Luckily, she was resting and I was in and out of the hospital in no time."

Deborah tried to hide what she was really feeling when she asked, "So, you were at the church all day?"

"Yeah, until about an hour ago." Eli emptied his pockets onto the kitchen island. Deborah looked closely at his cell phone and change laid out on the counter. She noticed that his wedding band was missing from his ring finger. Eli instantly stopped what he was doing as if he had just remembered something. "Oh, I left my briefcase in the car. I'll be right back, Deb."

As soon as Eli left the kitchen, Deborah grabbed his cell phone and searched his call log. She saw where she had called several times and then saw a call made to a number she didn't know. She quickly grabbed a pad of paper and scribbled the number. She slid the piece of paper into her front pants pocket just as Eli returned, briefcase in hand. He set it down. Deborah looked at his hand. He was wearing his wedding band. She looked him over very carefully and noticed his perfectly combed hair—almost *too* perfect.

A sinking feeling hit her in the pit of her stomach. She knew this feeling—it was a feeling that she had had many times in their forty years of marriage. She balled her hands into fists and started walking towards the powder room just off of the kitchen.

"Where are you going, Deb?" Eli asked.

She shook her head several times and just made it to the toilet before vomiting. Eli stood in the kitchen, listening. "Are you okay? Are the painkillers making you sick?"

Deborah emerged from the bathroom, wiping her mouth with a towel. Her eyes were red and watery. "I guess so, Eli. You know how sensitive I am to medication." She forced a smile, when all she wanted to do was to break into tears.

"Why don't you go rest on the couch and I'll just make a peanut butter sandwich for myself."

"I think that's a good idea, Eli. Get your own supper." She wondered if her last sentence sounded venomous, but decided she would blame it on her upset stomach if Eli questioned her. He didn't.

Kyle had just walked through the door of his apartment with two bags of groceries when his cell phone rang again. He looked at the caller ID and saw that it was Ruth. "Joe's pool hall," he answered. "Who in the hall do you want?"

Ruth recognized Kyle's voice and responded playfully, "I'm looking for the guy with the big stick."

Kyle chuckled, "Well, you're going to have to call back 'cause this guy doesn't have a big stick; but if you're looking for the guy with big balls, I can help you."

"Well...it's about time you grew some new ones!"

"They're getting there, Sis. What's up?"

"I just thought I would check in on my favorite brother in the whole world! How are you doing?"

"I'm not sure how sincere that statement is since I'm your *only* brother. But, I'm doing pretty well. And you?"

"Just been worried about you." Ruth hesitated before continuing. "Kyle, do you have a few minutes to talk?"

"Yeah. Is something wrong?"

"No. I just wanted to let you know that I called Mom today to check up on her. She seemed a little upset because she couldn't get in touch with Dad for several hours. Do you know what he was doing or where he was when she couldn't reach him?"

"He was at the office until about two or three today, and then he said he had some visitations to do. You know how that goes. Who knows what he was doing on his visitation? I don't ask and he doesn't tell."

"Okay…I don't want to go there right now. Just the thought is a little disgusting to me."

"Anyway, Mom called me before I left the office and asked if I knew where he was. I told her what I knew. Why?"

"Kyle, she was really upset—more than normal. I think it might have been the medication talking, but she said something to the effect that she should have listened to her mother."

"What??? She said something about Grandmother?" Kyle could hardly believe what he was hearing.

"What she said was her 'ignorant Hocking County mother knew what she was talking about'. Now, I may not have the words exactly as she said them, but I did hear her say Hocking County, but I didn't want to press the issue because she was so angry. But, I thought that might be of some help in trying to find out if her mother is still alive."

"Oh, she's alive still."

"Did you find her?" Ruth asked with astonishment.

"No. I just know that she's still living."

"How do you know?"

"Trust me, Ruth. I *know*. I can't explain how I know...I just do."

"I'll take your word for it. You always have had a knack for knowing things before any proof surfaces. OH! I almost forgot. You're not going to believe what I promised Mom. I told her that Naomi and I would attend the Mother's Day service."

"Wow! I'm shocked."

"I had to tell her something uplifting since she was so irritated with Dad. I guess she caught me at a weak moment."

"Did she tell you that they'd be beaming the show live to all of the cable outlets that carry them?"

"What? You're kidding me, right?"

"I wish I were. They've been doing it for the last couple of years. May is fund-raising month so they go live during the Mother's Day service to enamor the throngs of followers."

"Oh, great. Naomi's first exposure to a crazy charismatic service and it'll be beamed live across the nation."

Kyle laughed. "Not just the nation...but the whole earth!"

"Thanks for making it even more intimidating for me. I just hope Naomi doesn't start screaming from fear. Hell! I hope I don't make a scene myself—it's been so long since I've been a part of a Pentecostal service, I might be the one screaming! All I have to say is that you had better be there to support me. Mark refuses to participate in their 'mass hypnosis' as he calls it."

"I'll be there, Sis. I'm there every service. I don't have a choice."

"Good. Maybe we could get a glass or two of wine down before the service! They do use real wine for communion, don't they?" Ruth laughed as spoke. "Wouldn't that be a great headline? Earth Reaping Church pastor's daughter falls off of stage in a drunken stupor at special Mother's Day service."

"You don't have to worry about that. This is a grape-juice-only church. Even holy wine is a sin!" Kyle clucked. "Although, it would certainly be a ratings-booster, I'm sure. I tell you what...you stumble off the stage and I'll announce to the world that I'm gay."

The Ruth's laughter stopped. Kyle wondered why he had said what he said as the silence stretched out between them. "Uh...I'm kidding, Ruth. Just kidding."

Ruth's voice turned empathetic. "Its okay, Kyle. Really, it's okay. I guess you finally did grow some balls! So, are you coming out to me?"

Kyle felt his heart leap into his throat. His mind raced, trying to figure out what to say next. All that came out was, "Yes."

Ruth let out a deep breath and almost giggled. "I'm so happy to hear that you're not lying anymore. Oh, my god! I can't believe it. I am so proud of you, Little Brother! I've always known—always. I have been trying to get you to tell me ever since your divorce. Have you told anyone else?"

"Absolutely not. I can't believe I just told you. You can't tell Mom and Dad. Let me be the one to do that. Okay?"

"Can I tell Mark?"

Kyle knew that she would tell him anyway, so he said, "Sure. It's okay. I just have to figure out how to break it to Mom and Dad. I'm sure I'll be looking for another job as soon as I say something."

"Don't say anything until you find another job, Kyle. Once you secure a position somewhere else, then tell them."

"That's my plan, Sis."

"Are you seeing someone?"

"No. I don't want to risk exposing anyone to the family until I'm completely out and secure in another job." Kyle paused. "I know Mom and Dad are going to have a fit when I'm totally open about this. Dad's really going to shit since he's been paying for counseling for me."

"So, Dad's aware of this and he's been sending you to counseling? Ha! I love it! Well, here's what I think: Fuck 'em, Kyle. Fuck anyone who isn't supportive." Kyle giggled warmly at the support in his sister's voice. "Do you want me to keep an eye out for a man here?"

Ruth was enjoying herself and her voice was filled with excitement.

"That's okay, Sis. I think I can work on that by myself."

"I'm just offering. I'm here to be supportive and help find a man for my brother."

Kyle ignored the part about finding a man and replied, "I know you are, and I love you for that. If I need anything, you'll be the first one I call."

"I'm proud of you little brother. I really am. You're much stronger than you think. You're going to be just fine."

"Thanks. I love you, sis."

"I love you. We'll talk more later, right?"

"Sure thing. Bye."

"Bye, Kyle."

Deborah sat at the computer in the home office. It was after midnight and Eli was sleeping soundly in their master suite at the other end of the house. She logged onto the Internet and went to a website for reverse phone number lookup. As she waited for the web site to open, she pressed flat the piece of paper with the phone number she had copied from Eli's cell phone. She typed in the number and hit the search button. A few short seconds passed before a name and address appeared on the screen: *Joni Paisley, Gibbstone Drive, Columbus.*

Deborah crumpled the paper with her left hand and slammed her fist on top of the desk. Her eyes welled. She looked at the name again. She knew Joni very well. She was on the church Praise Team and was a frequent vocal soloist. In fact, Joni had just been featured on a recent telecast promoting her first CD. Deborah pictured the forty-year-old in her mind—her beautiful, long, wavy blonde hair that matched her equally striking voice, her petite build, and her piercing blue eyes.

Deborah shook her head and thought, *"Maybe I'm wrong. Joni did just release a new CD with the help of the church orchestra. Eli probably had a contract for her to sign or something. I just need to quit thinking the worst. Besides, I'm the First Lady of Earth Reaping Church and no one can take that away from me. Not only that, but I'm in demand for my own evangelistic ministry."* She closed the web page and checked her email. She saw that she had an email with an attachment from Pastor Dan White. She smiled when she realized it was the score for the Mother's Day service. She decided to wait to open the email until the following day and shut down the computer.

Helena was sitting in the kitchen of her old farmhouse in Laurelville, Ohio. Her friend and employee, D.J., was almost finished washing the dishes. D.J. was in her late sixties, but had the vigor of someone half her age. Helena clucked at her, "I told you to wait 'til we get home to do those dishes. You look awful silly in your Sunday best, doing dishes!"

D.J. looked at Helena and chuckled, "I can't stand coming home to a dirty kitchen. You'd think that after all these years of me working for you that you'd know me better than that. Besides, you know I gotta keep my hands busy when I'm nervous. Are you sure you want to go through with this?"

Helena looked her over. The full-figured woman looked very good in her black dress with the over-sized brown and black striped blazer. The pearl necklace she wore contrasted sharply against the neckline of the dress. D.J. wiped her hands on a dishtowel before fluffing her reddish-blonde hair with her fingers.

Not hearing an answer, D.J. said, "Well…I know you well enough that when you don't answer me it means that your mind is set." D.J. walked over and sat on one of the red vinyl steel chairs across from Helena. "Will the boy be there?"

"It's not time for us to meet face to face yet." Helena responded. "Hand me my staff, would you?" D.J. spotted the staff next to the back door just off the kitchen and retrieved it for Helena before sitting down again. "Give me a moment and I'll make sure he doesn't get there." Helena held onto the staff and closed her eyes. D. J. closed her own eyes and bowed her head. Helena raised her free hand with the palm facing out toward the north. She felt a warm flow of energy pulse in her palm. A closed mouth smile spread across her face and she started swirling her hand as if stirring an invisible bucket of water. After motioning for several seconds, she closed her hand into a fist and said, "And it is so."

"So be it," echoed D.J. Both women opened their eyes and looked at each other.

"It will just be me and the women today. Our two-spirited boy will have to find his way here."

"You amaze me, Helena. If I knew where one of my grandchildren was and that he wanted to get in touch with me, I would move heaven and hell to get to him."

"Well, you can't move hell if you don't believe in it." Helena's eyes twinkled at her friend.

D.J. raised both her hands to face level and swatted downward. "Always trying to get a rise out of me ain't you?" She laughed and continued, "I can't say I understand everything you do and know, but I do know that you're just about always right. The only thing I can think of that you've been off on is Debbie. Her marriage has lasted longer than either one of us thought it would."

"That's because she's refused to learn; but, I'm afraid her days of refusal are about over. The Universe has a way breaking our stubborn streaks when we won't listen.

"I told you that you should have taken a shot gun to Elijah the first time he stepped near little Debbie! The Lord helps those who help themselves." D.J. broke out in laughter at her own words. She noticed Helena look at the clock. "Should we get on our way?"

"Yes, ma'am, I think we should." Helena's voice turned tender. "Thank you D. J. for helping me and driving me around. My physical eyes might not be as good as they use to be, but my spiritual eye is seeing better than it ever has." Helena looked at D.J. and said, "You have a beautiful aura about you today."

"I've been waiting for you to tell me what color I am today. So what is it? I hope it doesn't look bad with my black!"

"The red looks great with your black," Helena responded. "It's a perfect color for today since it's symbolic of enthusiasm. Red makes things happen!"

"Oh, I have a feeling something is going to happen today. Is that why you chose the red dress you're wearing?"

Helena looked down at the outfit she had on before answering, "Yes. You should always wear red in a challenging situation because it gives you the upper hand."

"That's why I like being around you, Helena. I learn something new everyday!" The two women rose from the table and prepared to leave the safety of the rural getaway known as Serenity.

Eli stood in his studio at the church in front of the camera wearing a Joseph A. Bank signature gold collection Italian designed and tailored three-button wool navy striped suit. The white dress shirt was accented by the light blue tie marked with black diamond shapes which matched perfectly to the silk square in the breast pocket. The chestnut, lace-up dress-shoes were perfectly polished. He nervously fidgeted with the cufflinks on his shirt as he tried to compose himself before going on the air.

"Thirty seconds before the break, Pastor Eli," a voice from behind the camera said. "Your spot will go live and then will be ready for the live telecast thirty minutes after that."

Eli pulled on the bottom of his suit jacket and smiled into the camera. He loved the exhilaration of going live.

He only wished that Deborah wasn't the one preaching today so that he could be the only one in the spotlight, but he had bigger things to tackle later in the day. He looked at a large glass window and saw Deborah, Ruth, and Naomi watching him. He winked at the three generations before returning his gaze back to the camera.

"Ten seconds, Pastor...and five...four...three... two...one."

The light on top of the camera came on. "Praise God, Saints!" Eli enthusiastically bellowed into the camera. "Today is a special Mother's Day Service here at Earth Reaping Church in Columbus, Ohio, where we are coving the earth with the unadulterated word of the one true God. You are invited to participate in the fire that is falling right here in Columbus, Ohio and spreading throughout the world right from your own home. With your generous love gifts, we are going into the *entire* world with the Gospel message of Jesus Christ, our Lord and Savior! It is through the faithful remnant like you that we are able to do as Jesus commanded and reach an unpreached, unsaved world. Millions are finding salvation through this ministry because of your commitment to our mission! Our very own first lady, Pastor Deborah, will be delivering an anointed message straight from the breath of the Holy Ghost in just thirty short minutes. I know you won't want to miss this soul-saving, spirit-sanctifying, and fire-baptizing time in the Lord. Call a friend, your mother, your sister, your daughter and join us in thirty minutes right here on this station to hear a word from God to all ladies of the world! And, may God bless the women of this great nation today and every Christian woman throughout the Earth!" Eli's timing was perfect and the light went out on the camera.

The voice behind the camera commented, "That was great, Pastor Eli. Thirty minutes before the service goes live."

Eli walked out of the studio through the glass door where Deborah, Ruth, and Naomi stood. "How was that? Did I look good?"

"You looked like a televangelist, Dad," Ruth commented.

Eli bent over to talk to his granddaughter, "Isn't this exciting Naomi? Your Pappy is on TV and you will be today, too!"

Naomi was a very bright young girl and would often say things that one would expect from someone older than she was. The strawberry blonde six-year-old looked up at her grandfather, "I don't get it, Pappy. But, if it makes you happy, I guess it's alright by me. I'm just worried about that fire you were talking about. I hope no one gets hurt."

Eli straightened and looked around questioningly as if he didn't hear his granddaughter's concern. "Where is Kyle, Deb? I wanted him to look over my introduction for you one more time before we went live."

"We haven't seen or heard from him. I tried calling his cell phone, but it must be turned off because it rolled straight to voice mail." Deborah answered.

"That boy exasperates me sometimes. Doesn't he know how much this live feed is costing the church? He has a responsibility to be here! Of all days to be late!"

Ruth muttered to herself, but loud enough for her parents to hear her. "Great…I'm at the circus without my brother."

Eli shot Ruth a cold glance. "Try to be civil and present yourself as a godly woman for the sake of your mother."

Ruth's eyes danced with flames and she started to say something when Naomi tugged on her red dress. "Mommy isn't it exciting we're going to be on TV? And there's going to be fire, too!"

"It certainly is something. I hope there's a good sprinkler system in this church," she responded sardonically.

Deborah brushed off her daughter's sarcasm. "Okay, girls. The ushers have the front pew blocked off for our family. When the opening song starts, they'll escort you to your seats. Hopefully, Kyle will be here by then and he'll walk in with you." Deborah was in her element, orchestrating every detail. "You'll hear Pastor Dan announce you as the Basil children and there will be a round of applause. If you want to wave to the congregation, it would be a nice touch—they like to feel connected to our celebrity status. When you arrive at your seats, remain standing with the rest of the congregation as Pastor Dan announces my arrival. I will then announce your father. Just follow the lead of the service after that."

Ruth could not believe what she was hearing. She just shook her head and said, "Okay, Mom. I'll smile and pretend like I'm having fun."

Deborah raised her left eyebrow and pursed her lips before replying. "If that's the best you can do, then I'll just have to accept it."

Kyle awoke with a jolt and looked at the clock on the night stand beside the bed. His eyes wouldn't focus on the numbers, but he knew from the sunlight coming through his bedroom window that it was way past his normal time to get up. He tried to sit up, but felt a pressure that was almost impossible to overcome. His head swirled and he felt sick to his stomach. With effort, he focused his eyes on the clock. Ten-fifteen! "Dear God! Mom and Dad are going to kill me. I'm supposed to be at the church." He swung his well-defined calves over the side of the bed and with much effort pushed himself up with his arms. "What is going on? Did I drink something bad last night?" Kyle tried to remember what he had done the night before, but only remembered talking to his sister about today's live telecast before going to bed.

"You didn't drink anything last night," a voice answered. Kyle turned towards the sound at the foot of his bed. He jumped at the sight of an elderly man with long gray hair and a heavily wrinkled, olive complexion. He wore no shirt and his pants appeared to be of Native American style. He sat on the flat-topped foot board with legs crossed. A white mist surrounded him and although his eyes were dark brown, a beautiful light emanated from them.

"What the…who the hell are you?" Kyle demanded, nearly shrieking, in his typical morning bass tones. He reached for the sheets to cover his half-naked body.

The man gave a familiar smile that Kyle was sure he recognized as his grandmother's. "The more appropriate question would be who in heaven am I?"

Kyle stared blankly at the man. "I must be dreaming." He slapped his cheeks with both hands and shook his head. "Jesus! I'm awake!"

The man laughed heartily at Kyle. "No, I'm not Jesus. But, the elders and I have been watching you for quite a while."

"Great! It's not bad enough that I have dreams that seem real but now I'm hallucinating!" Kyle threw the covers back and slid out of bed before walking to the dresser and retrieving his cell phone. "You'll just have to wait because I'm really *not* seeing you. I have to call Mom and Dad to let them know I'm on my way to church."

"The battery is dead, Kyle."

"What?" Kyle asked the man absently as he fumbled with the phone. The man was right. Kyle couldn't get his cell phone to respond. "Shit!" Kyle tossed the phone on his bed and walked out of the room towards the bathroom. He was now rethinking the wisdom of not having a traditional land-line phone. When he entered the bathroom, he saw the man sitting on the closed toilet once again with his legs crossed. "Oh God—not you again! *Please* leave me alone and let me shower in peace!"

The man smiled and said, "I'm afraid your hot water heater went out during the night."

Kyle reached for the sink and turned on the hot water faucet. He passed his hand under the flow. "Shit! Shit! Shit! It's freezing!" Kyle turned to the man on the toilet. "What are you doing to me? Now I'll have to leave without showering!"

"I really don't think you'll be going anywhere in the next couple of hours, son."

"I think *you* should stop thinking and leave *me* alone!" Kyle screeched. He exited the bathroom and returned to his bedroom and opened the closet door. He started searching for a dress shirt, but not one could be found among the t-shirts and polo's. He yanked a pair of khaki pants and polo out of the closet in a huff. He pulled the pants on and slid into the shirt before walking to the dresser. His head moved back and forth searching for his keys. He flung his arms up in frustration. "Shit! Where the hell are my keys?"

"Apparently, you locked them in your car last night when you ran outside to pull some change out of your console to tip the pizza delivery man. Remember turning the dome light on in the car? Well, you left it on all night and now the battery to your car is dead."

Kyle spun around and glared at the man who was now sitting in the middle of the bed with his legs crossed.

"Okay!" Kyle yelled with tears in his eyes. "You have my attention. Who in *heaven* are you and what do you want from *me*?"

The man reached his hand towards Kyle and motioned for him to sit on the bed. Kyle hesitantly moved towards the man and sat on the edge of the bed. "You can call me Papaw, Kyle."

Kyle was trying to make sense out the total absurdity of the events happening before his eyes. "Are you... or...were you Grandmother's husband?" He ran his hands through his hair and held it back from his face while he tried to regain his composure. He felt pressure building in his head and rubbed his temples with his fingers. "I think I'm having a nervous breakdown."

"Take a deep breath, Kyle. Everything is as it should be." The man scanned Kyle with his eyes and Kyle felt a sense of love surround him. He took a deep breath as a sensation of peace filled him and the headache subsided. "I am your Great-Grandfather, Running Buck. Your grandmother is my daughter."

"Why am I seeing you while I'm awake? I just dream about Grandmother when I'm sleeping, but you're here in the flesh!"

"Not exactly in the flesh, son." Grandfather reached towards Kyle to touch him, but all Kyle felt was a pulse of energy when Grandfather's hand rested on his leg. "You see, your grandmother is still in the flesh and doesn't have all the liberties to appear to you while you're awake. Once a spirit crosses over, there are more options in how we appear, than just through dreams. The numbness you feel in your head is a result of our energies connecting to each other."

"You said something about the elders. What exactly were you talking about?"

Grandfather looked at the young man with intense wisdom. "My people call us Elders. Your Bible calls us a Great Cloud of Witnesses. Some refer to us as Masters or Guides. It's just something we do on the other side to encourage family members and loved ones on this side. And, today is a special day for many in your family."

"And that's why I need to get to church," Kyle's voice was filled with emotion. "Ruth hasn't been there in nearly twenty years. The service is being broadcast live and they expect me to be on hand!"

"Well, that's just not going to happen. Your time is here with me...not with your sister and not with your parents. They have their own special lessons to learn today of which you are not a part. They *expect* things from you that are not a part of your life purpose. You have allowed others' expectations of you to blind you for too long. It's time you stopped living up to their expectations and follow your purpose."

Kyle lowered his head and slowly shook it. "I'm not sure what my purpose is or where to begin, Papaw. I'm torn about who I am."

"You're not torn my beautiful two-spirited mortal. You are perfectly balanced. You just feel torn because the rest of your world is imbalanced. This modern world where you live has been built by a religious view that has removed everything holy from its natural setting. By subscribing to the religious and scientific dogma of these times, the majority of society—including most religious institutions—has become completely secular."

"I think my father would sharply disagree with you about his church being secular, although he would acknowledge that the culture is not spiritual."

Grandfather scoffed. "Your father's church is completely secular! It is pure capitalism governed by a despot! In Biblical terms, he has a form of godliness but denies its power. He is so blind to true spirituality that he has created a false doctrine that promotes himself and fills his bank account. His spiritual energy is so low that he is unable to recognize the wisdom that you carry naturally. It is such a shame. All indigenous cultures have recognized the giftedness in two spirit people. It only subsided as they were conquered and evangelized by western nations bent on dominating the riches of the earth."

"Okay. I've heard Grandmother tell me the same thing. But, I don't know what in direction to go. I'll loose everything in my current world."

"What you stand to gain is worth far more than what you will loose. Listen to your heart—to love—and you will be find balance and direction. After all, it is love that brought me here today."

Kyle looked questioningly at Grandfather. "I know nothing about you. How did love bring you here?"

"I didn't say *your* love brought me here. I said love. Your grandmother's love for you called upon me and I responded. All these things that happened to you today—oversleeping, your dead cell phone, cold water, no dress shirt, and the rest—all were perfectly orchestrated by the Great Spirit to keep you from attending church today."

"But, why?" Kyle pleaded.

"Your family is going to learn to live their lives without you there to make them happy. I know you've seen

yourself as the weak one of the family, but the truth is…
you're the strongest one of them all. You've had to be,
to fit into an unwelcoming world."

Kyle raised one eyebrow like his mother, "I'm not
sure I believe that I'm the strongest. Ruth has been the
trailblazer between the two of us."

"I won't argue that point with you…she certainly is a
pistol! She has a lot of your grandmother's traits which
she will discover in her own time."

"What do you mean? Is she going to find Grandmother before I do?"

A snicker slipped from Grandfather's lips. "Your
grandmother is going to find her."

"Today? Is that why I'm being held prisoner in
my own apartment?" Kyle regarded the man and felt
that the answers to his questions were affirmatives.
"So, Grandmother shows up at church today and I have
to miss it. That hardly seems fair!"

"Your journey is different, Kyle. Each of us has his
own labyrinth to negotiate. You will look back later and
understand why you did not meet your Grandmother
today. Divine order creates Divine appointments."

D.J. eased her white Lincoln into the parking lot of
Earth Reaping Church. "My God! I've never seen such
a parking lot for a church. It looks like a mall parking
lot. All these people…I just can't believe it. I've never
seen a church with parking lot attendants telling you
where to park. It's like a sporting event!" She stopped
the car beside one of the attendants, rolled down her

window, and asked, "Is there a place I can drop my dear friend off so that she doesn't have to walk so far?"

The man smiled at her and looked into the car at Helena. "Sure is, ma'am. Why don't you pull up next to the overhang there at the entrance of the church and park in one of the handicap spots." He pulled a piece of paper from his clipboard and handed it to D.J. "Just put that in your dashboard and the parking attendants will direct you to an open spot close to the entrance."

D.J. looked at the paper which read, "Priority Parking", and placed it on the dashboard. "I thank you now," she responded with glee. As she moved the vehicle in the direction the attendant had indicated, she said to Helena, "At least we get priority parking. Of course, they may regret that in a little bit."

Helena heard her but was deep in thought. Her eyes remained closed as they maneuvered through the parking lot. When the car stopped, Helena's eyes opened. "I need my staff, dear."

"I know, Helena. But before I get it…are you sure you want to do this? It won't bother me a bit to turn around and go back to Serenity without stepping a foot inside the church."

Helena looked resolved. "No, D.J., we're not turning back. If Jesus was able to clean the temple as he was directed, then I should follow through with the orders given to me. I've come to do a little house cleaning and I ain't afraid of a little dirt."

Ruth and Naomi stood in front of a pair of doors just outside of the church sanctuary with an usher named Charlie. Ruth's mother and father waited at their entrance point in a hallway just a few feet away. Ruth's stomach knotted at the thought of entering the sanctuary after being away from her parents' church for so long. The building they were in today was a different church than the one she had attended while growing up. The one she was familiar with had since been razed to make way for this monstrosity of a structure. Ruth eyed Charlie and thought he looked more like a bouncer than a saintly usher. He was well over six feet tall and the arm-seams of his suit jacket seemed like they would burst open at any moment from the size of his biceps. As she looked at his arms, Ruth giggled at the thought of the clothes ripping off this Incredible Hulk.

"Has anyone ever called you Hulk before?" Ruth asked Charlie ever so sweetly.

He looked at her with a cold stare. "I've heard about you and your smart mouth from your father. I'm not amused." He turned his back towards her and looked blankly at the closed doors leading into the sanctuary. "You just follow directions today and everything will go smoothly. If you don't…well, I'll just have to escort you out of the service."

Ruth straightened her back as if she had just been scolded by a parent. Involuntarily, she reached for Naomi and pulled her daughter closer. Naomi sensed the tension and stared wide-eyed at her mother. *I'm gonna kill Kyle for leaving me here in this carnival side-show,* she thought.

One of the doors opened just a crack and another usher said to Charlie, "On Pastor Dan's cue, bring her in." Charlie nodded. The thirty-member-orchestra began to play and the hundred-member-choir started to sing:

Can't stop praising His name

I just can't stop praising His name

I just can't stop praising His name

Jesus[9]

Then Dan White's voice bellowed, "Welcome, saints, to Earth Reaping Church in Columbus, Ohio. Today is a special Mother's Day Live broadcast and it is my privilege to be the first to welcome Pastor Eli and Deborah's daughter and granddaughter!"

Charlie looked at Ruth and Naomi. "Let's go. Follow me." As they entered the sanctuary, a roar of applause filled the room. Naomi held onto her mother's hand and waved with her free one. Ruth kept her eyes forward and felt the blood rush to her face. *This is humiliating,* she thought. They reached the empty front row, center-stage pew and Charlie motioned to let them know that they had arrived at their designated location. Once Ruth and Naomi turned to face the front of the church, Charlie moved into position at the steps leading up to the pulpit, facing the congregation with his hands clasped behind his back as if he were a secret service agent protecting the President.

The music and choir continued and Dan White announced, "And now...our very own First Lady and

Special Speaker today...Pastor Deborah Basil!" Deborah entered the stage from the left looking poised and confident. Again, another roar went up from the stadium-sized sanctuary. She smiled and waved as she moved towards the pulpit and took a hand held microphone from Pastor Dan. Her dark chocolate, double-weave wool jacket with patch pockets and two buttons matched perfectly with the straight skirt and brown peep-toe pumps. The light teal silk cami she wore under the jacket accentuated her now perfectly rounded breasts.

"Oh, hallelujah!" She called into the microphone as she bent towards the stage. The congregation responded with their own hallelujahs. "I feel the Holy Ghost in the House this morning! Woo!" Again, the crowd cheered and the music continued. "This is the day that the Lord has made! Let us rejoice and be glad in it! Huh!" Deborah accompanied the choir through one chorus with her hands raised above her head leaping in time to the beat.

When the chorus ended, she stopped her dance and spoke in an authoritative voice, "Now, let's welcome the founder and senior pastor of Earth Reaping Church... my husband...Pastor Eli Basil!" Deborah handed the microphone back to Pastor Dan and walked towards one of two high-back chairs that could be best described as a thrones, facing the podium just left of center. She stood in front of it clapping her hands as Pastor Eli entered from the same spot she had just moments before.

"Ooooh! Somebody in this house of worship better praise the Lord," Eli said into the headset microphone he wore. The crowd responded joyously and enthusiastically at the sight of the superstar preacher. "We are beaming live around the globe and I want to let the Devil know that there is a church in Columbus, Ohio that is on fire with the Holy Ghost!" The audience roared. Eli turned towards a camera and pointed directly at it. "Don't touch that dial! You may think that you just stumbled across this broadcast by mistake, but I have news for you: The Holy Ghost himself caused you to land on this station! I don't know what may happen to you if change the channel now...but if you stay with us...I can promise you that shackles will be loosed...sins will be forgiven...cancers will go into remission...and you will be filled with the Holy Ghost!" The roar in the building shook Ruth to her core.

Kyle looked at his great-grandfather and said, "It's started."

"Very good. You *feel* it don't you? You didn't even look at the time and yet you *know* that the events are moving forward."

Kyle seemed startled by the revelation and looked at the clock. It was just after 11:00. "I did feel it! Now that I think about it, there are a many times that I *feel* something about certain situations...almost like a premonition."

Grandfather nodded. "Of course. That's what I've been telling you this morning. Your energy field picks up things that most others miss. It's what makes you unique and is one of the attributes of two-spirited people."

"I don't have a good feeling about this."

"It's alright, Kyle. Everything will work out as it is meant to."

"Will my TV work or is it out of service like everything else?"

"It works."

"Can I watch the church service?"

"If you'd like."

Kyle walked from the bedroom to the living room, grabbed the remote, and turned on the television. He tapped the channel button until he found the church service in full swing with music.

Helena and D.J. stood in the huge entryway of the church as the music from inside the sanctuary piped through speakers in the ceiling. Signs pointed directions to the bookstore, coffee shop, and eateries. "Dear God! It *is* like a mall," D.J. remarked. "I see why Jesus turned over tables in the temple now. What would Jesus do with this vulgarity? Where do you get into the sanctuary?"

Helena pointed towards another sign with directions to the sanctuary. "It's that way, but I'm not going in just yet."

"Well, you really don't have to. Look over there…it's a TV showing the whole service!" D.J. was overwhelmed by the magnitude of the church. "I just can't believe my eyes. I can't believe people worship this way—if it is even called worship!"

"Oh, it's worship alright! They're worshiping the man...the church. Idolatry at its finest, D.J. But, all idols melt in the fire." Helena moved down the hall.

"Where are you going, Helena?"

"Stay here. I'll be back in a few minutes. I have an appointment with the man of the house."

D.J. looked at the monitor on the wall and seemed confused. "But...he's in the service. I can see him on the stage."

"He won't be for long. I'm just going to wait for him in his office." Helena methodically moved down the hall. The tap-tap sounded as her staff hit the marble tiles.

Papaw Buck was sitting on the couch with legs crossed next to Kyle watching the Praise and Worship service on the television. Kyle thought Pastor Dan looked especially attractive but tried to suppress his feelings. He thought about the kiss they had exchanged.

"Oh, yes. I know, Kyle." Grandfather spoke tenderly. "He too, has his own journey to follow. Fortunately, you have not joined paths with him. It is not meant to be that the two of you travel together."

Kyle turned to his grandfather with a confused look on his face. "How...?"

"Don't worry about the how, Kyle. You already know that what I've said is true; otherwise, you would have given into your inclinations in your office. You *felt* that it was wrong and you listened to that *feeling*. You did the right thing." Grandfather nodded at him.

The final song had been sung and Kyle knew that the offertory was next in the order of the service. His father walked towards the pulpit. "Praise the Lord, saints!" The congregation echoed hallelujahs, but it just was not a good enough response for the pastor. He grumbled angrily, "That was not a suggestion! It's a command!" The building thundered with praise at the urging of their omnipotent leader. "Now is the time that you get minister through your gifts to the Lord. As soon as I'm finished with the offertory, I am leaving on a Holy-Ghost-inspired trip to Washington D.C. to meet with several members of congress. These representatives understand the importance of family values and are sympathetic to our desire to return this country back to its Godly heritage, and support our latest organization, The Foundation for Biblical Ethics. I want you to sow a special seed today to help in our fight to take America back for God and support The Foundation for Biblical Ethics. I know this church is filled with obedient children of God. So, if you want to be obedient to God, I want you to take out your best seed right now." Eli paused for just a moment. "The Bible says to give and it shall be given to you. If you sow a seed to God, He will work in supernatural ways to multiply your seed. God told me this morning that there are twenty people who are going to give a thousand dollar seed today. I want everyone to search their hearts this morning and see if God is dealing with you to be one of those twenty."

Eli turned towards the camera and pointed into it. "You may be sitting at home right now and facing a financial challenge that seems like there is no way out of. But, I have news for you today: God can! God can bring you out of your mess today if you just take that step of faith and sow into this ministry. The Devil would like nothing better than for you to ignore the urging of the Holy Ghost right now so that the abortionists and gay rights advocates can take this country over and drag it to the pits of Hell! Don't let the Devil lull you into complacency. You can take control. The Bible says that one can chase a thousand and two can put ten thousand to flight. Imagine what we can do together in the face of the profane leaders of the organized minority that is hell-bent on eroding our founding fathers' morals! Now is your time to join up with the army of God. Call the number on the bottom of your screen with credit card ready and together we will rout the enemy!"

Eli looked at the ushers and nodded for them to start passing the offering buckets. "As the ushers collect your seeds, our very own Joni Paisley will sing the latest single from her newest CD. Don't forget to stop by the bookstore after service and pick up your own anointed copy of her CD." Joni entered the stage with microphone in hand and started singing. Deborah bristled. As Pastor Eli exited the stage from the left, he turned to catch one more glimpse of the soloist before heading towards his office.

Helena found the office area and went for the door with the nameplate that read: Pastor Eli Basil. The door was locked. She huffed indignantly, took a step back and tapped the door knob gently with the top of her staff. When she tried the door again, it .opened. As she stepped into the office, she noticed the beautiful hardwood executive desk with mahogany veneers. She looked around the office and saw the matching book-cases and a rich, leather love seat. She dropped into it with a grunt.

Eli had just left the stage and was going to his of-fice to pick up his briefcase and keys when he noticed that the door was open. He hesitantly walked into the office and looked around. There, before him was an old woman with a walking stick, sitting on the love seat. He didn't immediately recognize her and asked, "May I help you, dear?"

"I think it's me who can help you, Elijah." As soon as she spoke, Eli recognized the mother-in-law that he had not seen in nearly forty years.

"How did you get in here?" Eli demanded.

"Never you mind about that. You and I have some business to attend to."

"Well, Helena…I have to board my jet to D.C. and I don't have time for your nonsense. So, if you will ex-cuse me…" Eli moved behind his desk and started gath-ering his briefcase.

Helena stood and then swiped her staff towards the door. The door shut with a soft thud. Eli looked at the door and then at Helena with a perplexed expression. "This will only take a few minutes, Elijah; and then you can be on your way."

Irritated by the intrusion, Eli barked, "Be done with it old woman! Say what you must."

Helena smiled wryly. "I have a refresher Sunday School lesson for you. Remember the story of Nathan and David?" The blood drained from Eli's face. Helena didn't wait for a response. She walked towards the desk and stood before it. "Nathan was a prophet who paid a visit to King David and told him a story about a rich man stealing a poor man's only lamb to feed a stranger instead of using one of his own. Of course, David was angered and said that the man deserved to die. Then Nathan told David that the man was him." Helena paused.

"Well, I haven't stolen anyone's lamb to feed a guest."

"My child..." Helena oozed. "You know very well that the story was really about King David killing Bathsheba's husband so that he could take her as his wife."

"Enough, old woman!" Eli raised his voice. "I have to leave now."

Helena stamped her staff on the carpeted floor. "Not just yet, Elijah! I know what's going on and it won't be long before my daughter knows it too! I'm only here today to ask you to stop before you cause anymore hurt and pain to your wife...your children...yourself...and your parishioners."

Eli laughed maniacally. "You have too much time on your hands, old witch. And I have very little time for pagan practices and prophecies. Go back to your hills! I have a plane to catch."

"You've been warned, Elijah. I cannot make you heed the call of Spirit. I have done what I came to do. Good-bye." Helena turned and left the office. After she closed the door behind her, Eli bit his lower lip and shook his head as if to shake off Helena's words.

Inside the sanctuary, Deborah had just finished reading the scriptures from which she was forming her sermon for the day. She had read from the King James Version of the Old Testament Numbers 22:21-35. "I just love King James English, don't you?" Amen's reverberated throughout the auditorium. Deborah now wore the headset microphone and began pacing the length of the stage as she preached. "King James wasn't concerned about being politically correct so I've decided not to be politically correct either. That's why I've titled this sermon 'From Ass to Ass-ignment'!" Cheers and applause erupted along with amen's and hallelujah's. Deborah stood erect and smiled at the crowd's enthusiasm. "Now don't get all pious and act like you've never heard the word ass." She quickly turned and started walking towards the on-stage camera and pointed directly into it. "And don't you change that channel! You know that most of the television you watch has worse language than that." Ooh's and aah's filled the congregation. "If the word ass makes you uncomfortable, take it up with King James, not me! If this kind of celebratory message makes you squirm, maybe you would be more comfortable down the street at one of the frozen chosen churches! The point is, the Holy Ghost is supposed to make us uncomfortable at times! He is our moral compass and inner voice.

"You may be asking yourself why I've chosen this particular story to use as a Mother's Day message instead of a more traditional Proverbs 31 message. Well...I'm not a traditional woman and this isn't a traditional church." She crossed her arms over her chest with attitude, and nodded towards the crowd. She was rewarded with their appreciation. "Let me help you out with understanding this story. You see...Balaam is symbolic of manhood and the ass is symbolic of womanhood. Women, I want you to look at your man and tell him 'You can call me an ass if you want to, because I know I'm doing the Holy Ghost's work.'" Women all over the congregation turned and looked at their husbands and boyfriends and repeated what Deborah said.

"Now you may be wondering why I said it's okay to be called an ass. Well-huh...it was the ass that saw the angel of the Lord first-huh...not the *man* named Balaam. You see women; we are naturally more discerning than men are. True, they may be the ones in charge. They may be the ones saddling us up; they may be the ones pulling on the reins, telling us what direction to go in... but-huh! Ultimately...it is us women who see the spiritual direction and the righteous path!" Deborah bent towards the congregation and stamped her right foot as she furiously yelled in her best evangelistic tones.

Women throughout the church jumped to their feet, some with Bibles in their hands, screaming, "Preach the word, Sister!" And "I know that's right!"

"Some of you dear sisters have been roughed and tumbled by your Balaam...some of you have been battered and bruised...just like the ass who was struck by

Balaam three times. Let me speak a word of encouragement to you, dear sisters! There is coming a day when the Lord will open that man's eyes and he will realize that the ass he has been beating for all those years is really his own! When he thought he was keeping you tied down, you were just building character. Woo! I feel the Holy Ghost speaking through me right now! Someone had better praise the Lord in this house!"

Multitudes of people stood to their feet and started praising and rejoicing. Deborah looked towards the organist and nodded. He immediately started playing an upbeat tune and the rest of orchestra joined in as hundreds of people filled the aisles and the front of the altar, dancing and shouting.

Naomi scurried quickly along the pew to be near Ruth. Ruth suddenly flashed back to her childhood and remembered how Kyle had been frightened by the antics of the Pentecostal services. "My, times have changed," she said to herself. "They used to wait until the evening service to get wild." Naomi looked beggingly at her mother. "Its okay, Sweetie. They're not going to hurt us." She buried her face in Ruth's side so that she wouldn't have to view the chaos.

Deborah suddenly started speaking in tongues. The music stopped and crowd hushed. She prophesized for several minutes in the unknown language before trailing off to a whisper. Once finished, she stood in the center of the stage with her hands lifted towards heaven and her eyes closed. The congregation remained quiet, until a voice in the middle aisle started speaking.

"Oh, how Creator uses even the simplest creature to speak to those in power…" the voice said. Ruth looked over the bowed heads to see who was speaking. The crowd in the middle aisle parted. There stood an old woman in a red dress stood with a walking stick. Ruth looked at the woman and felt an instant connection to her. As she looked at her, she realized how familiar she seemed. —She saw the same face every morning in the mirror, only forty years younger.

All Ruth could muster was a labored whisper. "Oh, my god…Grandmother."

"How much longer will you allow Balaam to continue to manipulate you?" Helena continued. "It is time, my child, to refuse to carry your master any longer. For this day, an angel has appeared to open the eyes of the master." Helena raised her angelic staff into the air. "Open your eyes, my children, and see. Follow the lead of Spirit and reject the lead of your master. Open your ears and hear the assignment Creator whispers to you softly and tenderly. Come home. Come home. Ye, who are weary, come home!" She stamped her staff onto the floor.

Deborah's eyes popped open and looked directly at her mother. The color drained from her face. She looked for the head usher, Charlie. When they made eye contact with each other, she motioned with her thumb to exit the woman. Charlie quickly responded and briskly made his way up the aisle, latching onto Helena's arm. "Show's over, old woman," he said belligerently.

Helena squealed. "Let go of me you brute! I *am* Deborah's mother!"

"I don't care who you are! Pastor Deborah asked me to escort you out and you're going!" Charlie intoned in her ear as he pulled her out of the sanctuary of the church. The congregation erupted in confusion.

Deborah, leaning on the pulpit, looked like she was going to pass out. "Pastor Dan…Pastor Dan!" Pastor Dan ran to Deborah's side. "Play something…we're still live."

Pastor Dan turned and started singing into his microphone, "I command you Satan, in the name of the Lord, to pick up your weapons and flee…" The musicians and choir quickly joined.

Ruth couldn't believe what she had just witnessed. She jumped from the front pew and ran up the steps towards her mother. "What the hell are you doing? Was that really your mother?" Deborah could barely hear Ruth's voice over the sound of the choir and musicians. The last thing she remembered before passing out and hitting the floor was seeing Ruth's face spinning in front of her.

Several ushers ran to Deborah's aid. Ruth ran back down the steps. She grabbed Naomi's hand and said, "Come on, Sweetie. We're going to meet your great-grandmother."

The two left the sanctuary through the same door though which Charlie had pulled Helena. When they entered the hallway outside the auditorium, they spotted Charlie still tugging on Helena's arm while another woman swatted him with her purse.

"Leave Miss Helena alone, you jackass!" D.J. yelled between swats to Charlie's shoulder with her purse. "She's a frail woman!"

"This is private property and she's not welcome here." Charlie responded.

Ruth screamed at the large usher, "Stop it! Leave her alone!" Charlie released Helena's arm and D.J. took one more full-force swipe at the back of his head. He grunted as the purse struck him. He quickly spun around with his fist raised towards D.J.

"I ought to knock you out," he spoke angrily to her.

D.J. reached inside her purse and replied, "I've gotta Smith'n Wesson in here that's just begging for you to lay another finger on any of us women. And don't think I'm afraid to use it, sonny!"

Ruth wrung her hands together in a worried posture. "Ladies, why don't you come with me outside and we can find our cars and leave."

"That's the best idea I've heard from you all day, Ruth," Charlie acknowledged. With Naomi in tow, Ruth joined the two older women and they exited through the front doors.

Once outside the women stopped walking and turned to face each other. "Grandmother?" Ruth asked.

"Yes, dear. It's such a pleasure to meet face to face," Helena answered and held out her arms. Ruth welcomed her warm embrace and Naomi joined in the hug.

"Oh my god...I have so many questions for you. Kyle has been looking for you."

Helena soothingly responded. "I know, Ruth. Kyle will find me in the fullness of time."

"Where do you live? How can he find you?"

"Your mother needs you right now. Go to her and care for her." Helena moved towards the white Lincoln.

"But," Ruth responded indignantly, "at least give me your address!"

Helena stopped and turned back towards Ruth and Naomi. "Sweetie, you must learn to care for your mother in spite of her hypocrisy. The same love that you shared with me in your hug must be shared with her." D.J. and Helena got into the car as Ruth and Naomi watched. As D.J. backed the car out, Ruth looked at the license plate and noticed the Hocking County sticker.

Chapter 9

Kyle looked at the front page of the Monday morning edition of the *Columbus Dispatch*. A picture of his mother passed out next to the pulpit of the church was on the front page with the headline reading: *Mega-Church a Mega-Flop?* Half of the front page was dedicated to the previous day's service and the scuffle that took place in the middle of the sermon. It wasn't the first time the church had been in the headlines of the newspaper and, as usual, pastors and congregants would view the story negatively.

Pastor Dan had called Kyle and told him to stay away from the church because it was crawling with reporters from all the local news channels. Eli made a hasty return from Washington D.C. to help quell the shake-up that was reverberating into the local community. Eli had also called Kyle and blamed him for the disruption of the live service. Kyle didn't respond to his father's accusations, but seethed with anger.

Ruth had called while Kyle was on the phone with his father, but Kyle didn't dare interrupt him to answer the call waiting. When he retrieved her message, he found out that his mother was doing fine and that Ruth and Naomi were on their way back to South Point. Ruth told him about meeting their Grandmother and that the license plate on her car confirmed her belief that she was living in Hocking County.

Kyle lay the newspaper on his desk and sat in front of his computer. He decided to do an internet search on Hocking County. His first search led him to hockinghills.com. He scanned the front page and discovered that it was a destination area with nine state parks and 9,000 acres of state forest. He had no idea that such a large forest area was within an hour's drive of Columbus.

He found a tab for other links and clicked on it. On the next page, he saw a link to Logan, Ohio and clicked it. The pictures on the webpage looked quaint to Kyle. He saw a tab for news and thought it might be a link to the local newspaper. After hitting the news tab, Kyle found himself at *The Logan Daily News* website. He perused the site and saw a link to a story of interest. The link read: *Uproar at Columbus Mega-Church Has Local Connection.* Kyle quickly double-clicked the tab.

"Oh, my god! Grandmother!" Kyle exhaled as he looked at the story and a picture of his grandmother. He read the story eagerly:

Helena Crockett of Laurelville is the mother of Deborah Basil whose husband, Eli Basil, is the founder and senior pastor of Earth Reaping Church in Columbus, Ohio. During a live broadcast of their Mother's Day service at the church, Ms. Crockett interrupted the service and caused a commotion that caused her daughter to faint in the middle of her sermon.

Ms. Crockett is known locally for running a spiritual retreat on her thirty-acre-farm known as Serenity, in Laurelville. She has had run-ins with local churches over her "New Age" teachings, but this is the first time that she has confronted a church without first being targeted by the congregation.

Mrs. Basil was hosting a special Mother's Day service in which her daughter and granddaughter were featured guests. Ms. Crockett walked in and interrupted while Mrs. Basil was preaching and was escorted out of the church by an usher. Mrs. Basil then collapsed on the stage. She later was able to walk off on her own accord with the help of her daughter and an usher.

Ms. Crockett refused to answer any questions regarding the incident during an attempted phone interview with our staff. Earth Reaping Church was contacted for a comment, but no statements have been issued at this time.

When Kyle finished the article, he printed it and looked for directions to the Hocking Hills area. He found that it was less than an hour's drive from his apartment in Columbus. As he tried to decide whether to head to Logan or just call the newspaper and see if he could get an address for his grandmother, he heard a knock at his apartment door. He looked through the security peephole and saw his father standing outside. "Great," he muttered to himself.

Kyle opened the door and Eli marched in without saying hello. "I need a statement immediately to issue to the press. What have you come up with, Kyle?" Kyle looked dumbfounded by his father's statement. "I left D.C. hours ago! Surely, you've been working on a press release. I know you have enough sense to realize that we have to give them something."

"I haven't put anything together, Dad. I don't know what you want to say."

Eli's face was red with anger. "What do you think I pay you for? Give me something to explain that your mother is suffering from exhaustion due to her recent biopsy." Kyle raised his right eyebrow and bit his lower lip. His father grabbed his arm and yelled, "Don't give me your mother's look! Do what I tell you to do!"

Kyle tried to pull away, but Eli held firmly. "Let go of me," Kyle stammered.

"What did you say?"

"L-l-l-let…go of me!" Kyle found his resolution and spoke more forcefully. "I'm not writing anything for a press release. You do it. It's your church."

Eli tightened his grip. "Who do you think you're talking to? I am *your* father. I am the *pastor* of the church. And, I am *your* boss!" He gritted his teeth and moved his face close to Kyle's. "You will do exactly what I tell you to do! That's what I pay you for!"

Kyle pulled free of his father. "I'm tired of doing what *you* tell me to do. I'm not writing a lie for you! Mom had breast implants, not a biopsy. If you want to lie, do it on your own. I won't be a part of it!"

Eli was shocked, enraged. "I think you need a little time to think about what you're saying. Don't report to work for the rest of the week. You're on unpaid leave, starting today!"

"Fine. I need some time away from you, the church, and this family anyway!"

"Really? You want away from it all?" Eli's voice became more cynical. "I suppose you need some *fag* time to yourself." Eli's eyes narrowed to a squint and he spoke in a voice filled with disdain. "I know you haven't been attending your support group meetings *and* you made a pass at the facilitator. He told me all about it. God, you make me sick!"

"Yeah, Dad, I quit. But, I think your source got the story turned around! He hit on me!" Tears flowed down Kyle's face as anger, frustration, and indignation overwhelmed him. "The whole support group is just a lie set up to take people's money. Just like the lie you want to tell about why Mom fainted in church. They can't cure me, Dad. I'm gay...queer...a homosexual! No amount of prayer, or counseling, or casting out devils will change who God made me to be!"

Eli shook his head at Kyle. "You're no different than a pedophile, Kyle. Don't come back to the church, *period,* until you repent of your sins. You're fired! God didn't make you this way...Satan did. As far as I'm concerned, you're dead to me until you renounce this lifestyle. Stay away from me and your mother. You make me sick enough as it is...I can't imagine how your mother will react. No wonder Laurel divorced you. You are one demented piece of human flesh."

Kyle broke down in tears. "Get the hell out of my apartment, Eli! I wouldn't want the stench of my dead body to make you sick!"

Eli raised his right hand to his left side and gave Kyle a backhanded slap across the face. Kyle felt his head snap back.

"*Your* apartment? I think you forget who pays for this place!"

Kyle's temper flared. Grabbing Eli's shirt, he shoved him into the wall. Eli yelped in surprise.

"That's the last time you lay a god-damned hand on me...EVER!" Kyle released his father and opened the front door to his apartment.

Eli looked at Kyle. As he left the apartment and said, "You'll regret this, boy. I'll see to it." Kyle slammed the door behind his father and slid down the door in an emotional heap.

It had been two hours since Eli had left Kyle's apartment, as Kyle drove south towards Hocking Hills. Just when he thought he'd regained his composure, he'd remember his father's words of disgust and the tears would flow again. He knew his father had always been disappointed in him, but it was a stinging blow to actually hear it with such venom. Kyle felt his world shifting unmercifully beneath him. What would he do without a job or a place to live? The turmoil inside tore him apart.

He saw a sign for the Hocking Hills Market and turned off the highway to stretch his legs. As he pulled into the parking lot of the complex of white, green-roofed buildings, he looked around at the different shops. He saw a woman walking a dog in front of a store whose sign read: The Appalachian Arts and Craft Store. He parked his car and approached the woman.

"Hello. That's a beautiful dog. What's his name?" Kyle asked the short woman who appeared to be in her forties.

The woman lit up and replied enthusiastically. "Her name is Taylor. I'm Zoe."

Kyle returned her smile. "I'm Kyle. Do you live around her?"

"Yeah. Are you lost?" She regarded Kyle, taking his measure, then offered her hand.

Kyle shook it. "Well, I wouldn't say lost, but…"

"You're searching for something, aren't you?"

Kyle felt an immediate warmth towards Zoe, liking her immediately.. "Not exactly some*thing,* more like some*one.*"

"Oh, no…you may think you're looking for some-*one,* but you're really looking for some*thing.* Its okay, honey. You'll find it." She ran her free hand through her curly black locks and smiled confidently.

Kyle chuckled as he noticed a gentle glow about her spirit. "Okay, Zoe. You're probably right. I've just had a tough couple of days and was looking for a place to get away to."

"That bad, huh?"

"Yeah, it's been pretty bad. I just pissed my father off and he fired me, so I guess I'm looking for a job…a life…anything."

"Well, if you need something temporary I know the guy at the coffee roasting shop over there is looking for some help. I come in once a week as a volunteer to help him out, but he really needs more help than I can provide. Let me get him for you." She walked over to the entrance to the shop, opened the door, and yelled, "Hey, Moses! Get your ass out here." She turned back towards Kyle with a devious grin on her face. "We have a love-hate relationship. He's like the little sister that loves to torture me and I hate him in return!" She laughed with such veracity that her whole body shook.

"Sister? I thought you said the *guy* from the coffee shop." Kyle was a bit confused.

"Whatever," Zoe answered and waved her hand in front of her face as if shooing a fly. She carefully looked Kyle over again. "Oh, yeah…I think the two of you will like each other."

Moses walked out the door. "What the hell do you want, woman?" He was smiling as he asked. When he saw Kyle standing there too, he said, "Ooops! I'm sorry. I didn't know you had someone with you, Zoe."

Zoe took charge of the conversation which seemed a natural response for her. "Moses, this is Kyle. Kyle, Moses." Moses held out his hand and Kyle shook it. Kyle was stunned when their hands touched. He gave a cursory glance at Moses for fear of leering at him. What he saw made him tingle. Moses was three inches taller than Kyle with a very lean build. He had long, dark brown hair pulled back in a ponytail. His eyes were a deep penetrating hazel, his mouth perfectly sculpted by a well-trimmed goatee.

"Hello, Kyle." Moses said. Kyle looked into his eyes and felt an instant connection. Moses, too, was stunned with the depth of Kyle's blue eyes, and unable to say anything else for a moment.

Zoe watched the exchange between the men. "I thought so," she said with a smile.

Her voice brought Moses back to reality. Quickly he asked, "Thought what?"

"Oh, nothing! I thought the two of you would get along just fine. I gotta run, unless you need me here to keep the conversation going. It was so nice meeting you Kyle." She reached over and shook his hand and then hugged Moses. Zoe whispered in his ear, "Be nice to him. I think the two of you have a lot in common. If he needs a job, give him one!" She let go and headed to her Honda CR-V and jumped in with her dog. She honked as she drove off.

"I hope she didn't overwhelm you, Kyle. She is *quite* the character."

"She was fine." Their met eyes again. "Have we met before? You seem so familiar to me."

"I don't think so…maybe we knew each other in a past life." Moses gave a warm, hearty laugh. "Why don't you come in and have a cup of coffee. I roast all the beans fresh. Are you from around here or just visiting?" Moses held the door open for Kyle and they walked into the shop.

"Just visiting."

"Where are you staying? I know some great cabin rentals if you're looking for one."

"I just drove down for the day, from Columbus. I'm trying to find someone and a place she runs."

"What's the name? I know a lot of getaways here."

"Serenity. It's some kind of spiritual retreat."

"You're kidding…right?"

"No. My grandmother owns it."

"Helena is *your* grandmother? Really? Dear, God!" Moses was full of animation. "I know her! I actually live in a cabin on Serenity. Helena and I are very close.

I like to think of her as my own grandmother. Do you know anything about synchronicity?"

"What?" Kyle was overwhelmed with his luck.

"Synchronicity. It was a theory first put forth by the Swiss psychologist Carl Jung. In a nutshell, it's what we would call a coincidence that later turns out to have a deeper meaning—a Higher Power orchestrating events for a common goal."

Kyle's face lit up. "A divine appointment? So, God sent me here knowing that I would run into you because you live on my grandmother's property?"

"Exactly!" Moses enthused. "Do you drink coffee?"

"Yes."

"Have you ever had French-pressed coffee?"

"No…" Kyle's voice trailed off questioningly.

"It's the only way to drink coffee! You get the full taste of the coffee bean." Moses walked around the counter and pulled a French press from the shelf. "I'll make some of your grandmother's favorite. In fact, she likes it so much I call it Helena's Peaberry."

Kyle watched as Moses scooped the coffee beans and dumped them in a grinder. Once the coffee was ground, he poured it into the press, and then filled the coffeemaker with hot water. "It just needs to set for a bit. Then we can drink it!"

"So, did you grow up around here, Moses?"

"No. I just moved here a little over a year ago to open this business. I'm originally a farm boy from Illinois. I joined the military when I was eighteen, for four years. After that, I started working for corporate America. I spent fifteen years in that rat race until I decided that it was time to get out before it killed me. Now I'm here and loving every minute! I've never felt so at home. These hills are wonderful for the soul." Moses turned to the French press and gently pushed the lever. He grabbed a couple of mugs, he asked, "What do you do?"

"Well, I would like to think that I'm a writer, but up until today, I've been pretty much an administrative assistant."

"Really?" Moses handed a cup to Kyle. "Do you use cream or sugar?"

"No."

"Good. You can't taste the flavor if you doctor it up with cream and sugar." Moses raised his cup in a toast. "Here's to synchronicity." They touched their mugs together. Kyle took a sip. "What do you think? Is your grandmother right?"

Kyle savored the flavor. "Mmmm…yeah, it's really good."

"What company do you work for?" Moses asked.

"It's not exactly a company. My father is a pastor of a mega-church in Columbus and I worked for him. But, after today, I think I'm looking for a new job."

Moses' face became serious. "What church?"

Kyle was noticeably uncomfortable and answered flatly. "Earth Reaping Church."

"Oh, that's one of those crazy charismatic churches!" Moses chuckled. "That's cool—I'm just giving you a hard time. I was raised Baptist, so I understand a lot of the fundamental teachings of the church. So, your dad is Eli Basil? Wow! I've seen your father on TV. That's gotta be tough. What happened today?"

Kyle's uneasiness subsided with the commonality of religious upbringings. "Actually, I stood up to him for the first time in my life. So he fired me."

"Really? What was it about?"

Kyle hesitated. He looked Moses over again. Although he had just met him, he felt a kindred spirit and an accepting nature. "Honestly...I'm a little uncomfortable talking about it."

"That's okay. I completely understand having a fall out with a parent—and your church. My mother and I haven't spoken for a couple of years and I just can't find a church I'm comfortable with. The last time my mother and I spoke, she told me that as far as she was concerned I was dead to her and would see her in heaven." Moses was hoping that Kyle was experiencing a similar situation and thought by offering his own story it would help him to open up.

Kyle smiled and felt a sense of warm relief sweep over him. "I'm guessing we have similar situations."

Moses laughed. "What situation would make an evangelical parent disown his or her own son? Let's see there's divorce, but that's pretty widespread now. There are drugs or alcohol, but generally, parents will try to save you from that and won't go the disowning route. Hmmm...I can only think of one other situation, and since I don't see any reaction to the other possibilities, I think we *might* have something in common."

Kyle giggled nervously, but with some relief. "Okay... you nailed it...I'm gay."

"You're grandmother would prefer the term two-spirited," Moses said before taking a sip of coffee. "She always calls me her wonderful two-spirited helper when I do chores for her. Lucky for you, you have such an open-minded grandmother. She'll be a great support for you."

"The thing is...I've only met her once, when I was ten years old. It was a brief encounter. But recently, I've been dreaming about her."

Again, Moses laughed. "That sounds like Helena. I take it she has been *visiting* you in your dreams?"

"Oh, yeah...some very vivid ones. I tried to get her to tell me where she lived in the dreams, but all she would say is that I had to find her through the labyrinth."

"That's Helena. Well, you've found me! I live on her property and if you have some time today and can stick around, I'll be happy to take you to her after I close the shop."

"That would be great, Moses! I have all day and longer since I don't have to be at work tomorrow...or the next."

"Well, if you're looking for work, I could use some help around here, and your grandmother always has something for newcomers to do around her place." Moses' energy became somewhat flirty. "I do have an age requirement for working here, though. I'm not sure I can hire anyone under the age of thirty and I'm guessing you're about twenty-five or twenty-six."

Kyle blushed. "Thanks. I appreciate that, but I'm thirty-three. And...you're how old?"

"How old do I look?" Moses batted his eyes.

"Well, you said you joined the military at eighteen... spent four years there...then worked for corporate

America for fifteen before opening this place a year ago. So…I'd say thirty-eight."

"That's not fair. You weren't supposed to do the math! Besides…I asked how old do I *look*."

Kyle enjoyed the playfulness between them and answered, "Not more than forty-eight."

"Oooooh! You're supposed to suck up to the person who just offered you a job!" Moses replied. "I guess I'll just have to retract the offer."

"Did I say forty-eight? I meant twenty-eight. Yeah… definitely no older than twenty-eight!" The two men laughed together. "Thanks for making me laugh. It's a helluva lot better than what I was doing earlier today."

"See! Synchronicity at work, or as we were taught in fundamentalism 'all things work together for good'. Right?"

Kyle agreed. "I think I'm really starting to believe that scripture."

Chapter 10

Kyle was in his car, following Moses to Serenity down a winding road called Buena Vista. It was nearly six in the evening when Moses had closed Roasters, his coffee-roasting shop. Kyle was glad it was still light out, because he felt sure he would have gotten lost in the dark on the twisting road. The two men had spent the afternoon together, talking in between customers and found that they had many things in common. Moses had disclosed his own journey in accepting his orientation and the spiritual path he was on now. Although he would have judged Moses for his spiritual ideas just a month earlier, everything he said seemed to resonate with Kyle.

Kyle tried to concentrate on the road so that he could find his way back to Columbus, but he just could not keep the excitement at bay. Not only was Moses handsome but there was an attractive energy about him, and an understanding of Kyle's struggle to accept his orientation from a religious standpoint. The word 'synchronicity' echoed in his spirit as he thought about his grandmother refusing to tell him where she lived—and then running into Moses—a man with a similar background and a man who lived on his grandmother's property. "It just *feels* right," Kyle muttered as he drove. As soon as he uttered the sentence, he had a flash of his great-grandfather telling him to listen to his feelings.

The car in front of Kyle came to a halt at a stop sign, turned right, and then made an immediate left. "Wow. Will we ever get there? I hope I can find my way back," Kyle said to himself. Buena Vista ended at another stop sign and they made a right onto Middlefork Road. After two precarious S-turns, Moses made a left turn to stay on Middlefork. Not a half mile later, another left turn onto Union Road. This road wasn't paved like the previous roads had been, and was very bumpy. Kyle thought aloud, "I hope we're not on this road too long." He had no sooner spoken the words when Moses turned onto a graveled drive. A sign next to the drive read: "Welcome to Serenity…A Labyrinth of Trust, Hope, and Love."

Kyle's heart accelerated. He wasn't sure if it was because of the day's events or because he was finally going to meet his grandmother face to face. Unconsciously, he wiped his wet palms on his jeans. As they moved slowly up the gravel drive, Kyle looked at the old white farmhouse and felt a steady wave of love. He looked closer at the front of the house. There on the front porch stood the woman of his dreams with a staff in her right hand while her left waved at the two vehicles. Kyle swallowed the lump in his throat, barely able to wait to park his car. He watched as the woman made her way down the porch steps and along the sidewalk, then found a spot to park next to Moses' Jeep Wrangler.

Moses was already out of his car, grinning, when Kyle opened his own door. Grandmother was nearly at the parking area and she seemed to move faster than her legs should carry a woman of her age. "Grandmother!" Kyle barely choked out.

"Kyyyyyyle!" She squealed back at him. Kyle ran towards her as tears of joy streamed down his face. He fell into her arms just like the ten-year-old he was during their first encounter. Moses stood near the two, fighting back his own tears.

Kyle had never felt such a hug, or so loved. He couldn't get over how such a tight hug came from such a small lady. For the first time in his life, he felt settled and comforted. "Finally…finally we meet again," he said through his tears.

"Oh, yes, dear…you've found your way. I'm so proud of you." Helena pulled away from Kyle and looked at Moses with a smile. "I see you two have already met."

Moses spoke with a twinkle in his eye, "I don't know who the hell this crazy man is. I just thought he was some nut case following me out of Buena Vista. I figured if I needed protection you would take care of him for me, Helena."

Helena played along with Moses. "Well…I am known for taking in the crazies around here. I let you rent off me—don't I?"

"How is that living the *Tao*?" Moses retorted playfully.

Helena quipped, "Just because one is enlightened does not mean that one looses one's sense of humor." Both laughed heartily while Kyle tried to figure out what Moses meant.

Helena saw Kyle's confusion. "Moses is referring to the *Tao Te Ching,* an ancient Chinese spiritual text. It has eighty-one wonderful life-inspiring verses. It's required reading if you stick around Serenity for any amount of time."

"I look forward to reading it then, Grandmother."

"Come on boys, let's go inside. Supper is gonna get cold if we stand 'round out here chewing the fat."

"Oh, no, Helena. I don't want to intrude. I'll just head on up to my cabin."

"Don't be silly, Moses! D.J set the table for three tonight before she left for the day. I intend on having supper with two good lookin' men tonight. Don't disappoint an eighty-year-old woman."

"Three?" Moses asked. "You knew he was coming, didn't you?"

"You've known me for at least a year, Moses. Have I ever been wrong? What did I tell you this morning when you drove out of here?"

Moses cheeks flushed and he gave a sheepish look. "I'm not sure I remember."

"You remember alrighty! I'm just embarrassing you and you won't say what I told you."

"Maybe that's something we can talk about later." Moses quickly changed the subject. "What's for supper, anyway?"

Helena winked at Moses to acknowledge that she would drop it for now. "A good Appalachian supper— meatloaf, mashed potatoes, green beans, macaroni and cheese, warm bread, and cooked apples."

Kyle's face lit up. "Oh my god! I think I'm in heaven. Those are my favorite foods!"

Helena gave a cocky smile before adding, "Oh, I forgot about dessert—homemade brownies!"

"I love her brownies!" Moses said to Kyle. "They're killer brownies! She makes an icing for them that's to die for!"

"Okay, boys, git in the house and wash your hands. We can chat as we break bread together." Helena walked between the men, up the sidewalk towards the house. As they approached the back door, the aromas of Kyle's favorite foods filled his nostrils. A single tear slid down his cheek as he inhaled the enticing scents of home.

Kyle, Moses, and Helena sat around the table after finishing their meals, laughing and becoming acquainted with each other. Helena stood and gathered the empty plates. Kyle said, "I'll get those, Grandmother. Sit back down."

"No you won't. It's your first time at Serenity, so you're a guest. But, tomorrow night, you can do the dishes since the guest title won't fit you anymore! Did you get plenty to eat, such as it was, boys?"

"Oh, yes, Helena!" Moses cooed. "I'm stuffed."

"More than enough, Grandmother."

"I hope you saved room for brownies. I don't want them to go to waste." Helena said as she continued clearing the table. She walked over to the refrigerator to put some leftovers away. When she opened the door, she said, "Oh, for Pete's sake! I'm out of milk. Moses, could you and Kyle run into Laurelville and pick some up?"

Moses quickly agreed. "Come on, Kyle. I'll show you the big city of Laurelville," he said teasingly. The two men went out the back door and entered the Jeep. "Really, Laurelville's a quaint town. You'll love it!"

"How far is it from here?" Kyle asked as the headed down the driveway.

"It's just seven miles. Everything closes at eight o'clock so we're cutting it close." When they reached the end of the drive, Moses turned onto to Union Road in the opposite direction the one in which they had arrived. If Kyle thought the first part of Union Road was bumpy, he surely thought his teeth would rattle out of his head before they reached a paved road again.

"Is it a dirt road all the way there?"

"No. We'll hit 180 in a little bit." Moses paused and looked over at Kyle. "The combination of a big supper, my Jeep, and Union Road isn't a real good one, huh?"

"I'm okay. I'm just use to the paved interstate in Columbus." They arrived at a stop sign and a paved road. "Finally!" Kyle joked.

"Okay, Kyle. This is 180. If you turn left, it'll take you back to thirty-three, about fourteen miles from here. It's the easiest route to Serenity, but a little longer than the way I brought you."

Moses turned right and headed towards Laurelville. Within a few minutes on the smooth paved road, they arrived in the center of the village.

"This is Laurelville, Kyle." Moses dropped his voice and sounded like a tour guide. "On the right, you see the village gas station. After we make a right at this stop sign, you'll see the grocery store behind the gas station. Don't miss the village café on your left! They have some great home cookin'!"

"I see what you mean. It *is* quaint." They pulled into the parking lot of the store.

As they exited the car, Moses said, "Now, you might want to stick close to me in here. I don't want you getting lost." He laughed. When they entered the store, Kyle realized why. It was a very small grocery—but to him, it felt like home. They grabbed some milk and checked out. Moses chatted with the cashier and Kyle couldn't help but notice how friendly the locals seemed.

When they were on their way back to Serenity, Kyle asked, "What did Grandmother say to you this morning before you left for your shop?"

Moses tilted his head towards the side and exhaled. "I was hoping you would forget that conversation."

"Not me. I have the memory of an elephant."

"Well, that must be the only thing about you that's like an elephant because it doesn't look like you have an ounce of fat on you."

Kyle was flustered by the compliment, but said, "Thank you…but, I still want to know what Grandmother said."

Moses wiggled his jaw at being caught trying to change the subject. "Oh, she was giving me one of her predictions. That's all."

"One of her predictions, huh? And, the prediction was what?" Kyle pushed forward with the light-hearted interrogation.

"Are you always this curious?" Moses teased.

"Only when someone's evasive."

"Okay…okay…she told me that I was going to meet a very attractive helper before the day was over."

Moses looked sheepishly at Kyle. "There...are you satisfied now?"

Kyle smiled as his own face turned red. He wanted to say something, but he couldn't find the right words.

"And, if you're wondering if she was right...I would say she hit the bull's-eye." Moses added.

Kyle felt butterflies in his stomach. He tried to blame it on the bumpy road, but knew it was something he had never felt before—something that he had tried to create with his ex-wife, but never had. An uneasy quiet fell inside the Jeep.

"Well, this silence is awkward," Moses said. "I'm sorry if I'm making you uncomfortable."

"No, it's okay. I just don't know how to react. I'm extremely flattered..."

"But...the feeling isn't mutual?" Moses ventured.

Kyle laughed nervously. "Oh, no! The feeling is mutual...I'm just shocked that you find me attractive. When I first saw you, I thought I wasn't in your league."

By this time, they had pulled back into the driveway of Serenity. Moses stopped the Jeep abruptly and put it in park at the start of the drive. "Kyle, you don't know me very well. We just met a few hours ago, but there's one thing that pisses me off."

Kyle felt a bit uncomfortable with Moses looking directly at him. "I wasn't trying to piss you off. What did I say?"

"You said something negative about yourself. You didn't think I would find you attractive? That's insane and it's negative self-talk. Don't do that to yourself. You are a beautiful creation of God—physically and, what

I've learned in these few short hours, spiritually, too. Helena was dead-on...I did meet some *very* attractive today."

Kyle was overwhelmed. He felt his eyes water. "This has been an incredible day. I'll try not to do that again. Thank you. Your words mean a lot to me."

"Good. That's settled. Now, let's go eat some of your grandmother's kick-ass brownies." He put Jeep back in gear and headed up the drive towards the house.

Chapter 11

Open! Open!

The door has been closed for years

And I've only had my tears

As moisture in this arid place

To soften and cleanse my face.

This dank, dark, and dreary cell

Has at many times been hell;

Though I would fight to stay in,

I knew that lying was sin.

The ghosts, like clothes, drape around

This box which causes my frown.

I am pressed to live this way—

A morbid gloom without day.

The Labyrinth Home

A stale silence fills the air
As family, friends just stare;
"You are in your home!" they say,
While my faint soul fades away.

"Silence! Silence!" a voice sighs,
"This is not where you will die!"
The voice, a familiar ring.
It is my soul about to sing.

I will my flesh to react,
To face the spiritual fact
That I am what God has made.
It is past time to obey.

I push gently on the door
And my mind shakes at its core.
Is this just disparity?
Can I live Integrity?

"Open! Open!" my voice screams.

It is time to live the dream.

"Open! Open!" again, I cry,

"This cell is not where I'll die!"

—*Kyle*

Kyle set the pen on the desk in the upstairs bedroom at Serenity. He had spent the night and it was now six o'clock in the morning. He had been awake for thirty minutes, but felt the urge to write before going downstairs for coffee. He had found a black, leather-bound blank journal on the desk when he went to bed the night before. Inside the cover was a note:

For Kyle, may the labyrinth you travel be well documented so that others might learn from your experiences. Love, Grandmother

The aroma of fresh-brewed coffee wafted into the bedroom. Kyle pulled on his jeans from the day before and headed downstairs without putting on a shirt. When he entered the kitchen he saw Helena and Moses sitting at the table sipping from coffee mugs. Kyle quickly ran his fingers through his hair trying to arrange his frizzy curls.

"Good morning, Sunshine!" Moses enthusiastically bellowed. "Wow! That's some mop you have on your head first thing in the morning."

Kyle crossed his arms in front of him at the discomfort of Moses seeing him at his worst and wished that he had put on a shirt. "I wasn't expecting anyone else to be moving about this early."

"The early bird gets the worm! We're early birds 'round here," Grandmother said. "Moses has coffee with me every morning before he heads into Roasters. It's our time to discuss life and dreams and such. Did you sleep okay?"

Kyle noticed a clean mug sitting next to the coffee maker. "Like a baby. Is that mug for me?"

"Sure is. Help yourself." Helena answered.

Moses regarded Kyle as he poured himself a cup of coffee. He thought he should try to redeem himself for the comment about the hair. "That's what I thought. Not an ounce of fat on you! Is that a six or eight pack you have there, Kyle?"

"I think it's more like a four-pack right now. I need to get back to doing crunches again," Kyle answered with a bit of humor.

Moses wanted to feel the firmness of Kyle's abs, but decided not to in front of Helena. Kyle sat at the table next to Moses and took his first sip of coffee. Helena caught Moses eyeing her grandson's shirtless torso and smiled to herself. The three talked for about an hour before Moses left for work.

After eating breakfast together and cleaning the kitchen, Helena asked Kyle to join her on a walk to the pond. They left the house and made their way down the gentle slope behind it towards the pond. Kyle recognized it from his dreams. The spring air was refreshing and a light breeze tossed Kyle's curls.

"I love the morning sun. There's something almost magical about it, it makes me feel so renewed and warmed," Kyle said. "This property is beautiful, Grandmother. Did Mom grow up here?"

"Yes, she did." Helena stopped at a large rock next to the pond and sat on it. Her right hand held her staff. "Take a load off your feet, Kyle."

Kyle sat on the vibrant green grass and felt the wetness of the morning dew that hadn't yet dried in the morning sun. "I can't believe that I dreamed of this exact place. It's amazing." He pointed to the gravel drive that moved up the steep hill on one side of the pond. "Is that the drive to Moses' cabin?"

"Uh-huh. I'll let you make that trip yourself. At my age, the slope is little too much for me. His cabin is in the back corner of the property. You can't see it from here because of the trees. I had it built ten years ago and used to rent it on the weekends, but when Moses came along, I decided to let him stay year 'round."

"What do you think about him, Grandmother?"

Helena looked at Kyle intensely. "I sense you're trying to get my approval or insight into a future with him. Am I right?"

"Well, from what I gather, you seem to have a pretty good grasp of the future. I was wondering if you see anything working out between the two of us."

"Oh, I don't interfere too much in matters of the heart. That's for the two of you to discover."

"Is that another one of your veiled answers?" Kyle asked jokingly.

Helena chuckled. "You should know by now, Kyle, I rarely disclose everything about anything. It's not my place to use the gifts for my own empowerment or to manipulate others. Besides, the human will is a fickle thing. Take your mother for instance. I *knew* that she would marry your father in spite of my disapproval, but I didn't think that they would still be married today."

Kyle was surprised by her candidness. "Is the marriage what created the rift between you?"

"Your mother didn't want me interfering with her life. She knew I didn't approve of Elijah, but she had her own will and submitted it to him. I always believed—and still do—that she would retrieve her will back from your father. The day is coming."

"Why didn't you approve of their marriage?"

Helena remained silent for a few moments before answering. "Look at these hills, Kyle. Most people prefer to be on the tops of them to see all around and to be seen by those beneath them. They'll fight and claw their way to reach the top. They think there's power in the high places. I recognized that in your father at an early age. I saw that he would sacrifice anything to be on the top of the hill. You know from first-hand experience that he enjoys his perch. He enjoys everyone looking up to him, and he falsely believes that he's in the most spiritual place." She paused and looked across the pond before pointing. Kyle followed her gaze and saw three deer drinking at the water's edge.

"Kyle," Helena continued in whispered tones, "the spiritual places are really found in the low places. See the deer over there. They've come down from the hill to drink from the spring. Look at all these hills. They meet here in the valley where the source of life is. The peaks would not have any connection to each other if it weren't for the low places. And it's connection that honors Spirit, not separation, not titles or high perches." She paused and methodically continued. "This pond is feed by a spring that can only be accessed in this valley. The source of life and communion is here…not on the hilltop. The deer can't sustain themselves on the hill for long. They always have to come deeper into Mother Earth. Yes, the mountaintop experiences are exhilarating…but it's in the valley that one finds that his thirst is truly quenched and community flourishes."

Kyle listened intently. "I've never thought of it like that. I've always seen the mountaintop as the goal. Maybe that's because I've always seen my father either climbing it or at the top looking down." Kyle thought about what he was saying. "Yeah, actually, he is always looking down on people, including his own family."

"You're being forced into the valley now—as all of us have been or will be. Don't look at it as the Valley of Death. No. It's the Valley of Life. The valley is where you will find the strength of community and commonality. You've been afraid of the valley for many years, but it's your salvation. I know you've struggled, out of fear of not being on the mountain with your father, to accept the man that Creator designed you to be. But, know that your life source is in the valley. Water always seeks the lowest point. It's in the lowest point where cleansing and purification take place by the power of water. All life springs forth from water. Before birth, you're surrounded by water and it's the breaking of a mother's water that signals new life is about to emerge." Helena paused and scanned the hills and the pond.

She seemed inspired as the deer trotted into the woods. "Yes...do you see how this valley is a womb of Mother Earth? This is where you will find hope and new life."

Kyle was moved to tears and felt a warmth flood his entire being. "I just don't know what to do next, Grandmother. Dad has fired me from my job and told me that I'm dead to him. He even told me not to go near Mom. I really don't know what to do."

Helena bristled and stamped her staff. "Your father really pisses my pisser off sometimes." She then gave a soothing laugh. "He'll learn, though...he will learn."

"Is there something you're not telling me, Grandmother?" Helena didn't respond to his question. "Do you know about the affairs?"

Helena couldn't hide the shock in her face. Her eyes popped wide and asked, "*You* know about the affairs? I hadn't counted on you knowing."

"Yeah, I've known for a while. So does Ruth. I guess we've tried to hide it from Mom, but I suspect she knows—she's pretty intuitive, you know."

"She knows, Kyle. She just has to get to where you are and realize that the valley isn't such a bad place."

"Should I say something to her?"

"Absolutely not!" Helena scolded him emphatically.. "Deny your ego's urge to get even with your father by exposing him. The truth always has a way of leaking out...just like the water from this spring. Let the Universe take care of the revealing of your father's infidelities. Just because you have knowledge of something, doesn't mean you should be the one who announces it to the world." Her voice softened, "Surely you realize that your father is coming down so hard on you to deflect his own guilt."

"Yeah, I guess you're right."

"You are a *healer*. Don't use your gifts in the negative."

"A healer…is that why I feel my hands getting hot around people who are ill and during church services?"

Helena smiled enthusiastically. "Yes…yes…just like when you were ten and were a channel of healing for Ruth. You still have the gift. In fact, most people can be the channel, but there are a few who are *especially* gifted. Come here." She waved in her direction. Kyle stood and approached her. She took his left wrist in her hand and placed his hand just under her ribs. "I want you to close your eyes. Don't rest your hand on my body, but let it hover an inch above me."

Kyle did as instructed. Within a minute, he felt a tingling sensation in his fingertips and a slight vibration, before a pulse of heat left his palm. "Wow! I feel something like electricity."

"Yes, I feel it, too. Keep your eyes closed. Do you see anything in your mind's eye as you feel the warmth in your hand?"

Kyle kept his hand in place and his eyes closed. At first all he envisioned was an array of beautiful colors streaming through darkness. Then he saw what looked like intestines, but they were lined with black dots. Helena watched Kyle's mouth as it fell into a frown. "I'm not sure that I can see anything," he responded.

"Yes, you can, Ki. Tell me what you see."

Kyle hesitated and then felt an urging in his spirit to speak. "It looks like I'm seeing your colon and there are dark spots along it. It doesn't look good."

"Do you still feel the heat coming out of your palm?"

"It's subsiding."

"Good. When it's gone completely, say a prayer of thanksgiving before removing your hand." Kyle followed his grandmother's instructions.

When he was finished, he looked at Helena with deep concern. "Do you have cancer, Grandmother?"

"No, Ki. Not cancer. I have an occasional bout with colitis. What you saw was some scarring from that. You did very good work! I told you that you had a special gift of healing."

"Yeah, well...I'll never be able to use it in church as a gay man, so what good is it?"

"Quit looking to the hilltop. Your two-spirited gifts will be more than utilized here at Serenity! That's what breaks my heart about the Pentecostals and Charismatics, they put a wonderful emphasis on the gifts of the Spirit as found in 1 Corinthians Chapter 12 but then won't allow two-spirited people to practice in their churches. Somehow, they overlook the eleventh verse, which says that the Creator gives the gifts as he determines. Man cannot determine who can or cannot work his or her gifts. It's Spirit that determines who receives the gifts." She sighed. "You're always welcome to practice your gifts here, Ki."

Kyle smiled. "I like it when you call me Ki. It tingles when you say it."

"Well, Ki is a Japanese word for energy. Or you might recognize the Chinese word as *chi.* I think Ki is perfect for you!"

"Yeah, I've heard the term *chi* before, and Ki is a great short form of my name. You can call me Ki anytime, Grandmother." Kyle looked into the pond and saw bass and bluegill moving through the water.

"Well, I'm going to head up to the house," she said. "Why don't you walk around the property some." She stood up from the rock. "A fence marks the line on three sides and Moses keeps a path mowed around the entire perimeter. You'll find a labyrinth as you head up the drive to his cabin. I have some reading to do and then I'll fix some lunch. I gave D.J. the day off today since I knew you would be here, so I hope you'll enjoy a meatloaf sandwich. Do you like mustard on yours?"

"Mustard is great."

"Take your time. Let nature speak to you—she has much to teach you." Helena stood to go back to the house.

"Grandmother," Kyle spoke, "the labyrinth...what exactly is it? I mean I know what a maze is, but is there some significance to it?"

Helena chuckled at Kyle's inquisitiveness. "There *is* a difference between a maze and a labyrinth. A maze has many entrances and exits with multiple paths. It can be any shape. There are dead ends and you're forced to make choices. A labyrinth, on the other hand, is circular with one path that leads to the center. There is only one way in and one way out. In this way, there is no need to engage the logic part of the brain—you just follow the path before you. Serenity's labyrinth contains three sign-posts. The first one simply states 'trust' and it's at the entrance. The second one is located halfway through the journey has the word 'hope' inscribed on it. The final and greatest marker at the very center is 'love'.

"The labyrinth has been a sacred symbol to Gnostics, Pagans, and Christians. It's a powerful and spiritual tool that symbolizes the death of the ego with all of its addictions and the rebirth of the divine spirit. It's a visual reference to the earth-womb and designed for a slow meditative walk. When you walk through it, you'll see that there are several areas along the path to sit and meditate. I encourage you to take your time when you enter it, and learn what you can about your own calling and purpose in life. It's a wonderful way to slow the racing mind and quiet all the external influences, and awaken your inner spirit. Entering the labyrinth symbolizes going inward to receive. Exiting is simply taking what you've learned into the real world. It's quite simply a walking meditation—a spiritual path." When she finished with the explanation, she made her way back towards the house. Kyle followed her with his eyes for a while and then looked again at the pond before heading towards the drive up the hill.

Kyle decided to check out the cabin first and then come back to the labyrinth. When he reached the top of the hill, he turned and looked at the view. He could see for miles. He smiled to himself at the beauty of the trees coming to life on the hills around him and in the distance. He turned back towards the cabin and let out a sigh. The house in front of him was a traditional, two-story log home with a stone chimney on one end and a green metal roof. The front porch had a swing hanging from the rafters and a matching end table made of western red cedar. He walked around the side of the house and found a screened porch on the back side. A gas grill sat next to the porch and from the looks of it, it had never been used. Kyle wondered if Moses cooked, or ate with Grandmother all the time. A humming sound caught his attention and he looked around. He found the source of the noise and was delighted to see a hot tub. He was just thinking about pulling his clothes off and jumping in when he heard, "What the hell are you doing?"

Kyle jumped and spun around in a scream, "Oh, shit!"

Moses stood in front of him, holding his stomach, and laughing. "Oh, I'm sorry. I didn't mean to startle you. I was just trying to see who was snooping around my house."

Kyle tried to get his wits about him and nervously laughed. "Yeah, I see how sorry you are. Somehow the laughter negates your apology."

"You should have seen yourself jump!" Moses couldn't keep from laughing. His eyes watered.

"You scared the shit out of me, Moses! What was I supposed to do, fall asleep?" Now, Kyle was laughing at himself, trying to imagine what he must have looked like screaming like a girl.

"Well, I'm guessing that wasn't your 'butchest' moment."

"Enough already," Kyle pleaded. "What the hell are you doing home? I thought you were at the shop all day."

"Zoe stopped in and decided to volunteer today. She thought I could use a day off for some reason. I parked down at your Grandmother's because I thought you'd be with her. She told me that you came up here so I thought I'd surprise you."

"Congratulations...you succeeded in surprising the shit right out of me."

"Did you see the hot tub?"

Kyle nodded.

"Were you thinking about hopping in?"

"Well, I was...but I think I need to change my underwear now!"

Moses smiled and raised his eyebrows flirtatiously at Kyle. "The only rule I have about the hot tub is "no clothes allowed."

Kyle replied sarcastically. "I suppose you've had scores of men just bite on that line haven't you?"

Moses seemed offended by the remark. "I was just kidding, Ki. Honestly, I've never had anyone else in the hot tub with me."

"Did you just call me Ki?"

"Yeah...is something wrong with that?"

Kyle chuckled. "Not at all. That's what Grandmother is calling me. I really like it."

"Well, it doesn't matter whether you like it or not, because that's what I'm calling you from now on." Moses' eyes shimmered with excitement. "So, was that comment about "other guys" your way of finding out if I'm seeing someone?"

"Actually, I was just trying to be cute…but, since you brought it up…are you seeing someone?"

"I'm available." Moses was purposefully coy.

"And?"

"And…what? What else do you want to know?"

"Have you ever dated anyone? How many people have you been with? Do you have children? Do you want children? Do want a relationship? Do you…"

Moses cut him off. "Hold on there, Mr. Lawyer. Am I on trial or something? I can't remember all the questions if you fire them off in rapid succession. First, I've had two semi-serious relationships in my life. I told you about the one guy yesterday that lasted for about a year. We never lived together—thank god! Before him, I was engaged to be married. I was thirty. We called off the wedding two days before it was scheduled. I told her about my inclination towards men and we decided that marriage wasn't right. So, I don't have children. I've been a very active uncle to my nieces and nephews and love them like my own. I'm crazy about my sister and her family in Indiana—she has two boys and her husband's a really neat guy. One of these days, you'll get to meet them. I know you'd love them right from the start. And as far as a relationship …" Moses paused for dramatic effect, "I think I'm finally ready to be in one. I feel like I've come into my own and that I'm a whole person. So, yeah, finding another whole person who isn't looking for someone to fill in their own gap would be great."

"Sounds like you have your feces neatly consolidated," Kyle mused.

"What?"

Kyle smiled at Moses and chuckled. "You have your shit together."

Moses laughed. "Oh, I get it—must be the writer in you, waxing poetic."

"Grandmother is going to have lunch ready. I should head back down."

"I'll walk with you." Moses wrapped his arm around Kyle's shoulder in a brotherly fashion and started towards the drive. Kyle felt the warmth of Moses' spirit in the firm embrace and placed his own arm on Moses' shoulder. As the two headed down the drive towards the old farmhouse, Kyle felt a comfortable friendship blossoming between them just like the Lilies of the Valley that fragrantly lined the gravel road.

Chapter 12

Kyle sat in the middle of the labyrinth at Serenity, peacefully watching some ants scurry about their business as he held onto a piece of paper. A fall gust of wind shook the tall grasses around him as he pondered the events of the last five months and how so much had changed for him. When he had returned to his apartment after a week's visit to Serenity in May, he discovered that his father was evicting him. He should have known that was coming since the church owned the apartment complex that he lived in, but it had caught him completely off guard. He was allowed to take a few personal effects and his computer, but the furniture and everything else had to stay. His grandmother graciously opened her home to him and he had settled into the slower paced life of Serenity and the surrounding Hocking Hills. He worked at Roasters with Moses most days, and Helena utilized his healing gifts at Serenity whenever she had a class or retreat. Although he wasn't getting rich, and, in fact, was making less money than he had ever made in his life; he felt more secure and comfortable than ever.

Ruth had made the trip several times over the summer to visit Kyle and their grandmother. She was thrilled that Kyle was making it without the assistance of their parents. Mark and Naomi had joined her on a couple of the visits and just loved the surroundings of Serenity. Helena said that Naomi was a natural at seeing into the spirit world and that Ruth should bring her to visit more often for some training. Mark was impressed with Helena's perspective on spirituality and agreed that they would indeed encourage Naomi to seek out spiritual growth. Ruth and Kyle continued to talk on the phone at least once a week.

From a spiritual perspective, Kyle was being exposed to schools of thought that he never would have explored before the transition to Serenity. He was now seeing Universal Truth in all great religions. When he had first begun his spiritual quest, he had initially rejected his own religious upbringing and wanted nothing to do with Christianity. Helena scolded him several times about not "*throwing the baby out with the bath water*" and encouraged him "*to hear with his spiritual ears the teachings of Christ and not the dogma or hierarchy of a particular denomination.*" He now felt at peace with the ideas with which he had been raised and was able to focus on the positives of Charismatic Teachings, including their celebratory praise, their emphasis on the gifts of the Spirit, and even their understanding of the Laws of Attraction and Reciprocity.

In the past five months, Kyle had emailed his mother several times explaining that he was happy and felt at peace with God for the first time in his life. He looked down at the paper in his hands and read the most recent reply from her one more time:

> *Kyle,*
> *"You speak lies and the truth is not in you." You are the exception to every rule you apply to others. Every*

time I have written you it has been an effort to win back your love. You have spit on it!!! You do not love me. You DID intend to hurt me, even kill me emotionally. I will no longer be controlled by you. YOU are judgmental! Your GOD does not exist! Christian pagans create their own gods and call them Jesus in total disregard for GOD's Word. Your GOD is not the GOD of the Bible because you do not believe the truths written in it. Once you were my son. I still love my son. But you have left that station. I will miss my son deeply; however, I have been accused by you the last time! I have answered dearly and live daily with the consequences of every sin I have committed since becoming a Christian. The HOLY SOVEREIGN GOD OF THIS UNIVERSE and my HEAVENLY FATHER ALONE will be my judge. He describes himself as merciful, loving, forgiving and above all faithful. You are none of these!! I will no longer allow you to judge me with the rules you do not live by, or respect. I exercise I John 1:9 every single day by confessing my sins and GOD hears and answers me. Do not EVER communicate with me again in any form—Ever— unless you are begging my forgiveness and speaking with respect! Your e-mail address is removed from my records. I will see you on Judgment Day before the throne of God where all will be perfectly clear. My only hope is that you return to the fold before that Day of Reckoning. In the meantime, I have a son who has left me forever. It saddens me but when Satan takes away, God often gives even more than we have lost! Your Mother

"I thought I might find you here," Moses said as he approached Kyle. Kyle folded the email and smiled at him. He was glad to see him. Their relationship had deepened over the last few months since first meeting in May. "Your grandmother said you left out of the house in a bit of a huff after getting an email from your mother. She said you didn't want to talk to her about it and that she saw you heading in this direction."

Kyle handed Moses the printed email without saying a word. When he had finished reading it, he asked, "Are you okay?"

"Honestly…I'm numb. At first, I was pissed…but really…did I think her response would be different this?"

"What can I do to help?" Moses moved closer to Kyle and put his arms around him.

Kyle melted into his arms. "Hugs are wonderful," he sheepishly responded. At the warmth of the hug, Kyle started weeping.

Moses held Kyle's face in his hands to make eye contact with him. "Look at me, Ki. You are a wonderful human being. I'm so amazed at how open your spirit is and at how sensitive you are to everyone's needs here at Serenity. I've never met anyone so gifted, except for maybe your grandmother. Your mother just needs time. Don't let her or anyone else bring you down. I wish I had half the talent that you have and half the ability to share love the way you do. You are *wonderful*, Ki. And that's why I love you."

It was the first time Moses had uttered those words to him. Kyle sensed an almost tangible healing balm surround him. Kyle's tears of sadness turned into tears of joy as he started giggling. "I love you, too, Moses!" Their faces moved towards each other and their lips met in their first tender kiss.

Moses pulled away from Kyle and looked directly in his eyes. "I've wanted to do that for so long. Your lips are so full and beautiful. God that was nice!" Moses leaned over and they kissed again. This time the kiss lasted much longer and Moses gently pressed his chest into Kyle's until they were lying on the ground together.

When Moses pulled back this time, the evening sunlight around his head looked like a halo to Kyle. "You're an angel," Kyle sighed as he brushed the loose hair from Moses' face.

Moses touched Kyle's nose with his index finger. "I think you should get back to your grandmother's and let her know you're okay. I have some chores to do at the cabin and then I'll be down for supper. I'll see you in about an hour, Ki." In spite of his desire to stay with Moses and in his warm embrace, Kyle agreed to go back to the farmhouse.

As Kyle approached the back of the house, he noticed D.J. shaking rugs outside. She smiled at him and asked, "Are you okay?"

"I'm doing better, D.J." Kyle knew D.J. well enough to know that when he stormed out of the house earlier that she would question his grandmother about his mood. He assumed that his grandmother had shared the email with her.

"I hope you don't mind...and I know it's none of business, but..." she paused and took a deep breath after shaking a rug, "I just want you to know. If you were my son, there's nothing that you could do that would make me stop loving you. My boys have done things that I'm not proud of and wished they'd never done, but I still love 'em. If you ask me, I think Debbie has been brainwashed by your father! Hell, I wouldn't be surprised if he wrote that email and then sent it from her account. Your grandmother wouldn't want me telling you this, but if it were me and I received an email like you did, I'd march myself over to the Logan Daily News and have them print up an obituary and then send it to her." D.J. was noticeably agitated. Her normally pale cheeks were flushed red. "Now, that's what I'd do! I'd be happy to have a son like you."

"Thank you," Kyle said warmly.

"I'm serious!" D.J. answered. "Some people don't have the sense God gave a goose. I just about had a conniption when your grandmother told me what Debbie said to you! I was so mad I took a wash rag and beat the dryer to get the tension out of me."

Kyle chuckled. He knew full well that anytime D.J. was enraged, she'd beat the dryer with a towel. He had watched her do it several times since his arrival to Serenity. Most times it was over her adult sons that depended too heavily on her and she would arrive at Serenity in a huff. "Are you *feeling* better now?"

"Now I have one of my bad headaches. Would you have time to lay your hands on my head and do that magic stuff you do to help make it go away, Ki?"

"I can do that for you, D.J. but it'll cost you." Kyle said with a grin.

"Well, I just made a fresh batch of chocolate chip cookies. Would that pay the bill?"

Kyle's face lit up. "I think that is a perfect trade!" The two went into the house and D.J. put the rugs back in place. Kyle went into the living room and waited for D.J. to follow. When she entered the room, she took a seat in the recliner. Kyle placed his hands just over the top of her head and closed his eyes. Silently he prayed, *"I ask for the healing angels to manifest in this place and I open myself as a vessel of pure light and love. May the love of God flow through me into this beautiful creature of light."*

Kyle felt the familiar warmth in his hands. He intentionally visualized the color green because of the color's effects on the autonomic nervous system. He had recently studied the effects of color on the body and its ability to heal. Kyle knew that green was great to use for high blood pressure, anxiety, and headaches. In fact, his grandmother had told him that she knew he was a natural healer because his aura had a strong green hue to it. It was Helena that had taught him that the heart chakra was associated with the color green and was the bridge between the spiritual and natural world. Kyle focused his attention in the area of his heart and visualized seeing green grow from inside him, engulfing his body, and channeling through his hands.

Kyle heard D.J. make a cooing sound and opened his eyes slightly. With his eyes just barely open, he was able to visually see the color green emanate from his hands. Slowly the color surrounded D.J.'s head. Kyle felt a slight tingling sensation in his hands as the physical healing manifested. He had learned through experience that the tingling sensation only happened when a physical healing took place. If he was performing a spiritual or emotional mending through energy work, all he felt was the gentle warmth. Sometimes the prickling sensation was uncomfortable for him if the individual had serious ailments, but this time is was not so painful. Soon the quivering stopped in his hands and the heat subsided. He said a silent thank you and removed his hands.

"Oh, my! That's so much better, Ki." D.J. enthused. "I love that magic touch of yours. I'm telling you, I could feel a fire start at the top of my head and move down my neck!" She moved her head back and forth.

"Do you feel better?" Kyle asked.

"One hundred percent better!" She jumped up from the recliner and gave Kyle a big hug. "Thank you much, dear! You really have a gift there, Ki—one *any* mother should be proud of!" With a wink, a nod and a pat on his shoulder, she strolled out of the living room and returned to her work in the kitchen. "Ki, if you want a cookie or two before supper, I won't tell your grandmother."

Kyle moved into the kitchen and was about to grab a cookie when he heard Helena say, "Yes, but you don't want to spoil your supper. Save them for dessert, young man."

Kyle turned towards the living room and saw Helena standing near the door to her room. "How long have you been there?"

Helena gave a jovial look of scolding and said, "Long enough to know that I can't leave you two alone for very long, or else there'll be trouble!"

"Ah, Helena, you know I wouldn't do anything with Ki that would get him in *too* much trouble." D.J. clucked.

Helena walked towards Kyle and put her arm around his waist. "Good work, Ki. I watched the whole treatment. I saw you used the color green in the healing. It's amazing to watch your aura change colors as you work. It's usually a thin blue with the green point right at your heart chakra, but when you're doing a healing it grows in thickness and swirls with the primary color your working with. It's just magnificent to watch!"

"There you go with that aura stuff again, Helena. I sure wish I could see people's auras…it just sounds like a wonderful thing to glimpse!" D.J. said wistfully.

"I keep tellin' you to meditate and concentrate. I'd be happy to do some training with you, D.J. They're very helpful in learning people's true intentions no matter what their words might be saying."

"Well, one of these days, Helena, I'm gonna take some time and let you train me. I just have a few things on my chore that have to get done first." She broke into a cackle. Kyle and Helena to joined her in laughter. "But right now, I need to get out of here and head home for the day. Do you need anything else before I go?"

"No. You get home to your husband, and tell Leo I said hello," Helena answered. D.J. folded a dish towel and hung it on the front of the stove before giving

Helena and Kyle a hug. She headed out of the house and left in her white Lincoln.

Helena asked Kyle, "How are you doing? Better?"

"Yeah, I'm feeling a little better."

"The best cure for your own hurt is to always reach out to others in pain. That's what's so great about the Universe and its healing energy...when you act as a channel for healing, you receive healing too." Kyle nodded and smiled warmly at Helena. "And, I couldn't help but notice a bit of pink in your aura, too."

Kyle blushed and tried to change the direction in which Helena was headed. "Well, I read that pink is useful in raising energy and healing. Besides...if it appears in your aura it means you've obtained the balance of spiritual enlightenment and worldly being."

Helena narrowed her eyes at Kyle to signal that she wouldn't be easily rebuffed. A tender laugh seeped from her lips. "I see you've been studying your book of colors, but I don't think that's symbolic of what I saw. I'm sure that since you've been reading about colors that you also know that pink reveals the beginning of a new relationship. It is the color of friendship, purity, and *love*—a sign of a new *relationship*!"

Kyle heard the screen door open on the back of the house and Moses walked in. "What's for supper?" he asked. Kyle looked at Moses. He felt Helena's eyes on him.

"Yes...yes...your pink is certainly glowing now," Helena said with a twinkle in her eye. Moses looked at Kyle questioningly, but thought it would be best not to ask what she was talking about.

Kyle was in his bedroom at Serenity, sitting at his desk writing in the journal his grandmother had given him when he arrived. The feelings from earlier in the afternoon swept over him as he thought of the embrace and first kiss he and Moses had shared. After supper, the two men cleaned the kitchen and spent time with Helena, telling stories and laughing. When Moses was ready to return to his cabin, Kyle had walked outside with him where they had shared another kiss and a warm embrace. Kyle watched Moses walk up the hill to his cabin until he was out of sight.

Kyle down his pen and read his poem:

Let

Let his eyes ensnare me—

I am stilled by their charm.

Let his eyes capture me—

In them I feel no harm!

Let his laugh beckon me—

I am calmed by its tone.

Let his laugh entice me—

My heart, no longer stone!

Let his arms embrace me—

I am warmed by his touch.

Let his arms surround me—

It is never too much!

Let his heart overcome me—

I find health in its glow.

Let his heart empower me—

There is life in its flow!

Let his love ignite me—

I am wooed by its call.

Let his love engulf me—

I surrender my all!

—Kyle

Kyle closed the journal and undressed for bed. He lay on his side and positioned a pillow against his back. He wondered what it would feel like to have Moses' arms wrapped around him in bed. Slowly, he drifted off. As he slept, dreams of a future with Moses filled him with love. Despite the hateful email he had received from his mother earlier in the day, he was at peace.

Chapter 13

After the church incident on Mother's Day, the local media had been investigating everything about Earth Reaping Church. Accusations about financial mismanagement related to their home and vehicles surfaced after an investigative report exposed Helena as Deborah's mother and that she operated a New Age retreat. Eli had been very adept at deflecting criticism from the local media. Things had settled down. He had even been able to use the situation with Kyle as a springboard to continue his battle against same-sex marriage.

Deborah turned the story of her mother's intrusion into the service as a call against the growth of New Age spiritualism in the religious broadcasting community. She had appeared on several nationally televised religious talk-shows to promote her crusade against the growing battle between the New Age Movement and traditional Christian values. Deborah even told people that her mother had influenced Kyle to join forces with her, and that her heart was broken over the loss of her son to a cult. The controversy had actually led to a windfall in donations to Earth Reaping Ministry.

While the ministry of the church was acquiring a harvest of donations and a furry of growth, the marriage between the two pastors was withering. Deborah had become increasingly suspicious of the relationship between Eli and Joni. Eli had been working more and more at the church since Kyle had been let go. He said

it was because he was picking up Kyle's former respon-
sibilities and couldn't complete his work and Kyle's in a
normal workday. Deborah sensed the he wasn't telling
the truth. In fact, her dreams were filled with visions of
Eli's infidelities and she knew from past experience that
when her dreams repeated, she should pay attention.

This night was the last straw. Deborah was furious as
she closed her cell phone after failing to reach Eli for
the last three hours. She was sitting in her Hummer in
the church parking lot next to Eli's parked car. There
was only one other car in the lot and she knew exactly
who owned it—Joni Paisley.

Deborah contemplated going back home, but she
was boiling with anger. She decided to go inside. She
entered the church and crept quietly through the halls
to the office area. The door to Eli's office was slightly
ajar and she heard voices coming from inside. Deborah
leaned close and listened.

"Tell me what you want, Joni," Eli said in a strained
voice.

"I want you to end it with Deborah!" she seethed.
Deborah's heart thumped in her ears like a drum as she
listened to the conversation.

"I've told you, Baby, it's complicated. I don't know
how the church would survive if we divorced."

"Don't give me that crap, Eli. You know as well as
I do that there are many other televangelist who have
divorced and are still on the air. Do I need to name
them?"

"I know, Joni. I know." Eli took a deep breath and
after a moment, continued. "I've been thinking about

using the incident with her mother as an excuse. It's been a few months since it happened. Kyle's run off to be with her and I could say that Deborah's starting to return to her roots of Pagan worship. I think that would play well for me."

"Then what are you waiting for? Do you want to spend the rest of your life with that dried up prune, or do you want to continue to have my sweet honey? From my perspective, I can't imagine why you'd want to stay with her when you could have someone as young as me."

Deborah couldn't take anymore. She slammed the door open. It hit the wall with a thunderous crash. Joni was sitting on Eli's lap in the chair behind his desk. Both Eli and Joni jumped to their feet instantly. "Eli Hershel Basil!" Deborah screamed as she marched to the front of his desk and rested both hands on the edge of the wood. "Do you really think I'm that easy to get rid of? Do you think I'd let you just tell people that I melted into the sunset to follow some Pagan Religion? Do you? Do you?"

"Uh-Deborah…you…ummm…you…misunder-stood. Joni and I were just going over some music for…"

"Save me the lies, Eli!" Deborah faced Joni and pointed in her direction. "And, do you think that you're the *first* tramp that he's slept with?" Joni looked shocked and scared by Deborah's rage. "Please! You're just another whore in a long line of whores that have come before you. Do you really think you can take him away from this church? Do you really think that he can divorce me and run off with you? I'm sorry, but this is *my* church and no slut is going to take my place!"

Joni stammered and tears welled in her eyes. Deborah enjoyed the power she felt as she stood before the two adulterers. The fear and tears from Joni fueled Deborah's rage. She laughed maniacally.

"Let me enlighten both of you about this church, the house, and everything else you think you own, Eli. Half of everything is mine!" Deborah turned back towards Eli. "Do you really want to hand half of your empire over to me? Let me make myself clear...I will NOT go quietly into the sunset. If you want to start divorce proceedings, I'm ready! Bring it on, Baby! *You* will loose this church! I'll make sure of it because I'm the one with the Biblical reason for divorce. And, trust me, I've kept a record of all the other harlots. *I'm* the one with the connections to all the religious talk shows. Who do you think the people will follow, you, or the wife who faithfully stood by her cheating husband for forty years?"

Eli's face turned blood red; he reached across the desk and grabbed Deborah by the shoulders. "Are you threatening me, Deborah? This is my empire, not yours! *I* built this church. *I* bring the people in every week. *I* raise the funds to support every last ministry. *I* am the pastor!"

"Let loose of me, Elijah or I'll call nine-one-one, or would you rather see spousal abuse added to the front-page headline!" Eli released Deborah with a shove. She stumbled backwards before regaining her balance and readjusted her outfit. "I've had it Eli! This is the last time! Do you hear me? The last time I hang my head and keep my mouth shut!" She stormed out of the office and slammed the door.

Deborah left the church, got into her Hummer, and drove with screeching tires out of the parking lot. Her thoughts turned to the email she had sent Kyle earlier in the day and wished that she hadn't sent it. Even still, she decided that she'd drive to Hocking Hills and try to gain Kyle's allegiance against his father.

Kyle and Zoe were with Moses in his cabin on the hill with a low fire burning in the fireplace of the great room. Helena had been leading a group study over the last month on Native American Shamanism. This evening Helena sent them to Moses' cabin to practice drumming and journeying on their own. They had each made by hand their own drums from raw elk hide in a previous class with Helena. Moses had hand-painted a snake on his drum in honor of his power animal. Kyle and Zoe's drums were unadorned. As a ritual, they smudged with sage and said a prayer before entering into the journey state.

"Okay, boys," Zoe said, "I'll drum this first round and the two of you journey to the lower world with the intention of discovering any blockages you may have in fulfilling your life purpose."

Kyle and Moses agreed and reclined on the floor on individual blankets. Moses covered himself with a blanket against the cold he always felt when participating in journeys. Zoe started beating her drum and the two men entered the lower world in their preferred ways.

Helena was sitting at the pond in a meditative state when she felt the drumming start in the cabin. Although her ears could only hear the trickling spring that fed the pond, her spirit quivered with ecstatic joy from the vibrations of the drumming on top of the hill. She looked at the full moon and took satisfaction in knowing that it was in its fullest power. Staff in hand, she unconsciously rocked back and forth and prayed.

"Father…Mother…Spirit, I ask for your guidance and wisdom tonight as my own child, Deborah, comes to confront me about Kyle. May I have the strength to face intimidation, and where I am weak, I ask that my angels and guides encourage me. I am not looking forward to this confrontation, but I know that it is for the higher good." Helena paused, set her staff aside, and opened her palms face up in front of her. "I am just a vessel, Great Spirit. Although I am fearful in my mind and weak in my body, I trust your wisdom and ask that you fill my essence with peace. Yes…yes…I feel that gentle pulse. I invite the elders and helping spirits to assist me in my assignment tonight. And…yes, Daddy…I would especially like to see you." She picked up her staff and looked at the angelic face on the top of it. "Creator, I ask that you fill me with love and that all that I say tonight be guided by Your Light. And it is so."

Deborah had been driving for nearly an hour after her blow-up with Eli at the church. She was now on the twisting road, driving towards the childhood home that she had not been to in over thirty years. Her speed was slower than most of the locals drove because she was unfamiliar with the turns. As she rounded a bend in the road, an opossum ran in front of her Hummer. She just missed it. She shuddered at the sight of the creature and had a flashback to her early childhood with her grandfather explaining his understanding of the animal that she thought must surely be the ugliest one in Hocking Hills:

"Debbie, the possum might be ugly but even it has much to teach us." He told her. "You've seen them play dead. They can do it at will. That means there are times when you have to will yourself to do what is right even if your mind is telling you to retaliate. Sometimes you just have to play dead and then scurry off when no one is paying attention. Anytime a possum crosses your path, ask yourself if what you're about to do is what the Great Spirit wants you to do."

Deborah shook off the memory and continued in the direction of Serenity. Her thoughts returned to her anger with Eli. She knew that she needed Kyle to help her if Eli was serious about a divorce. She was sure Kyle would run to her side because Eli had always been hard on him. Just then a large buck with a huge set of antlers leaped across the road in front of her. This time she hit the brakes hard and felt the thump-thump of the anti-lock system catch. The hummer stopped within inches of the buck. They stared at each other for a few seconds before he ran off into the woods. Once again, a memory of Deborah's grandfather came to her:

"Now the deer reminds us to stay connected to our children because a newborn fawn hardly moves in the first few days of life. When you have children of your own, don't take them in public right away so your energy will stay connected to them and so they won't be bombarded by unfamiliar people. If a buck with a set of antlers crosses your path, he is saying that you should pay attention to your inner thoughts. The antlers are symbols of the connection to your intuitive abilities. You should listen to the still small voice inside of you, not the voice of your ego."

"Dear, God, take these pagan memories from me!" Deborah screamed as tears ran down her cheeks. "I know you're doing this to me, Mother. It won't work! I'm on a mission from God and Kyle is coming home with me tonight!" She almost missed the drive to her childhood home before the Serenity sign caught her eyes. She turned into the drive and made her way along the gravel. As she reached the end of the drive, the Hummer's lights cascaded down the gentle slope towards the pond. She saw Helena.

Deborah's wrath churned inside as memories of her mother telling her not to marry Eli flooded over her. She thought that she had put her mother behind her until she had showed up at church when Kyle was ten. Deborah regretted ever letting Kyle out of the car that evening to greet her. Then Deborah thought about Helena interrupting the Mother's Day Service earlier in the year. Just an hour earlier, she was faced with the fact that Eli was cheating on her again and contemplating divorce. She had always known in her heart that he was unfaithful, but seeing and hearing it personally for the first time made it a harsher reality.

"It's your entire fault, Helena." Deborah whispered as anger boiled over. She grabbed the Bible from the passenger seat, opened the door to the SUV, and slid out in a rage. "Helena!" She shrieked as she slammed the door to the Hummer.

Zoe, Moses, and Kyle had just finished discussing the first journey when a strong wind rattled the metal roof of the log cabin. "Do you want to get on the road, Zoe? It sounds like a storm's blowing in." Moses said.

"Let's do one more journey. I want you to drum so that I can journey this time." She answered.

"Okay, one more. Why don't you take time to just visit with your guides or power animals this time Ki, and Zoe can set her intention on discovering any blocks for her life purpose."

"Works for me," Kyle answered.

"Cool. Let's do it," Zoe chimed.

Moses began to beat the drum. As he always did on the journeys, Kyle envisioned the pond on Serenity in his mind's eye and dove into it. Within the dark water was the familiar light. He swam towards it. He felt the liquid membrane at the light's source and gently pushed through it. Kyle looked around and saw that he was in a beautiful wooded area with a stream flowing, crystal clear, and lush green foliage everywhere.

"Skye!" Kyle called. He looked for the beautiful chestnut horse that always greeted him upon entering the lower world. Something gently nudged Kyle's neck and he recognized Skye's soft nostrils. Kyle giggled at the horse in a warm hello.

"Would you like to ride?" Skye asked.

Kyle didn't answer, but quickly swung his legs onto the horse's back and wrapped his hands in the mane. Skye quickly worked up to a full run and Kyle felt the horse's muscles move powerfully with each stride. The faster Skye ran the less separated from him Kyle felt. Within moments, Kyle felt at one with his power animal—the two had morphed from separate entities into one. Kyle felt Skye's mane as if it were his own, bouncing as he ran. Kyle now knew the meaning of strength and grace, perfectly balanced, that Skye had spoken of during their first encounter when he was just a boy of ten. Skye slowed to a slow trot and they separated into two entities again.

Kyle looked around. They were in an open field surrounded by pine trees.

"Ki," a voice said behind them.

Kyle turned. A giraffe spoke to him. "Have you come to speak to me?" asked Kyle.

The giraffe responded in poetry:

> *"Emerging from the thicket of brush*
>
> *With dainty legs ever so gingerly,*
>
> *My long neck scans the horizon.*
>
> *What a view!*
>
> *I can see for miles into the distance.*

Though my hoofs are grounded,

My head is above the fray.

I have a clear vision

Of what is in this expanse

And with this knowledge

I am comforted.

While I may be standing in the midst

Of ever shifting earth,

I catch a glimpse of fertile lands—

They are just within a short journey.

I know my strong legs

Will carry me to this destination.

As I move toward Eden swiftly,

My potent neck aids

My seemingly deft legs.

And, once arrived at my destination

I am reassured that my premonition was correct.

It is Eden.

I did glimpse heaven.

I am Giraffe."

Kyle laughed appreciatively and asked, "Is there something I can learn from you?"

The giraffe was noble and tender in his response. "I am here to help you see into the future. My long neck enables me to see great distances. If you look close, you will notice that I have three horns—the two blunt, long ones and a third just above my eyes. The third bump is placed in the area of the brow chakra or third eye. This is the psychic power source. Thus, my neck is the bridge between the physical and spiritual realms." He lowered his head. "Please, climb onto my neck"

Kyle climbed onto the giraffe's neck. His strength amazed Kyle as he smoothly lifted his head high into the air, as if the one-hundred-sixty-pound man were a feather. The giraffe started toward the line of pine trees and stopped where they began. Kyle looked over the tops of the trees. He was amazed at the difference in weather and daylight between the two sides. Although their side was a warm, sunny, mid-afternoon day, on the opposite side of the trees was dark. Kyle felt the cool temperatures of an autumn night. Lightening flashed and the wind howled on the darker side.

"What am I seeing?" Kyle asked the giraffe.

"Look closer, mortal." The giraffe responded.

Kyle looked more intently at the scene. He realized that he was looking at the pond on Serenity. His gazed at it. The more he peered into the darkness the more things began to take shape. First, he noticed his grandmother, staff, in hand. Then he saw his mother standing in front of Grandmother, reaching towards her forehead. Although he could tell they were speaking to each other, he couldn't hear a word over the howling of the wind. A blast of air shook both women. Helena caught herself with the staff to keep her balance. His mother tilted and dropped the Bible from her left hand. Kyle watched as Deborah knelt to pick up the book and then jumped in front of Helena, shaking the Bible in her face.

The heated debate continued and Kyle noticed that a beautiful white light surrounded his grandmother in spite of what appeared to be an angry exchange. Suddenly, Kyle realized that the birds in the trees were singing the most beautiful song he had ever heard. He listened intently and soon it seemed that the trees, hills, and grasses joined in the song. The more they sang the whiter the light around his grandmother grew. As the song continued, Kyle noticed that his own spirit seemed to pulse with the rhythm of the cries from creation. It was as if every cell and molecule in his body absorbed the music and resonated with it perfectly. The connection he felt between himself and all of creation was intact for the first time in his life. He no longer felt like a separate entity, but rather a small portion of the whole universe.

Kyle briefly looked above the tops of the trees and saw the radiant beings in human form, their feathery wings and brilliance indicating that before him was an angelic host. One creature floated towards him and softly brushed the sides of his head with its wings. The softness Kyle felt was other-worldly. Immediately after the sweeping wing grazed him, the lyrics to the song being sung throughout the cosmos, echoed in his heart:

Love never gives up.

Love cares more for others than for self.

Love doesn't want what it doesn't have.

Love doesn't strut,

Doesn't have a swelled head,

Doesn't force itself on others,

Isn't always "me first,"

Doesn't fly off the handle,

Doesn't keep score of the sins of others,

Doesn't revel when others grovel,

Takes pleasure in the flowering of truth,

Puts up with anything,

Trusts God always,

Always looks for the best,

Never looks back,

But keeps going to the end.

Love never dies.[10]

A solitary tear rolled down Kyle's cheek at the simplicity and familiarity of the lyrics. The song of extravagant love germinated within him, blossoming in cascading flowers outward. It resonated around and through him. He saw the beauty of life in the dark landscape around him.

He watched as his grandmother started slowly moving up the gentle slope towards the farmhouse. Deborah ran up behind her and spun her around by the shoulders. Words again were exchanged. Then Deborah kicked the staff out from under Helena's grasp and she fell to the ground careening down the hill until her body stopped with a thud at the pine tree in front of Kyle and the giraffe. His mother ran towards her SUV and a bolt of lightening just missed her forcing her into the side of the Hummer. A second bolt streaked in front of Kyle and the giraffe causing the hair all over Kyle's body to stand on end. The bolt of electricity hit a branch directly over his grandmother. It broke from the tree and fell onto Helena.

The rain fell in a torrent. The place where his Grandmother's body rested was now covered with the limb from the pine tree. Through the pine needles, Kyle saw her white silky hair stained with blood creating a mesh between her hair and the fallen limb of the great pine.

Suddenly, a great vortex descended on Kyle and pulled him from the neck of the giraffe of the lower world. He spoke a quick thank you to both the giraffe and Skye. Kyle felt his body move through the physical plane of earth into the spirit plane of the upper world. His great-grandfather's face appeared in the midst of the stars of the heavenly realm and said with urgency, "Go to your grandmother, quickly!"

Moses felt a quickening in his spirit, telling him to end the steady beat of the drum and move with the faster rhythm to signal Kyle and Zoe to return to the physical world. Kyle's heart pounded with the quickened pace. The thumping reverberated in his ears and he felt his spirit thud into his body on the floor the cabin. The sound of his heart matched the rhythm of the drum. Then the call back from the drum was complete.

Kyle's eyes popped open and he sat up immediately. "Grandmother!" he screamed.

Chapter 14

Deborah was hysterical as she drove her Hummer. She had somehow taken a wrong turn on the dark, winding roads from her childhood home and found herself on the road through the 5,000 acre Clear Creek Metropark. Her tears made it too difficult to drive. She decided to park so that she might regain her composure. The beauty of the park was veiled by the dark rain of the night. She parked next to a large, green, waste management dumpster and rested her head on the steering wheel. A loud thump on the hood of her SUV jerked her to attention.

Deborah screamed in horror as a pair of eyes watched her intently. She blew the horn of the Hummer to scare the raccoon, but it stayed on the hood. "Go away!" she screamed as loudly as she could. Her scream made the creature lean against the windshield. It regarded her closely. Deborah shivered. She turned on her wipers in an effort to drive the animal away. The raccoon was unfazed and leaned away from the windshield. He followed the wipers first with his head, back and forth, and then tried catching them with his paws. Deborah didn't dare put the vehicle in gear for fear that the creature might scratch the paint if it tried to hang to the moving SUV.

"Get off my car!" she screamed again.

"Why do you yell at your teacher?" a voice inside the Hummer asked.

Deborah looked in her review mirror and saw the face of her grandfather.

"Dear, Jesus!" she squealed. Papaw Buck laughed. His reflection disappeared. Deborah looked to her right. There sat her grandfather in the passenger seat. She repeated herself, "Dear, Jesus!"

"That's exactly what your son said the first time he saw me!" Papaw Buck laughed again. "Trust me… I don't look anything like Jesus."

"Oh, God!" Deborah whispered. "She's either put a spell on me or I've gone completely mad."

Her grandfather looked at her sternly—the look he would give her as a child when she hadn't done what he'd told her to do. "Oh, Little Debbie, pull yourself together. You were mad back at Serenity. Now just regret everything you've done today. There is no spell… other than the one you've created for yourself."

"I'm not talking to you! You don't exist. You're a figment of my imagination."

"I remember a time when your imagination created many paradises. Remember that, Little Debbie?" Papaw Buck looked at her lovingly. "In the past you used your gift of prophecy for the good of all. Now you use it to benefit yourself." He saw that he had touched a soft spot in his granddaughter. "You've been acting like you're a teacher with nothing left to learn. Do you think the deer and possum were coincidences tonight? Those lessons you learned as a child still apply today. You ignored Raccoon as he was trying to teach you too."

Deborah's spoke weakly through her sobs, "Please, stop. I can't take much more right now."

"No. I won't stop. You have been so busy preaching over the years that you've forgotten how to listen. Raccoon is speaking to you about the mask you've been wearing. You're a master at your disguise. You've even gone so far as to physically alter your body."

Deborah placed her right arm across her breasts as if to hide them. "Our followers expect to see youthfulness and beauty—it is a sign of prosperity. It's my job to look presentable on camera. "

Papaw Buck's eyes narrowed. "And...what exactly is your job? A thief? A manipulator? I'd say if anyone is practicing witchcraft it is you, my Dear. You seem to use raccoon medicine for personal gain. Your facility in persuading others to give of their riches to your husband's ministry is not an honorable use of your gifts. You've made yourself into something that you're not by joining forces with a selfish anti-Christ. Raccoon is asking if you're hiding your true self. The answer seems clear. The answer is *yes*."

Deborah sat in silence as she contemplated his words. "Oh, Papaw Buck...I'm miserable. I don't know what to do. Eli...Kyle...Mother...It's all too much at one time."

"You've used raccoon medicine today in self-defense. You've been quite ferocious. It's time to balance. Discard the mask of the raccoon and lay the old self to rest. Awaken Little Debbie—the one who enjoyed time spent with me at Serenity; the one who used her curiosity to learn from nature and then taught those lessons to others." Papaw Buck reached towards Deborah and placed his hand just below her rib cage. "This is your center. It will enable you to be sensitive to the changes that are occurring. It is your personal power center and it will direct your will appropriately."

Deborah closed her eyes and felt her abdomen quiver. A feeling of self-confidence surged through her body and she felt a breaking away of dependency on Eli which had undermined her self-worth. As the energy surrounding her diminished, she opened her eyes to find herself alone in the SUV. The raccoon was gone.

Kyle fled from the cabin and ran down the drive with Moses and Zoe close behind him. Neither Moses nor Zoe knew why Kyle had screamed for his grandmother and then sprinted out of the cabin, but they felt an urgency to follow. The rain fell hard as they ran. Kyle lost his footing and would have hit the gravel had Moses not caught him.

"What's going on, Ki?" Moses asked in the brief pause as Kyle gathered himself.

"It's Grandmother! A tree has fallen on her and she needs our help!"

"Where? How do you know?" Moses questioned urgently.

"At the pines...between the house and the pond." Kyle's breath was labored. "Papaw Buck spoke to me during the journey and said to get to her immediately!"

By this time, Zoe had caught up with the two men and overheard the conversation. "Dear God! Let's find her!"

The three ran down the drive. The rain hit Kyle's face like tiny needles cutting into his skin. A shiver ran over him as they reached the pines and saw the downed limb. "Over there!" Kyle pointed.

It took both men to move the heavy tree branch off Helena. "Grandmother!" Kyle called.

Moses scooped Helena in his arms in a swift motion. "Let's get her inside," he said. They were half way to the house when Zoe said, "Her staff! Get her staff, Kyle!"

Kyle ran back down the hill and searched for the staff. It took him several moments to find it. He grasped it, and a surge of energy swirled around him. The next he knew, he was inside his grandmother's bedroom where Moses had laid her on the bed.

Zoe wrung her hands, trying to hide her distress. "Put the staff next to her," she said as her tears bubbled out of control. "I'll grab a towel for the bleeding." Kyle hadn't noticed the blood until Zoe mentioned getting a towel.

"Oh, god! Grandmother *please* wake up…*please!*" Kyle begged.

Zoe returned and applied the towel to the wound on Helena's brow. Moses covered her with a wool blanket. Kyle held her hand.

Moses leaned towards Kyle and said, "Ki, pull yourself together and do your thing. Stop the bleeding. Do what she's taught you to do."

"I don't know if I can," Kyle stammered.

"Ki…you can. Use your extravagant love. Bathe her in light and love. I know you can do it. You are a healer, Ki!"

Kyle wiped his eyes and then rubbed his palms together several times. Zoe removed the towel from Helena's head. Kyle placed his hands over his grand-mother's brow but didn't touch her. He closed his eyes. He mumbled something inaudibly and drew a symbol with his tongue on the roof of his mouth. Instantly, he felt the familiar warmth of universal energy heat his hands. His fingers trembled as waves of energy filtered through them towards his grandmother. The warmth was replaced with a tingling sensation that Kyle recognized as a physical restoration. He knew his grandmother had sustained a serious injury based on the level of pain he sensed in the tingling of his fingers, and the knife-like pangs in his own skull. A solitary tear feel from his right eye as empathy and compassion for Helena swept through his spirit.

Moses and Zoe watched, amazed, as the blood changed from a steady stream to a trickle and then stopped all together. Kyle's pinky fingers twitched outward. He knew it as a signal, telling him to place his hands on either side of her head. He covered her ears. Once again, the warming sensation built until his hands tingled painfully.

Zoe held her hands over her mouth in a prayerful position as the tears ran. Kyle placed his hands over Helena's heart and felt a burst of love channel through him into his grandmother. Kyle's body quivered from the divine blast. His skin prickled.

"Mmm," Helena cooed, as her breathing became even and deep.

Kyle moved his hands into prayer position and gently kissed his index fingers. He opened his eyes and saw that the bleeding had stopped. Helena slowly opened her eyes. She looked directly into Kyle's and a smile spread across her face. "Thank you, Ki," she whispered softly. "That felt wonderful."

Moses placed his hand on Kyle's back and Zoe leapt with joy, her hands still in a prayerful position at her mouth. "Oh, thank god," she said.

"How are feeling, Grandmother?" Kyle asked tenderly.

"I feel like a tree fell on me," she chuckled. "You did a wonderful job, Ki. I'm so proud of you." She reached her hand for his and grabbed it with strength surprising in someone who had just experienced what she had.

"Can I get you anything, Helena?" Moses asked.

"I'd say a man, but the only two around here have eyes for each other." She grinned at the men. "I guess I'll settle for a shot of Jack Daniels instead. I need a little something to warm the insides now."

"Coming right up," Moses said.

"Don't forget everyone else! We've all been out in the cold rain and a little Jack will warm and settle us all."

Zoe said, "I'll help. Jack for everyone!" She followed Moses out of Helena's bedroom.

"I'm so glad you're alright, Grandmother. I was so scared. I wasn't sure I could help."

"There is no fear in love, but perfect love drives out fear[11], Ki. You were able to tap into love in spite of being afraid. You did a great job."

"What about Mom?"

"Don't worry about her, Ki. I have a feeling she's at a crossroads. Her arrival here was her way to lash out at someone over whom she felt power. She confronted your father tonight about his indiscretions."

"Did she tell you?"

"Not verbally...but, I saw it. She's scared...she feels as if she's lost the men in her life, and doesn't know how to deal with it. She's used fear and intimidation for years to get what she's wanted, but those weapons fail over time."

"Will she be alright?" Kyle was genuinely concerned about her.

"Oh, yes. We'll send love her way. Okay?"

Kyle nodded in agreement. Zoe and Moses returned with shot glasses of whiskey. Kyle helped Helena sit up and she took a glass. She held it up in a toast and said, "To love...friends... and family!"

"To love!" The three answered and they clanged glasses together before shooting the whisky down their throats.

Moses wrapped his arms around Kyle from behind and whispered in his ear, "I'm proud of you, Ki. You did a great work tonight." Kyle melted in the embrace.

Deborah entered her home in a state of utter calmness. Although the incident with her grandfather in the SUV had initially shaken her, she now felt a sense of comfort in knowing that one man was still near her. She hadn't thought about what she would say to Eli upon her return, but was sure she could handle any situation without returning to the rage that had consumed her earlier in the evening.

The house was unusually quite. Deborah knew that Eli was home because his car was in the garage, but it felt strangely empty. She walked through the house searching, but didn't call out for him. In the kitchen, she noticed a solitary glass sitting on the counter that hadn't been there when she'd left earlier. A tingling sensation went through her body and the hairs stood up on the back of her neck. Her heart pounded loudly in her ears and she shut her eyes to collect herself, and shake the unusual feeling. With her eyes closed, a vision of dripping blood appeared. Deborah inhaled loudly and opened her eyes. She noticed a light on in the powder room off the kitchen. She went to turn it off.

As she drew near, the pungent odor overcame her. She gagged. Her hand covered her nose and mouth. In the bathroom, she saw the source of the stench. She screamed. Eli lay face down on the floor. He was covered from the waist down in urine, feces, and blood. The room spun. Deborah fled. She grabbed the cordless phone in the kitchen and dialed nine-one-one.

"Nine-one-one, what is the nature of your emergency?"

"This is Deborah Basil. My husband's collapsed in pool of blood. I don't know how long he's been here—!"

"I'll get an ambulance to you immediately. Is he still breathing?"

"I think so...I don't know...I can't handle the smell—just *hurry!*"

After Zoe and Moses left the farmhouse, Kyle ensured that his grandmother was comfortable before heading to his room. He undressed and climbed into bed. Tossing and turning in a fitful sleep, his mind replayed the scene of the limb crashing onto his grandmother. He sat up in bed, startled and looked at the clock. It was just after midnight. He felt wide awake. Sliding out of bed, he tiptoed down the stairs to check on Helena. He paused outside her bedroom and listened to her steady snores. Satisfied that she was sleeping soundly, he returned to his room and lit the lamp on the desk. Taking his journal and pen in hand, he began to write.

The Long Night Fought

When nightmares rage within

my head, your arms begin

their calm embrace. I find

health for my tortured mind.

When dark clouds swarm around

my life, your light abounds

that much more. I am warmed

as our strong bond is formed.

When dreams force me to scream

aloud, your soft voice beams

with strength. I am soon soothed

by your love, pure and smooth.

When torments rip my soul,

your gentle touch makes me whole

again. I am drawn near

to you without fear.

When morning song arrives

to us, I am alive

with you. Your love has brought

me through the long night fought.

—Kyle

Chapter 15

The next morning Kyle made his way down the steps as quietly as he could in case Helena was still sleeping. At the bottom of the stairs, he noticed the familiar voices in his grandmother's kitchen. It was his grandmother and Moses participating in their early morning coffee ritual. This time, though, the voices were muted, as if talking in secrecy.

"I was just wondering what you thought about it," Moses whispered. Kyle froze. He felt that he should go back upstairs and not interrupt the conversation, but was curious.

"If the timing were different," Helena began, "you would have my blessing without reservation. I think he needs more time. I think you should wait until the New Year. He's about to face another obstacle and after that he'll have closure. I want the best for you *and* Ki, but you have to let him mature. A whole person looks like a closed a ring. His circle has almost closed now, but isn't quite complete. Remember, it's two complete circles that make the number eight and the number eight holds special symbolism. In Buddhism, the number eight represents the path of spiritual perfection; in Native American Earth Count, it symbolizes Natural Law; the Greek Goddess of love Aphrodite had eight rays on her star; and Jesus gave eight Beatitudes in his Sermon on the Mount. You see, each individual must be a completely closed circle before joining with another;

otherwise, you never reach spiritual perfection as a combined unit. The entire universe operates in a cyclical motion and enlightened relationships reflect this action. If two people join before they are realized, theirs becomes a co-dependent union, which is not of Spirit. Let Ki close in his own time so that you have a whole partner and not a partner with a gaping hole."

Moses nodded. "I appreciate your wisdom and insight, Helena. Sometimes when I see something that I want to do, I rush into it and think I can make everything work."

Helena chuckled. "I know, Moses. I remember what it's like to feel those butterflies and the euphoria of falling in love. I'm not so old that I can't remember how I felt the first time I laid eyes on Wesley, Deborah's father."

Kyle listened intently as his grandmother spoke about his grandfather. She had never mentioned him, and Kyle was keenly interested in learning about his mother's father.

"Woo! Lordy!" Helena continued with a deep exhale. "He was something else! I was sixteen years old and he was nineteen. Looking back, I see what children we really were...but, you can't tell teenagers a thing. His family didn't want him marrying a half-breed, as they called me, and they did everything they could to stop us from seeing each other. He promised me that we would elope after his military training before he shipped off to war. Our hormones got the best of us and I became pregnant the night before he left for boot camp. He was killed in a military exercise the last week of training." She paused and Kyle heard her sip her coffee. "I believed at that time that he was my soul mate, and never looked for another man. Of course, I had a tough go of it in those times as an unwed mother and Deborah always resented me because she didn't have a father."

"Helena, I'm sure you did the best you could," Moses offered.

Kyle decided it was safe to make his entrance at this point and noisily walked through the living room into the kitchen. "Good morning, Grandmother!" He bent and kissed her forehead as she sat at the table. "Good morning, Moses!" Helena and Moses returned Kyle's greeting as he poured himself a cup of coffee.

"How are you feeling this morning, Grandmother?"

"A lot better than last night!" she said cheerily.

Moses smiled at Kyle and said, "How are you this morning?"

"I'm good," he answered.

"Any good dreams last night?" Moses asked.

"I had some weird ones."

Helena's interest was peaked. She leaned toward Kyle and asking, "And what did you dream about?"

"One of them was about Dad. He was standing in the church alone—no one was there and he was calling my name over and over. That's all I can remember about that dream. In the next one, all of us were at the church sitting in the front row and there was a casket at the front."

"Who do you mean '*by all of us*?" Moses asked.

"You, Grandmother, Ruth and her family, and me—we were all sitting together. Flowers were everywhere.

I can still almost smell them. Grandmother, you stood up and sang the old hymn, *Softly and Tenderly Jesus is Calling*—just like in my dreams when I was a boy."

Helena leaned back and crossed her arms. "What do you think it means?"

Kyle looked perplexed. "The only thing that I can think of is that it's symbolic of the church dying since in the first dream the church was empty and in the last one there was a funeral."

"Hmmm," Helena's eyes narrowed and almost closed. She raised her right hand to the middle of her forehead and patted herself three times.

Kyle had seen her do this before when she was in deep thought or sensing something. "Do you think I'm right about my interpretation, Grandmother?"

"There's a Native American saying that says, 'to die is to walk the path of the dream without returning,'" she answered quietly. She then rubbed her nose and said, "My nose is itching…someone must be coming for a visit."

Kyle and Moses looked at each other questioningly.

The silence was broken by the sound of a vehicle on the graveled drive. Moses hopped up from the table and looked out the window facing the driveway. "Hey, it's Ruth!"

"What's she doing here?" Kyle wondered aloud.

Helena bowed her head for just a moment and placed her fingers on her forehead again. Kyle looked at her questioningly as she looked up with a serious look on her face. Her eyes pierced him with an abundance of love as she nodded.

Moses opened the back door with his usual enthusiasm and jokingly called to Ruth, "Hey, Ruth! You look like hammered shit! What the hell are you doing here?" When he saw the look of dread on her face Moses wished that he hadn't teased her. He quickly added, "I'm sorry, Ruth. What's wrong?"

Ruth entered and removed her jacket. Kyle stood from the table and walked towards her. "Ruth? Are you alright?" Without waiting for a response he wrapped his arms around her in a tight hug. Ruth burst into tears. "Sis, what's wrong?" Kyle's heart raced through an eternity of silence.

"Child," Helena held out her arms towards Ruth, "come here and sit a spell. Would you like some coffee?"

Ruth pulled away from her brother's embrace and nodded in silence. Moses grabbed another mug, poured some coffee, and placed the cup in front of Ruth as she sat at the table. The two men took their own places with Kyle closest to his sister.

"Ruth, what's going on?" Kyle asked.

"Let her catch her breath, Ki," Helena spoke gently. "Take your time, Ruthie."

Ruth spoke hesitantly as she tried to quell the storm of emotions inside her. "Last night Mom called me from the hospital. I guess she came home and found Dad passed out in a pool of blood in the bathroom."

"What?" Kyle asked in astonishment. "Is he okay? What's wrong with him?"

"No...he's not okay." Ruth started weeping and put her face in her hands. Kyle placed his hand on her shoulder. When she had composed herself, Ruth placed her hands on the table. "He's sick, Kyle—really, really sick."

"What is it?" Kyle questioned.

Ruth's shoulders shook. Helena reached across the table and placed her hands over Ruth's. Ruth felt a sense of warmth course through her body and center in her heart. She looked at her grandmother and smiled through her tears.

"It's cancer...prostate cancer...and it's spread to his spine."

"Oh my god!" Kyle whispered. "Is he conscious?"

"He was when I left the hospital. Mom's an emotional wreck. I wanted her to call you but she said she just couldn't bear to do it right now. Dad was calling your name, Kyle, when he was in and out of consciousness. I think you should go see him."

Kyle thought of his dream during the night of his father saying his name repeatedly in the empty church. "Can they do anything for him?"

"They're talking palliative care only. They've said he has six weeks to live, at most." Ruth started shaking again. "The social worker's going to meet with Mom later this morning to discuss Hospice care." They sat in stunned silence as Ruth's words sunk into their spirits. "I told Mom that I was coming here to tell you and she said she wanted me to come back later today to help her make decisions about Dad's care."

"Do you want me to go back with you, Sis?"

"No...yes...no...Mom told me it was okay to tell you, but she didn't want you around. I'm sorry, Kyle. I'll talk to her some more. I think you should see Dad."

Kyle looked down at the floor. "He probably doesn't want to see me anyway. The last time we talked he said I was dead to him."

"I think prayer and meditation would be an excellent way to encourage Elijah and ourselves." Helena announced. "Why don't we start right now?" The four held hands as they sat around the table. Helena lead the prayer, "Holy Father...Mother...Spirit...we are your children and we honor you in this time. Our physical minds question as we try to grasp the gravity of the situation which faces Elijah and our family. Although we have heard the physicians' report, we know that only You know the outcome of these circumstances. It is not our place to question or to judge...but it is our mandate to love and send light towards Elijah, his church and followers. We open our minds to receive insight from the Universe. We open our eyes to see the beautiful complete canvass that Mother Earth has painted for us. We open our ears to hear what Spirit speaks to us in this time of trial. We open our mouths to speak Holy Wisdom. We open our hearts to be a channel of Divine Love to all that we come in contact with. We open our bellies to be a river of life. And, we remain grounded to our connection with each other and Mother Earth. We cover this situation in Light and Love and release it to your Will...And it is so!"

They continued to hold hands for several minutes with their heads bowed even after Helena finished praying. Ruth meditated on seeing light in the Valley of the Shadow of Death. Kyle asked for guidance on how to act in the best interest of his parents. Moses was moved with empathy for his dear friends. Helena connected to her guide and saw what the rest of the year would bring...she smiled with sad satisfaction.

Ruth had returned to Columbus and Moses had headed into Roasters for the day. Kyle stayed home with his grandmother. Once again, they sat around the kitchen table. "I'm not sure what to do, Grandmother."

Helena looked at Kyle with tenderness. "You will, Ki. Open yourself to receive the wisdom of your next move with your parents."

"If I could, I would go immediately and visit Dad, but he told me he never wanted to see me again—Mom, too. They both said I was dead to them!"

"Ki, you have to put their harsh words aside and allow love to manifest in their lives through you. Do you remember when you were a child and you said that you would never be the son that your father wanted?"

Kyle thought back to his dream as a boy and remembered instantly. "Oh, yes. And your response was that I was the son he *needed.*"

"That's right."

"Well, I'm not sure how he needs me when he doesn't even want to see me."

"Ki, you've lived here for a few months now and you've heard me teach about lessons we have to learn in this lifetime. Your father still has a couple of lessons to learn before he crosses over and you are intricately entwined in his studies. You each have something to learn from this. You've said yourself that you feel as if you found a home when you arrived at Serenity, right?"

Kyle nodded.

"Every man, woman, and child arrives on Earth looking for home—everyone is looking for serenity and it's not just this physical location. You could have found your home anywhere if you had just looked inward for it. Your father is no different. He's been searching for home his entire life. Oh, he's masked the search with dogma and rules. He's convinced himself that by others needing him, he's arrived, but the truth is…he's still searching. And, you…well…you have to settle your ill feelings towards your parents before you can call yourself a whole being. You have to forgive them for their actions and words. What do you think I would do if your mother walked through that door right now?"

Kyle looked at his grandmother and chuckled. "I'd hope you wouldn't go for a walk with her down by the pine trees."

Helena smiled at his humor. "Well, I might be a little hesitant to do that," she giggled with sarcasm. "Seriously, if your mother walked through that door right now, I would welcome her with open arms and infuse her soul with as much love as I could—even though she caused harm to me last night. That's love, Ki. It moves only when we allow it to. I prefer not to block the flow of Divine's greatest gift. Creator has been very gracious to me and I try to acknowledge it by sharing it with all. It's an irony that as we open to love and surrender our egos, that we complete the sacred circle and become whole. All of creation finds home in love and joyously sings its song."

Kyle remembered his journey and the birdsong he'd heard. "I think I've heard the birds sing of love…during my journey last night when I saw the situation unfolding between you and Mom."

"Yessssssss," Helena dragged out the word as she exhaled. "How did you *feel* when you heard the song?"

Kyle thought for a moment before responding. "I felt as if I had arrived home…that my spirit sang the song although I didn't know the words. It was as if my soul's identity was in the words. Almost like my DNA vibrated to the rhythm of each syllable."

"Yes…yes…yes!" Helena squealed with delight. "That's the feeling I'm talking about! You've experienced it once. Now that you've heard the song and felt its power you can give it to anyone…or anything."

"What do you mean?"

"Ki, what you felt during your journey as the birds sang can be duplicated within your spirit at any given time. All things are encoded with the song of love—even the rock I like to sit on at the pond! In fact, Jesus himself said that if we keep our praise quiet the stones will cry out." Kyle nodded in recognition of the well-known Biblical reference he remembered from his Charismatic background. "You know everything vibrates with energy and that energy is *love.* You must be able to give that to anyone or anything."

"But, how can I if Dad rejects me?"

"Ah…so you're afraid of rejection?" Helena asked inquisitively.

"I don't know...I guess."

"Go get *The Message* by my chair in the sitting room." Kyle did as his grandmother asked him and returned with the modern Bible translation. "Now, find 1 John 4:18 and read it out loud."

Kyle thumbed through the book quickly and found the verse she wanted him to read. " *There is no room in love for fear. Well-formed love banishes fear. Since fear is crippling, a fearful life—fear of death, fear of judgment—is one not yet fully formed in love.* " He looked at his grandmother when he had finished reading and waited for her to respond.

"Okay, Ki. Now I want you to close your eyes and listen." Kyle closed his eyes, took a deep breath, and exhaled. Within moments he heard the barely audible thump-thump of his heart ringing in his ears in the midst of the stillness.

"Take a few deep breaths and continue listening to the sound of your heart, Ki." Kyle did as he was told. What was once a faint sound seemed to reach a crescendo with the disconnection from his physical surroundings.

Helena continued, "The heart beats without any effort on your part, pushing vital nutrients to every organ of your body. You don't think about making it work...it just does what it's designed to do. It's a perfect work of the Creator and functions without fear. Your thoughts of rejection from your father or mother or anyone else is a blockage of the outflow of love and healing that you have to offer to all you come in contact with. The heart has been used as a symbol of love for millennia because it functions without judgment. Well-formed love acts the same way...without thought...flowing to all...uninhibited and unafraid. Isn't it about time you abandon the impulsiveness of immature fear and return to a fully-formed love?"

A feeling of relief dissolved within Kyle. He slowly opened his eyes and saw that his grandmother was smiling gently. "Yes, Grandmother...I get it. I see what you mean."

"Then take the knowledge you've gained and apply it. The application of knowledge is true wisdom, Ki."

"So, how do I apply this knowledge?"

Helena gave her usual chuckle. "Ki, you don't need me to tell you what to do. You left the world of black and white when you left your authoritarian upbringing. Everyone knows what's right and wrong...they don't need someone else to tell them." She stopped for just a moment before continuing. "Ki, look inside yourself and listen to Spirit speak to you. When you take time to listen, you'll know what to do and why your father *needs* you."

"It's a lot easier to function when you have rules telling you what to do and someone telling you what your next move should be," Kyle said.

"True," Helena acknowledged, "but then the intentions aren't pure. When you do something because it's what you're told to do, how much love is in it?" Helena looked at the ceiling and closed her eyes for a moment. "You know what we should do tonight?"

Kyle smiled when he recognized that she had a spiritual solution to his dilemma. "I bet you're going to tell me."

"I think a soul retrieval is fitting for you!" she gleefully answered.

"What's soul retrieval?"

"It is a practice rooted in Shamanism. Soul retrieval allows you to get back a part of yourself that has been taken away from you. It's known as soul loss. Sometimes people steal them from you and sometimes you freely hand them over. When this happens, a hole remains inside you that allows your energy to leak away. I think that in the relationship between your father and you, he has a part of your soul. I want Moses to participate in this...in fact, I'll have him journey for you while I drum. Your only function will be to lay there and let the Universe work."

Moses, Kyle, and Helena sat together in the living room of the farmhouse after cleaning the kitchen and dinner dishes. Several logs burned in the fireplace as they each smudged with sage and Helena said an audible blessing. The heat and crackling from the hearth warmed the bodies and souls of them all.

"Moses, during this journey you'll use your spirit guide to help you retrieve any pieces of Kyle's soul from his father. Ask your guide to help you."

"Will Eli readily hand it over?" Moses asked.

"He could, or you may have to bargain with him to get it. It really depends on the state that Eli is in right now. Sometimes other souls are ready to return the pieces of their victims and will just hand them over. Other times, you have to use cunning and manipulation to retrieve the parts. You'll know once you come face to face with Eli in the other world. Your guide can help if you must use trickery. Okay?"

"I think I understand,"

"Now, as soon as the drum brings you back, I want you to cup your hands and blow the soul fragments into the top of Ki's head and then into his chest. Ki, you just lie still after the drumming and let Moses finish the work. You might need to lie still a few minutes after he returns the pieces, so take your time before you sit up."

"I can do that," Kyle answered.

"And I'll do my part, Helena" Moses said.

"Okay, boys, lie on the floor with your shoulders and hips touching and I'll begin drumming when you're comfortable." Kyle and Moses relaxed on the floor with their shoulders and hips resting next to each other. Moses placed his hand on top of Kyle's and gave a gentle squeeze.

The drumming started. Kyle took a deep breath and relaxed. He felt the waves of each drum beat surround him and vibrate his spirit. Brilliant lights in a rainbow of colors flashed before his mind's eye. Then he saw his great-grandfather kneeling over him as he lay on a dirt floor in what looked like a teepee. Grandfather Buck took a feather and lightly waved it over Kyle's body, chanting in an unknown language. Kyle let go of all thoughts as euphoria swept through his essence.

Moses found himself with his veiled guide in surroundings that looked like an ancient, open-air Roman temple. Although Moses never saw his spirit guide completely, he always felt his presence near him in his journeys. Moses made his way through the temple awe-struck by the towering white stone arches and beautiful violet tapestries blowing in the breeze. A thick purple material blocked one of the arches and Moses pulled it aside. He stepped through.

On the other side of the archway, Moses walked into what appeared to be an empty arena. An ornate stage sat on his right, rising about six feet. Sitting on the bottom step leading up to the stage was Eli. He looked frail and withered. He didn't notice Moses, so Moses approached Eli.

"Eli?" Moses questioned.

Eli lifted his head to look at Moses. "Yes, have you come to watch me? I used to put on a magnificent show before the crowds stopped coming."

Moses was moved with empathy by the sadness in Eli's voice. "Why did the people stop coming?"

"Because they found out I was a fake and was stealing from them. The emperor has judged me now and my last show here will be with the lions."

"The lions?" Moses asked.

"You know...I'm being fed to the lions. I suppose that will bring back the crowds. It's not much solace that my last show will draw the largest crowd and I won't be able to enjoy the cheers and feel the rush of performing."

Moses thought for a moment and asked, "Is there something you haven't accomplished that you would like to before your final show?"

"I have some things that I need to return to their owners." Eli looked forlorn and reached inside his robe.

He pulled out a chalice with a downward-pointing triangle, etched with gold in the glass, and held it up as if inspecting it for defects. "This belongs to my wife. It used to pulse with a beautiful light and was filled with the sweetest honey I had ever tasted, until I took it from her. I'm going to give it back to her when she comes to visit me before my sentence is carried out. I hope it pulsates and fills to over-flowing again when I return it to her."

Eli placed the chalice back inside his cloak. "I really do love her...I always have..."

"You said you had a few items. What is the other one?" Moses asked as gently.

Eli stood. Moses thought he was going to run from him, but he turned and reached to an upper step. When he turned around, Moses saw that he held a beautiful ivory scepter topped with a dove as the finial. "This belongs to my son. I would like to return it to him, but I'm afraid that he won't come to see me before my execution. I can't give it to his mother to return to him because she might keep it for herself. I really want him to have it back...he doesn't even know I have it...I took it from him when he was so young." Eli's voice cracked and he started to cry. "I've failed again. I just couldn't help myself. This scepter is so beautiful...and the power that comes with it so desirable. I thought I had to steal it to gain authority; but, it doesn't work for me."

Moses felt moved by the sincerity in Eli's voice. "Eli, I know your son."

Eli's face brightened as the tears traced lines in his face. "Really? Will you see him soon?"

"I'm on my way to see him now. I would be honored to return the scepter to him."

Eli handed the rod to Moses without hesitation. "Could you tell him something for me when you return this?"

"I can." Moses answered.

"Tell him I'm sorry I took his scepter and withheld my love...he was just so gifted...so different from me."

Moses heard the call-back of the drum begin. "I'll tell him, Eli. I'll tell him. This is an honorable act. Thank you for your cooperation."

The drumming stopped and Moses was back in the living room at Serenity. He turned and leaned over Kyle. Just as Helena instructed, he cupped his hands on top of Kyle's head and blew. He immediately moved to Kyle's chest and repeated the process. When Kyle felt the last breath blow over him, he envisioned a dove landing on his chest. Helena nodded towards Moses in acknowledgment of a job well done. Kyle stayed in a restful state for several minutes until his vision of the dove dissipated. Slowly, he sat up and with a newfound confidence.

Helena smiled at both men. "And, how was that, Kyle?"

"Invigorating!" he enthused.

"Your countenance is different, Ki. You look like a new man!" Helena looked at Moses. "Would you like to share what happened on your journey?"

Moses was eager to share his experience and the message Eli had wanted to send to Kyle. After giving every detail of his journey, he looked at Kyle and noticed he had tears in his eyes. He put his arm around him and gave him a comforting hug.

"Very interesting…powerful medicine here," Helena mused. "Moses, you did a wonderful work today."

"I'm curious about why it was a scepter that Eli had taken," Moses wondered aloud.

Helena was ready with an answer. "Remember, boys, when you journey there is much symbolism. The scepter is an emblem of royalty, authority, and power. It comes from the Greek word skeptron. The Roman scepter was usually ivory with a golden eagle on top, but during the advent of Christianity it was topped with a cross. It's interesting that his one was topped with a dove."

Kyle interjected, "Interesting is right! After Moses blew into my chest I had a vision of dove resting on me!"

"Really?" Moses asked excitedly. Kyle nodded affirmatively.

"Wonderful! Wonderful!" Helena was enthusiastic. "The dove is symbolic of the feminine energies of Peace and Prophecy. Its song is tied closely to water since it must return to springs at dusk to drink. Water is, of course, a feminine energy, too."

"You mean, Dad tried to suppress my two-spiritedness by stealing my power?"

"Oh, I get it completely," Moses said. "Your father took your birthright—the scepter—and beat you with it through fear and intimidation so that you wouldn't be able to manifest the Divine feminine nature of Peace and Prophecy. He thought he could keep you from being gay if he stole your power!"

"Very good, Moses!" Helena filled to overflowing with excitement at her student. "And, now, Ki, you have these pieces of your soul returned to you. Not only are they returned, but your father handed them over willingly and that in itself is significant."

"What do you mean?" Kyle asked.

"What it means is that your father is settling things before he crosses to the other side. It's a very good sign that he's learning the lessons he was required to learn in this lifetime."

"What about the Deborah's chalice? Should I have done something with it?" Moses questioned.

"You did the right thing, Moses. Deborah isn't here for you to return it to her and we don't have her permission to do a distant healing. It sounds like Eli will try to return it to her on his own." Helena nodded as if she had already seen the future.

"He's dying, isn't he?" Kyle asked.

Helena looked intently at her grandson, "What do you *think?*"

"I think he knows that death is near. He told Moses that judgment was coming in the form of hungry lions. I think that was symbolic of the presence of cancer in his bones since lions can snap human bones with their jaws. And, it seems that he would be willing to see me but thinks I won't come. I guess I should try to visit him."

Helena nodded in approval. "You're gaining the wisdom of the elders, Ki."

Chapter 16

It had been three weeks since Eli's diagnosis of cancer. He was at home with Hospice care with a ready supply of morphine to help with the intense pain. Deborah sat in a chair next to the bed watching him sleep as she worked on a sermon with her laptop. His color was quite pale and his hair, visibly gray at the roots without the aid of hair color that usually masked its dull tint. His breathing was slightly labored, but steady.

Eli dreamed in his morphine-induced sleep. He was on top of the hill behind the old farmhouse at Serenity. He recognized the place where he and Deborah would sit together during their courtship as teenagers. Eli surveyed the magnificent view and felt oddly comforted at on the property of Serenity.

"It's a wonderful view, isn't it?" said a voice from behind Eli.

Eli turned and saw a man, nearly eight feet tall, with piercing blue eyes and thick wavy blond hair, standing behind him "Who are you?" Eli asked, intimidated by the imposing creature.

"I am Micha'el, Eli."

Eli noticed a soft, pulsating light emanating from the man. Although there was a sense of intimidation, he felt comfortable with the Being. "Are you an angel?"

"Yes."

"Am I dead?" Eli questioned.

"No, Eli. You're still alive."

"Oh, thank God! I haven't been able to talk with Deborah to ask her forgiveness. I don't want to die until I have things settled with her and the children."

"You need to hurry, Eli. There isn't much time." Micha'el said urgently.

"I know…it's just so hard to talk to Debbie with all the medication. I'm either out of it when she's around or she's gone when I'm alert. Can you help me?"

Micha'el smiled warmly. "I can do my best, now that I have your permission to help."

Eli looked pensively at the angel. "Would it be possible to see my son before I die?"

"I will do my best now that I have your permission," Micha'el repeated with a nod. He reached his arm towards Eli and gently waved his hand in an upward motion in front of Eli's face.

Eli awoke with a jolt and made a guttural sound with his breath. Deborah looked up from the laptop to see what had startled Eli. The room slowly came into focus and he felt lucid for the first time in weeks. He turned his head and saw Deborah sitting next to the bed. He smiled and said, "Debbie, I'm so glad you're here."

Deborah leaned forward and set the laptop on the floor. "You're awake. Do you need more pain medication?" she queried with a tone of exhaustion.

"No. I don't want any medication right now. I want to talk to you."

"You really should rest, Eli. I'm not sure we have anything to talk about," she said coldly.

Eli's eyes watered slightly. "Yes, there is Debbie. I need to apologize to you. I've hurt you over the years and I am truly sorry. You've always been my first and only love. Would you forgive me?"

Deborah looked at her husband pitifully and raised her eyebrow in its signature pose. "Elijah Hershel Basil, you have done a lot of hurt to me with your infidelity. I certainly don't have the strength within myself to forgive you. What I would really like to do is take a knife to you and cut your manhood off! But, it appears that God has already judged you."

Eli felt her cold stare, but shrugged it off. "I've been wrong over our years together and I really am sorry, Debbie."

"Why did you do it, Eli? Why?" Deborah's anger was building. "We're not talking one time...but, you cheated over and over again. If I was your only love, why?"

"Because...I was afraid of you and insecure in myself." Eli took a deep breath and moaned in pain. "The pain I feel now is because of the hurt I caused you...I realize that. I just ask that you forgive me."

"You have no idea of the pain you've caused me!" Deborah's voice was venomous, but she reluctantly added, "I will forgive you...but, only because it's my duty as a Christian to forgive. I just find it a little insincere that you confess your sins on your deathbed!"

"I know, Debbie. I should have been man enough to do this earlier. I am truly sorry and I deeply regret what I've done to you." Tears ran down Eli's face. "I've never been as strong as you. Your strength, sweetness, and beauty captured my heart on our first date. Do you remember that night?"

Deborah, indeed, remembered their first date. Her mind wandered to the Friday night meeting of the Pentecostal Young People's Association, the PYPA that they attended as a date when she was a senior in high school. Eli had grown up in the Pentecostal Church in Logan, but it was Deborah's first time ever in a church. She remembered that her mother hadn't been happy when she had attended a youth group associated with an organized religion, but had allowed her to go anyway because she didn't want to interfere in her spiritual exploration.

The evening started with the PYPA's theme song. The lyrics of the song wafted through her mind like the aroma of fresh-baked apple pie:

"We are the members of the PYPA

We are in this battle and we're her to stay

Routing out the devil

Seeking souls to save

We are the members of the PYPA."

Deborah had been amazed with the exuberance of the teenagers in the meeting room and found their energy contagious. The jubilance of the songs radiated among the group in a way she had never known since her family's spirituality was practiced at home with nature. She thoroughly enjoyed the drums because it reminded her of the drumming her mother would do during their own practice.

After the singing, the youth leader had given a message about the sinful nature of man and Hell. Deborah had never heard of Hell from a theological perspective or the idea of original sin. The speaker's words were very persuasive and filled her with fear of eternal damnation. At the end of his lesson when he asked if anyone wanted to give their life to Jesus, she ran to the altar to escape an eternity in the lake of fire. Her mother had been less than impressed when Deborah returned home, ecstatic with a new-found faith.

"Do you remember it, Debbie?"

Eli's question returned Deborah to the present She looked at Eli with warm recognition as the bitterness of her hurt melted. "Yes, Eli. I remember it alright."

Eli smiled at her. "Well, as I remember it, your mother wasn't very happy with you when you came home and told her you had dedicated your life to Jesus."

"I think she was unhappy with me trying to evangelize her," Deborah gave a gentle chuckle. "What was I thinking? Did I really believe that someone who had practiced shamanism for as long as she had would change her ways? Oh, I was young and naive." Deborah's last sentenced seemed to reverberate between them.

Eli looked seriously at his wife, "Debbie, you've never been naïve. Your gifts with the Word of Knowledge and Word of Wisdom have always impressed me. I always knew that you were aware of what I was up to. I abused your gift of grace and I'm sorry."

Deborah's heart softened as she listened to Eli's kind words. She wept softly. "I'm so scared, Eli. You've always been near, even when you were running around. I just don't know how I'm going to do it without you."

"You'll do better than I would without you. You can't help it…it's in your name…" Eli's voice trailed off as he looked at the foot of his bed. "Oh, there's Micha'el again."

Deborah followed Eli's but saw nothing. "Eli, what are you talking about? Who's Micha'el?"

"You know…Micha'el…he's an angel. He's helping me right now."

"Eli, there's no one there," Deborah said. "I think it's the morphine talking."

Eli smiled reassuringly. "Oh, he's here. You just can't see him because he's the angel that will take me to Jesus. You'll see him when it's your time." He paused as if listening to something. "He wants me to tell you about your name. Deborah means bee, and a bee can accomplish the impossible. You'll do just fine without me. You'll pollinate many flowers and build your honeycomb, as you should. He says all honeycombs are constructed in a hexagon, which symbolizes the heart, and the sweetness of life found within your own heart. You'll finally be able to be the mother you've always wanted to be. The sweetness I've stolen will be returned to you." He broke off in tears.

Deborah moved from the chair to the bed and wrapped her arms around Eli as he wept. "I'm so sorry you're going through this. And I'm sorry for what I said before. Please forgive me." Eli nodded, comforted by the love he felt in his wife's arms and from her words.

For the first time since his return from the hospital, Deborah stayed in bed with him through the night.

Ruth sat at the bar in her parents' kitchen watching her mother flit between rooms as she prepared to go to the Ann Taylor shop at Easton Town Center. The cordless phone rang and Ruth looked at the caller I.D. "Mom, its Kyle. Do you want me to answer it?"

Deborah emerged from the powder room just off the kitchen and flipped her short hair with the left hand. "If you want to talk to him, go ahead. I have to get to Easton."

Ruth looked at her mother condescendingly, "He's *your* son. Have you talked with him yet?"

"Ruth, I *really* don't have time to discuss this right now. Are you going to talk to your brother or not?"

Ruth set the phone back on the counter and hopped down from the barstool. Facing her mother, she scolded, "You're doing a serious disservice to Kyle and Dad by not talking to him. He wants to know how Dad is doing. Can't you put aside your anger towards him for the sake of Dad?"

Deborah placed both hands on her hips and quipped, "I believe *I* am the parent here, not *you*." The phone finally stopped ringing. "Besides, that's why we pay for voicc mail."

"What is your beef with Kyle, Mom? Is it because he's gay or because he's living with Grandmother?"

"Ruth you really have no business getting involved in this." Deborah made as if to move past Ruth, but Ruth blocker her.

"I think it *is* my business. Dad has been asking for Kyle. Kyle has been asking me about Dad. You won't take Kyle's calls, so I'm left in the middle. I'd say that it *is* very much my business since you have put me in this position."

Deborah, shocked, glared at Ruth coldly. "I *really* don't want to talk about this with you, Ruth. I have to get to Easton."

"Mother," Ruth was forceful, "you have plenty of outfits for church tomorrow. We *are* going to talk about this right now! Now we can do it as two sane, grown women or we can yell and scream at each other. Either way...we are going to discuss it now."

Deborah recognized the determination in Ruth's eyes. She relented. "You're so much like your grandmother," she said with exasperation and took a seat on one of the bar stools.

Ruth sat on another. "I'll take that as a compliment since I think she's a really neat woman. Let's start with Grandmother since you brought her up. What is the problem with her?"

"You wouldn't understand, Ruth. You attend a high church that's far more liberal than the way you were raised."

Ruth looked confused. "High church? What do you mean by that?"

"I mean your denomination is structured along a hierarchy and is considered a mainline denomination. You have a specific order of service and the service doesn't flow with the movement of the Spirit." Deborah shook her head as if she weren't explaining herself well.

"You're more accepting of other peoples' religious practices. Your father and I believe in a strict interpretation of The Bible."

"Come on, Mom! Don't drop back to 'for the Bible tells me so'. Answer the question about your mother."

Deborah sighed. "Your grandmother is open to many things spiritually, but when I committed my life to Jesus and subscribed to the views of Pentecostalism she threw a fit. I believed then, and still do today, that what she practices is clearly spoken against in the Word of God—the same with your brother. Both of them are an abomination in the eyes of God. The only redemption for either of them is to accept Jesus Christ as their Lord and Savior and turn from their wickedness. The Bible is *very* clear about that!"

"Didn't Jesus teach to love one another?" Ruth asked. "Where is the love in cutting both of them off from your life?"

"Yes, Jesus did teach about love. And, I can still love the sinner and hate the sin. That's what I'm doing in both of their cases."

"I disagree with you. I don't think it's humanly possible to love the sinner and hate the sin. From my perspective, your hate of the sin is played out in your treatment of both of them. I think that if you asked them, they wouldn't be feeling much love. If you love them, how can you cut both of them out of your life?"

Deborah was defiant. "I haven't cut them out. Both of them know that when they confess their sins to Jesus I'll welcome them back into the family with open arms. I told Kyle that in my last email, and I told Helena the same thing when she objected to your father and me getting married."

"So, you won't have anything to do with either one of them until they meet your conditions? Hmmm… sounds like someone is playing God." Ruth's tone was sarcastic.

"I'm just following the laws of God. If you associate with the devil, sooner or later he'll ensnare you."

Ruth rolled her eyes. "Dad needs to see Kyle before he dies. I think you need to allow that to happen."

"As I've said, Kyle is welcome in this house when he returns to the arms of his Savior. Until then, I don't want him in this house."

"What are you going to do when Dad dies? Are you going to exclude Kyle from the funeral, too?" Ruth screamed angrily as control slipped away.

"Calm down, Ruth. I've thought that through. It's fine with me if he attends the funeral. After all, it'll be held at the church, and what better place to return to Jesus then at church? Your father will want an altar call at his service, so I think that it'll be a good time to reach Kyle. With his father's passing, maybe he'll realize that his lifestyle will only drag his soul to Hell."

"Please don't use the lifestyle phrase with me. The truth is your son, my brother, is *gay*. There's no such thing as a gay *lifestyle*. I know many gay and lesbians and none of them have the lifestyle that you have, Mother. A lifestyle is how you spend your money; it isn't one's sexual orientation. Many Christians would find *your* lifestyle to be a bit over the top."

"Are we finished here, Ruth? I really need to get a new outfit for church tomorrow." Deborah stood and walked towards the powder room. "You're going to stay with your father tomorrow while I'm preaching, right?"

Ruth watched her mother disappear into the bathroom. "Yes, we're finished. And, yes, I'll be here for Dad tomorrow." Ruth shook her head in annoyance and decided to give Kyle a call as soon as her mother left.

Ruth leaned over her father and brushed his hair into place with her fingers. Eli slowly opened his eyes and seemed to stare past his daughter before focusing on her face. "Are you okay, Dad?" she asked.

Eli made a feeble attempt to smile, "I think so, Ruthie." He looked directly into Ruth's eyes and seemed to be searching her soul. "You do love me in spite of myself, don't you?"

"Yes, Daddy, I do."

"What? No smartass comment from my little girl?" Eli chuckled.

Ruth looked surprised. It was the first time she had heard her father curse. "Well...shit, Dad, if I had known morphine would allow you to cuss I would have snuck some into your coffee when I was a teenager!"

Eli continued, "Oh...shit...damn...this pain really pisses me off!" They both started laughing and Eli grimaced in pain again. "Oh, fuck! Don't make me laugh, Ruth...it hurts too much."

They continued laughing and Ruth's eyes filled. "Thank you, Daddy. It's nice to see the human side of you."

"I just wish I'd let you and your brother see more of it. I'm sorry I was so hard on the two of you..." his voice trailed off as he took a painful breath. "I wish I could make it up to my little girl." Eli patted Ruth's hand with his own.

"Oh, Daddy," Ruth's eyes welled up with tears and she hugged him, "it's okay. I haven't heard you call me your little girl since I was ten. I couldn't ask for anything more." She pulled away from her father.

Eli stretched his hand towards her face and wiped her tears. "I always hated to see my little girl cry, but it warms my heart now. I thought you hated me. I guess not. Thank you." His face contorted in pain, "Oh, shit!" His thumb pressed the morphine release button. "Kyle...I want to see Kyle...can you get him to come?"

"I just talked to him, Daddy. He is coming in the morning while Mom's at church."

Eli's eyes brightened for just a moment and then closed. "Good" he muttered, "tomorrow is good...I can tarry for one more day to see Kyle..." his voice trailed off as he entered into the respite of the narcotic.

Chapter 17

Eli felt Deborah's lips touch his forehead and heard her whisper, "I'll be back after church, Hon. We'll pray for you. Ruth is here if you need anything." He slipped back into unconsciousness and found himself dreaming of Serenity. He stood at the pond and heard the singing of birds. He listened intently and noticed that it wasn't just chirping noises the birds were making. The more he paid attention, the more he realized that he knew the song. He sang with them.

Well, some glad morning when this life is o'er,

I'll fly away.

To a home on God's celestial shore,

I'll fly away.

When the shadows of this life have gone,

I'll fly away.

Like a bird from prison bars have flown,

I'll fly away.

Well, just a few more weary days and then,

I'll fly away.

To a land where joy shall never end,

I'll fly away.

Oh, I'll fly away, O Glory,

I'll fly away.

When I die, Hallelujah, bye and bye,

I'll fly away.12

"You really like that song, don't you?"

Eli turned towards the questioning voice and looked surprised. "Grandpa Buck?" Buck nodded in acknowledgement. "Of course I do. It's one of my favorite Gospel Hymns. We just don't sing it much anymore. It's been replaced by choruses."

"Yes, I know," Buck replied. "Out with the old, in with the new. Everyone's always looking for a new move of Spirit. They seem to forget that Spirit is the same yesterday, today, and forever." Buck paused to let his words sink into Eli's heart.

Eli looked at Buck intently and a warm smile broke across his face. "I'm starting to see that things aren't as black and white as I thought. I guess that happens when one is about to step into death. Or have I already? Is that why I'm seeing you?"

Buck smiled at Eli, "You're close, son, but you're not here yet. You have another lesson to learn before your son comes, if you're open to it."

"I want to make things right with Kyle. I'm open to hear what you have to say."

Buck looked carefully at Eli. "I sense you have an open spirit now. I think that it will be good to share some native traditions. My people view anyone with some degree of homosexuality as two-spirited—meaning that they are both male and female in one body. These people were considered the wise ones, with a keen understanding of Spirit's ways. Spirit is neither male nor female *and* both male and female at the same time. Two-spirited people are physically one gender, but spiritually both. They are the healers, teachers, artists, spiritual leaders of the community. They are more spiritually attuned than other humans."

Eli interrupted. "I feel that now, but I ran Kyle out of the church...and the family."

"You did Kyle a blessing by running him off. He would have left of his own accord at some point. Two-spirited people see through the religious dogma. Eventually, most two-spirited people must leave their early indoctrination when they realize that it is not the way of Spirit. Two-spirited people know Truth innately—they do not have to be taught Truth."

"Will Kyle forgive me?"

Buck's eyes pierced Eli's. "Do you love your son?"

"Yes...he's my son...of course, I love him."

"Then tell him...he's right over there." Eli's head turned. He looked where Buck pointed. He saw nothing but the rolling hills of Serenity. "Open your eyes, Eli. He's right in front of you." The hills and pond were suddenly filled with a light so intense that Eli had to squint.

Eli opened his heavy eyes. His bedroom came into focus and he saw Kyle and Helena standing next to his bed. Helena leaned on her staff as she looked down on

Eli. For the first time in all the years Eli had known Helena, he sensed the love surrounding her and surrounding him. "Helena," Eli muttered, "I was just talking with your father."

Helena's face filled with light as she smiled. "I know. He's sittin' on the foot of the bed. It should bring you great comfort to know that he's here with you." Kyle turned his head towards the end of the bed and noticed Grandpa Buck sitting with legs crossed engulfed in a brilliant white light.

"It does, Helena...and I'm glad you're here. I've wanted to apologize for being such an ass to you over the years."

Helena chuckled at Eli's choice of words. "Most people have a misconception about the ass, Elijah. They think it is stubborn and unruly. But, its symbolism is really about wisdom and humility. Why do you think Jesus' entry into Jerusalem on Palm Sunday was on a white ass? Because it showed that Jesus was victorious in transfiguring his life and awakening his soul wisdom." Eli nodded as the words resonated in his spirit. "The ass teaches us not to hold on to the past and your previous stature. Instead, listen to your inner wisdom and act with humility."

"Thank you for sharing your wisdom with me, Helena. I just wish I had been more open to your understanding of God and his creation before I reached this point. I'm sorry for the pain I've caused you."

"I forgive you, Elijah." Helena reached towards his head. "May I?" Eli nodded and closed his eyes. She placed her left hand just above the crown of his head and felt the flow of warm, pulsing heat. She prayed in whispered tones, "Creator...Maker of all Things...we thank you that this child of yours is still learning, even now at this point in his journey. We thank you that he is covered with humility and is listening to Spirit. May he be filled with Your light and love and the love of his family. And it is so."

"Amen," Eli answered as he opened his eyes.

Helena looked warmly at Eli. "Yes...the ass is a perfect animal totem for you at this time. What a connection to Spirit I felt when I laid my hands on your crown!" She looked at Kyle. "I'll leave you two alone now. Peace to you, Elijah." She started walking out of the room.

"And, to you, Helena," Eli managed to say as she left the room. He looked at Kyle and patted the edge of the bed. "Sit, son." Kyle looked pensively at his father and then sat on the bed.

Eli smiled apologetically and spoke with a raspy voice, "I know the last time we talked you said I would never lay a hand on you again. I apologize for being so rough with you." He reached his hand towards Kyle leg. "Is it alright?"

Kyle nodded as his father rested his hand on him. "Dad," Kyle began, before his emotions overcame him. He bowed his head and placed his hand over top of his father's. The serene silence was broken by the sound of Eli weeping as Kyle stroked his father's pale hand. Kyle did his best to suppress his emotions but the reality of that which was passing was too much. He wept.

As Kyle's tears fell on their hands, his father said, "Thank you...thank you for coming, son. I was afraid you wouldn't make it. But Micha'el said you would."

"Who's Micha'el, Dad?" Kyle asked as he wiped the tears from his face.

"My angel...the one who is taking me to see Jesus. I want you to know that I've been waiting for you before I go to heaven. It's important for me to tell you that I waited for you. Oh!" Eli winced in pain.

Kyle leaned towards his father. "It's okay, Dad. I made it. I'm here."

"I was wrong...about you. Pope John Paul II once said 'the worst prison could be a closed heart.' He was right. I have been closed-minded when it comes to who you are." Eli sucked in a painful breath. "But, I understand now...and I feel free from that prison. I feel free to love my only begotten son. I am so very sorry for hurting you. Can you forgive me, son?"

Kyle looked at his father's gaunt face and nodded. "Yes, Dad, I forgive you."

Eli closed his eyes and smiled at his son's response. "You're a better man than I ever was." Kyle shook his head at his father and bit his lower lip. "Yes. Yes, son, you are. You have every right to curse me now and withhold your forgiveness. I'm not sure I would have been able to forgive if the situation was turned. You are an amazing creation and I am so proud of you, Hoss. You found your foundation in God much earlier in life than I did. I just wish I would have found home before now." He wheezed as he finished his sentence and moaned in pain.

"Dad, you don't have to talk to me. It's okay." Kyle's tears flowed. "I'm sorry for crying. I know you never cared for a cry-baby."

Eli patted his son's leg. "Cry, son, cry. Your heart speaks volumes with your tears. You've always been able to speak from your heart."

Kyle chuckled as he wiped his nose. "Well, if tears are a sign of an open heart then mine must rarely close."

Eli laugh quietly, and then groaned. "I would never accuse you of having a closed heart—at least of your own accord. I think I closed it for you...I regret that." He sat up and lifted his arms towards his son as if reaching for an embrace. Kyle leaned over his father and they hugged. With his mouth next to Kyle's ear, Eli whispered, "This is my son, whom I love; with him, I am well pleased. Listen to him!"[13]

Kyle recognized the scripture quote and shuddered with ecstatic joy. Tears poured down both men's faces as they clung to each other and rocked back and forth. "Thank you, Dad. I love you, too."

Eli slowly pulled away from his son in tortured agony. "I want you to have something, Hoss. In the night stand...open the top drawer." He pointed towards the side of the bed using his last bit of strength.

Kyle opened the drawer and saw a framed black-and-white picture. He gently lifted it from its spot and looked at it closely. Kyle ran his hand over the glass and recognized a younger version of his father holding him on his shoulders. Kyle guessed that he must have been about three. "I've never seen this, Dad."

Eli laid back into his pillow. "Do you see it over your head?"

"See what?" Kyle asked as his eyes peered closer at the picture.

"The Holy Spirit over you...in the tree."

Kyle noticed the tree behind them and looked at the branch directly above his head. Although the picture was faded with age, there appeared to be a white dove sitting just above Kyle's head. He smiled, remembering the dove from the soul retrieval and said, "Yes, Dad. I see it."

"It's yours. I want you to take it with you." Eli closed his eyes and moaned. He tried to reposition himself to relieve the pain but caused more instead. "Your hands, Kyle. Would you...lay them on me...and...take the pain away?"

"I'll do my best, Dad." Kyle placed the frame at the foot of the bed. He briskly rubbed his hands together and placed them on either side of Eli's face. Kyle's own eyes closed as he said a silent prayer for the highest good to be accomplished in his father. The warm heat quickly built in his hands as he stood quietly. The tingling sensation Kyle felt in his fingers was almost unbearable. A bolt of pain shot through his body from the base of his spine to the top of his shoulders. Kyle heard his father whimper in relief. With that sound, Kyle experienced a depth of empathy greater than any he had ever felt during energy work. A solitary tear slipped from Kyle's left eye and his hands trembled next to his father's head.

A brush of air swept across Kyle's face and his hands seemed to float involuntarily towards Eli's belly. They hovered just above Eli's navel and once again, Kyle felt a tremendous heat pass through his hands. Another puff of air, like feathers, swept across his face. He heard his father say, "Yes, Micha'el, I'll tell him."

Kyle felt the heat diminish and slowly opened his eyes. He withdrew his hands, and feeling light-headed, he placed his left hand on the bed for balance. "You said something, Dad? What was it?"

Eli placed his hand back on his son's leg. "Thank you, son. The pain is bearable now. I only have a few moments left..." Kyle looked intently at his father. "Peace, Kyle. Peace I leave with you, My peace I give to you; not as the world gives do I give to you."[14] Eli inhaled with a rattle, exhaled, and said, "Let not your heart be troubled, neither let it be afraid."[15]

Kyle held his father's hand. "Thank you, Dad. I honor your peace. I love you."

Eli took another rattled breath and spoke as he looked directly in his son's eyes, "You are loved..." Eli nodded at the foot of his bed and smiled. The air stirred again around Kyle and a white feather floated from the ceiling. It gently landed on the framed picture. He turned towards his father just in time to see his eyes close as he slipped into his final coma.

Ruth stood in the hall outside her father's room, watching the scene unfold, trying not to sob. She had never witnessed her father so tender towards Kyle. She was overwrought with emotion. A hand touched her back and she heard her grandmother say in a soft whisper, "Here's a tissue, Ruthie. It's beautiful isn't it child?"

Ruth nodded in response as she wiped her eyes.

Kyle walked into the hallway and wrapped his arms around the two women. "Thank you, Sis, for letting me see Dad. I've never experienced such a sense of pure empathy in my life—it was sickening and encouraging at the same time."

"I'm so glad you were able to come." The three pulled away from each other and Ruth saw the picture and feather. "Did you see that feather float from the ceiling? Where did that come from?"

Kyle looked down at the picture and feather. "I think it was from the angel Dad was talking about. I actually felt the wind from the fluttering of wings in there. I'm sure angel wings brushed my face."

Helena stretched her hand and pointed towards the feather. "Let me have a look at it, Kyle." He handed the pure white feather to her. She turned it in her hands, looking at it closely. "Powerful medicine...yes, powerful medicine," she said in hushed tones almost to herself.

"What do you mean, Grandmother?" Kyle asked.

"Feathers are powerful medicine in that they're symbols of rising from the mortal world of gravity into the spiritual plane of freedom. It's both balance and the wind at the same time. Look," she rotated the feather in front of her grandchildren, "this is a contour feather with the down feathers attached. Contour feathers allow air to flow over a body to allow for flight and down feathers are for protection. Hence, this is your symbol to take flight, Kyle, knowing that you'll always be protected. The way in which you described your empathy towards your father was interesting, because down feathers are excellent in developing the gift of empathy. Keep this feather with you and it will help you to discern whether your physical feelings are of your body, or are the manifestations of those around you.

Yes...yes...yes...powerful...powerful medicine!" Helena handed the feather back to Kyle.

Kyle looked at his watch. "Sis, we better get going before Mom gets home Thank you again for letting us visit." He hugged Ruth. "I love you, Sis."

"I love you, too, Brother."

Helena hugged Ruth again.

"I love you, Grandmother." Ruth replied.

"I love you, too, Ruthie."

"Let us know about Dad's condition, Sis."

"I will." They walked through the large house and to the front door. As Kyle and Helena walked outside, Ruth said, "Be careful! I'll call with any news!"

Kyle helped Helena into his car. He turned to his sister standing at the front door and waved with sign language "I love you." She returned the symbol as he hopped inside his car and drove off the compound.

Kyle drove in silence on the drive between Columbus and Lancaster. Helena sat with her eyes closed in silent prayer. Kyle was happy that there was little conversation because it gave him time to reflect on the events of the morning. He had just exited the main highway and was making a left turn onto State Route 159 from U.S. Route 22 when he noticed a cat that had been hit by a car lying motionless on the edge of the road. His emotions bubbled over and he started to cry. Helena opened her eyes and looked at her grandson. "Ki, do you want to talk?"

Kyle shook his head, not so much as to say no but more to shake the emotions. "I don't get it, Grandmother. I just don't understand. You laid your hands on Dad. I laid my hands on him. I felt the energy go out of me. I felt healing channel through me and he didn't get better. I don't understand."

Helena looked lovingly at Kyle as if he was a boy of ten and not a man in his thirties. "Ki, every *body* has to die."

"But I felt the energy, Grandmother!" Kyle said impatiently.

Helena's tone was soothing despite his childish response, "Yes, you did feel healing energy flow through you. I felt it, too. But, we are not the authors of our lives or the lives around us. And, you need to understand that in *death* there is perfect healing. This shell that we have become so attached to—the body—is shed in death. No more sickness…no more addictions…no more *dis*-ease."

"But *you* said that I was the son my father *needed*. I thought you meant he needed me to heal him. I expected him to spring out of the bed after I laid my hands on him!" Kyle said pleadingly.

"Ki, listen to me and stop wallowing in self-pity." Helena said. She was much more direct with him in her tone. Kyle unconsciously straightened his back as he continued driving. "Don't you see the healing you brought to him today? I know you're not so naïve that you don't understand that healing can be body, soul, or spirit. The healing that's needed most isn't necessarily a physical healing. Your life…your love brought peace to your father this morning. That, my child, is a much more miraculous healing than any *body* could ever experience! Your presence there this morning allowed your father to complete his journey home before crossing over. I think Elijah spoke eloquently about finding home and that it was *your* life in which he rejoiced because you've found home at an earlier age then he did."

Kyle kept his mouth closed as he let his grandmother's words sink into his spirit and then reverberate within his heart. Helena let out a stifled huff from between her closed lips and pointed her finger at him. "Healing...yes, I would say that your father found perfect health today through the universal love you channeled. And, that is home, Ki. Unconditional love is the only home that every spirit is searching for in this labyrinth we call life. There are many paths...many twists and turns. Sometimes there's confusion when we end up exactly where we started, but the trick is to learn that you followed your physical eyes and not the urging of your spirit, which is the higher wisdom. Your father understood this today with you. What you experienced with Elijah was a sacred moment—a flow of unconditional love between father and son! It was a miracle, indeed. You would never have expected to experience this a month ago."

Kyle smiled at his grandmother and her wagging finger. She dropped her hand and patted his leg. "Thank you, Grandmother. I think I get it now." He grabbed her hand and gave it a squeeze.

"Wholeness is the state of universal love, which is our home, Ki. Remember that...always."

Chapter 18

That evening, Ruth sat on the bed next her father while Deborah soaked in the hot tub just outside the sliding glass door of the master bedroom. Eli hadn't been alert in the three days since Kyle's visit. She looked at the clock on the nightstand. Eleven. A deep sigh escaped her as she watched her father's pale, gaunt face desperately suck in a breath with a deep rattle and then expel the air in a sigh. Ruth winced, feeling as though her father's pain were her own as his lungs fought for oxygen. She gently caressed his hand and noticed the coldness of his skin.

A solitary tear fell from Ruth's left eye. She absent-mindedly wiped at her cheek and found herself singing a hymn from her youth in the small Pentecostal church in Flatwoods, Kentucky. *"I'll fly away, O Glory, I'll fly away. When I die, Hallelujah, bye and bye, I'll fly away."* She stopped singing and brushed her father's brow. "Daddy, it's okay if you want to fly away. I just want to let you know while no one else is around what a Daddy's Girl I've always been. Now, I know, no one would believe me…but, it's true. I have always looked up to you for approval…and attention…although I guess that some-times I went about it the wrong way…" Ruth trailed off with a chuckle. "…but I guess that was the smart-ass in me, right?" Eli's head twitched and the corner of his mouth pulled up almost in a smile as he inhaled again.

Ruth leaned close to her father's ear. "You don't have to stick around here for anything else. You did a great job with Mom, Kyle, and me. We felt your love in your words over the last week. We'll be okay. We love you. This is as far as I can take you on this journey. Let your angel and Papaw Buck take you the rest of the way, Daddy. They know the way." She kissed Eli's cheek as another tear feel from her eye. She continued singing the hymn.

"We always come back to our roots in times of tribulation, don't we?" Deborah stated. Ruth, startled by the sudden intrusion while she was singing, stopped in mid-chorus, and looked to see her mother standing near the bed in her white, Egyptian cotton robe.

Ruth tried to keep her sarcasm in check and responded flatly, "I know how much Daddy likes that hymn. I'm just trying to honor him."

"I think the best way to honor him would be to return to the spiritual foundation he laid for you when you were a child and start attending a charismatic church." Deborah replied snidely.

Ruth's reply was sardonic. "I'll look into that when I have the time, Mother. How was your soak in the tub?"

Deborah raised her eyebrow at her daughter. "This is really no time for sarcasm. I'm just trying to make a point about where you'll spend eternity."

"I get the point." Ruth's eyes narrowed as she looked at her mother. "Shouldn't you put some clothes on? I'm sure it must be hard on your back without your girls having any support." Deborah huffed at her daughter and hastily walked into the master bathroom suite.

Ruth returned her gaze to her father. "Sorry about that, Daddy. I guess some things will never change. Mom's controlling and I'm still a smart-ass." Eli's jaw dropped open and the corner's of his mouth seemed to smile as he took a labored breath. Ruth waited to hear the exhale, but all that followed was a long slow release of air.

Silence.

Ruth moved closer to her father. "I love you, Daddy."

Silence.

Tears filled her eyes, but no sobs left her lips.

Silence.

She leaned over and kissed her father on the cheek.

Silence.

A rustling sound came from behind her.

"Ruth." She turned and saw her mother fully dressed with her mouth drooping open and a look of shock on her face. "Is he…gone?"

Ruth nodded in response.

"Oh, God! No!" Deborah screamed and sank towards the floor.

Ruth jumped up from the bed and caught her mother. With her arms around Deborah, Ruth cradled her mother as her sobs filled her ears. Ruth rocked Deborah like a mother with a child and whispered soothingly in her ear, "It's alright. Daddy just flew away. He went home. He's free. He's finally free."

Eli watched his daughter comfort his wife from above. He looked to his left and saw Papaw Buck floating next to him, surrounded by a white light. Eli turned his head to the right and saw Micha'el smiling. "Is this it?"

Micha'el nodded. "Easier than you thought, huh?"

"I feel wonderful!" Eli answered. "This warmth is amazing. It feels just like when Kyle laid his hands on me, except I feel it coming from the center of my belly and flowing outward."

"God is good!" Micha'el declared.

"All the time," Papaw Buck concluded.

"What now?" Eli asked.

Micha'el gave a hearty laugh. "What else do you want? Should I call up my buddies in the choir to announce your arrival in a fanfare of music?"

Eli sensed that Micha'el was joking with him. "Nah…save it for someone else. I had plenty of that as a pastor."

"I'll say!" Papaw Buck chimed. The three roared with laughter.

"Can I see Kyle one last time?"

"I don't see why not. You're not scheduled to arrive for another thirty seconds." Micha'el replied and then winked at Papaw Buck. "Take him to see *his* son and then we will go to *Our* Father."

Kyle had been asleep for about an hour in his room at Serenity. He was lying on his back when he felt something alight on his face. His right hand reflexively brushed at it as he stirred.

"Hoss!"

Kyle sat straight up in bed and his eyes popped wide open. He gasped. He turned his head, searching the room. Although he didn't see anything, Kyle felt a presence that was undeniably his father's.

"Hoss!" He heard the voice again and turned his head from left to right. Kyle felt a divine peace flood his spirit and chills shook his body. He felt the curls on his head relax as they always did when he was in a meditative state. Closing his eyes, he inhaled deeply through his nose. The scent of Old Spice aftershave filled the room and then he exhaled with a smile. The memory of his father's love of Old Spice when he could afford any cologne on the market warmed his heart. The electricity in the air slowly faded and Kyle lay back on his pillow. Sleep returned easily to him as the smile gently faded from his lips.

Kyle got out of bed and pulled on a pair of flannel lounge pants and a grey t-shirt when his cell phone rang from the desk in his room. It was early morning. He looked at the time as he walked towards the phone; it read six o'clock. He picked up the phone and saw the caller I.D. read, "Mom & Dad Home." Flipping the phone open, he hesitantly said, "Hello."

"Kyle, it's Mom…."

There was a pause and Kyle drew a slow breath. He tried to read her tone for some idea as to why she'd called. *"Surely Ruth would call if something happened to Dad,"* he thought. *"Is Mom calling because she found out*

Grandmother and I were at the house and now she wants to chew me out for sneaking in to see Dad?"

"Are you there, Kyle?" Her tone was subdued and slightly irritated.

"I'm here, Mom."

"It's your father…he passed away during the night."

Upon hearing the news, he instantly remembered the dream from the night .before. Kyle's emotions boiled just below the surface, but he contained himself and responded with a flat, "Okay."

"Ruth and I were with him when he passed peacefully. *I* just wanted to call and let you know."

Kyle noticed the emphasis his mother put on the word "I". He was surprised that she was calling with the news and slowly asked, "What can I do?"

"Nothing…right now." She paused as if trying to decide whether to continue or not. "I would like to ask if you'd be interested in saying a few words at the funeral. I know we've had our differences recently, but I thought you might like to be the spokesman for the family since Eli always thought you had a way with words. If you're not comfortable with it, that's okay."

"I'll do it, Mom. It would be an honor." Silence filled the space between them for what seemed like an eternity.

"Well," Deborah finally continued, "I'll call later with the funeral details. Okay?"

"Okay…and, Mom…"

"Yes?"

"Thanks for calling me…thanks for asking me to be a part of the funeral."

"Okay, Kyle. Bye."

"Bye, Mom." With the good-byes said, Kyle slumped onto his bed and started to cry. He knew he had to share the news with his grandmother and Moses, but needed a moment alone before interrupting their morning coffee ritual.

Kyle walked into the kitchen and saw Moses and his grandmother sitting at the table, sipping coffee. Their conversation stopped when he entered the room, and they looked at him questioningly. He stood silently with his head bowed for a few seconds searching for the courage to tell them.

"Ki?" Moses uttered.

"Dad's gone," he whispered.

"Oh, Ki," Helena muttered as she closed her eyes.

"He's gone." Kyle repeated and started to cry.

Moses rose from his seat at the table and embraced him. "We're here for you, Ki."

Kyle melted in the strong arms of Moses and wept. Moses put his lips close to Kyle's ear and whispered tenderly, "I'm so sorry, Ki. I know how hard this is, but I'm here with you. What can I do to help?"

"You're doing it," was all Kyle could say through his tears. He held onto Moses as if his life depended on it.

Helena stood and made her way to Kyle. She reached up, softly twisting his curls in her fingers. "Yes, Ki, Moses and I are here for you. You're not alone as you mourn. You're surrounded by our love and a host of angels right now. You're in a safe place where you can grieve without fear."

Moses let go of Kyle when he felt the tears stop. "Sit down and I'll pour some coffee for you." Kyle and Helena sat at the kitchen table while Moses took a cup and poured the coffee. "Helena's coffee is sure to comfort!" Moses said as he set the mug in front of Kyle.

"Thanks," Kyle said, and mustered a smile.

"Did Ruth call to tell you?" Moses asked.

"Actually, Mom called." Moses and Helena looked at each in surprise. Kyle noticed their expressions. "Yeah, I was shocked, too."

"How did the conversation go?" Moses asked.

"Short. Cordial. She asked me to say a few words at the funeral and I said I would."

"Maybe Deborah's coming around," Helena mused, in a whisper.

Kyle's lips turned in a crooked smile. "Well, she certainly didn't gush over me or anything like that, but at least she called and asked me to be a part of the funeral. She said she'd call about the details later." Kyle seemed to loose his train of thought and his eyes filled again. "You know...I think Dad came to say good-bye last night."

Helena leaned onto the table with her elbows. "What do you mean?"

Kyle told them about awakening in the middle of the night and hearing his father's voice calling to him. "I felt his presence in the room. It was strangely comforting...almost hypnotic, so I just went back to sleep."

Helena nodded. "Yes...many times loved ones will say a final good-bye if you're not with them when they pass. It's a final act of love. Cherish that moment, Ki. It's your father's present to you!"

"I was just telling your grandmother that Zoe is working for me today so I don't have to go into the shop. Do you want to catch a matinee with me?" Moses asked Kyle.

"I don't know if I'm up for a movie."

"How about grabbing lunch then?"

"I don't know."

"Ki," Helena said with a bit of exasperation, "Moses is trying to ask you out on a date. Now, I know you just lost your father, but I think it would be wonderful if you got out of here for a while. Besides, if you don't say yes to him, I know an old woman that would love to go out with a tall, dark, and handsome gentleman caller."

Kyle's somber mood broke and he giggled. "Okay, Moses. I'd better say yes before my grandmother moves in on you. I guess I *should* get out of here for a little while."

"Good!" Moses beamed with pride. "Then it's settled. I'll pick you up at eleven-thirty. That should give you enough time to do something with that mess on your head."

Kyle reflexively ran his right hand through his hair and tried to straighten the morning frizz. "What do you mean mess? Don't you like my bed head?"

"I'm sure it would be just beautiful if I were waking up next to it."

Kyle's eyes popped out of his head. Helena noticed his embarrassment and gave an ornery chuckle. "You're smooth, Moses, but I have a feeling you're going to have to do better than that to win my grandson's heart." Kyle squirmed uncomfortably. "Isn't he cute when he's embarrassed?"

Moses noticed Kyle's uneasiness. "Oh, he's cute alright, Helena...*very* cute!"

"You're getting better, Moses. Keep it up and you might just catch him!"

"Hey, you two! I'm sitting right here," Kyle chimed in sarcastically. "Can you save this talk for when I'm not around?"

Moses and Helena laughed. Helena caught her breath and said, "Oh, Ki, it doesn't bother me. I may be old, but I ain't dead yet."

"Well, it makes me a little uncomfortable talking about this in front of my grandmother!"

Still giggling, Helena replied gleefully, "I know... that's what makes this so much fun for me!" Kyle shook his head in surrender and joined in their laughter.

Kyle and Moses had enjoyed a delicious lunch at The Inn at Cedar Falls in the original 1840's log cabin. It was Kyle's first time at The Inn and he was awed to see his meal prepared in the open kitchen by the chef. Conversation between the two was light-hearted, as Moses had intended. When they returned to Moses' cabin he started a fire as Kyle watched him. Once Moses was satisfied that it would burn properly, he sat with Kyle on the chocolate-colored, leather loveseat.

"Move closer to me and I'll keep you warm," Moses playfully urged as he reclined the footrest on the loveseat. Kyle shifted his body towards Moses and felt his warm arm wrap around his shoulder, squeezing it tightly. "Thanks for going to lunch with me today. I really enjoy spending time with you, Ki."

"Thanks for taking me. It was nice." Kyle's voice drifted off dreamily.

"Do you need a power nap now, with such a full stomach?"

Kyle yawned and snuggled closer to Moses. "I might be able to catch a few nods."

"Here," Moses said as he spread a blanket over them both. "Get cozy." Moses pulled Kyle closer to him and gently rubbed his head before lightly kissing his brow.

In the warmth of Moses' embrace, Kyle's sadness overcame him once again, and he started to cry. "I'm sorry, Moses," he said through his sniffles.

"Hey," Moses gently put his hand under Kyle's chin and lovingly looked in his eyes, "it's okay. I'm all right with your grief. I just wish I could take the pain away from you." Moses brushed Kyle's tears with his thumb and tenderly kissed his lips.

Kyle nestled his head into Moses' neck. "I'll be okay."

"I wish I could keep anything from hurting you, Babe. I wish my love was enough to keep you safe from everything."

"I feel plenty safe right now, Moses. Your arms are like heaven to me." Kyle shuddered nervously before kissing Moses.

Moses' hands caressed Kyle's face as they kissed. Slowly, he moved his hands down Kyle's neck, along his shoulders, and then to his chest where he began kneading it. In hushed tones he said, "God, Ki, you feel wonderful." Moses moved his tongue along Kyle's neck while his hands moved to his waist. In one swift motion, Moses pulled Kyle's lithe body onto his so that Kyle was straddling his lap facing him.

"Mmmm," Kyle quietly breathed as they continued kissing.

Moses' fingers slipped under Kyle's shirt and onto his back causing Kyle to slightly arch at the electricity of the skin to skin contact. Goosebumps covered Kyle's body as Moses' strokes made their way from his back to his chest. Kyle felt light-headed from the kissing, the touching, and the arousal of the contact. Moses tenderly slipped his finger into Kyle's belly button and whispered, "That's nice—a hard six-pack and a delicious belly button." Kyle's stomach danced involuntarily with the embrace.

Kyle enjoyed every moment of their exchange. The air was electric with their desire. His nostrils filled with Moses' musky scent. His passions urged him forward and his partner's fervor carried him. How he wanted to surrender to his love!

Moses pulled away from Kyle and held both hands in front of his chest. "We should stop. This isn't what I intended. I'm sorry."

Kyle looked confused and thought he might just break down again. "What? Did I do something wrong?"

"No, no, no, Ki!" Moses was emphatic, but kind. "I feel like I'm taking advantage of your emotional state. I don't want to do that."

"So...if I said I was okay with it..."

Moses cut in before Kyle could finish. "Trust me. I know that you're with what we were doing." Moses placed his hands on Kyle's thighs with a grin and looked down at his hands. "Yeah, I felt that."

"And?" Kyle queried.

"And, as much as I'd like to continue, I guess I'm a little old-fashioned."

"I'm not sure I understand." Kyle moved off Moses, onto the loveseat and sat facing him with his legs pulled to his chest.

Moses sensed he was making Kyle insecure with his aloofness. "Okay, Ki. I apologize. I'm not very good at this. I guess I'm feeling a bit anxious."

"Not good at it? You seemed to be pushing all the right buttons for me."

Moses chuckled and dropped his head into his hand before looking directly into Kyle's eyes. "Thank you, but I'm not talking about that." Moses inhaled deeply before continuing. "Ki, I don't want to just fool around and then go our separate ways. I want a commitment before we get physical with each other."

"A commitment?"

"Look, you're under a lot right now with your father's death and I don't expect an answer today or even tomorrow, but..." Moses seemed to loose what he was going to say next.

Kyle was apprehensive in the silence and finally asked, "But, what? What are you trying to ask me?"

"Oh, I can't believe I'm screwing this up!" Moses said to himself as he slapped his own legs. "I'm trying to ask you to marry me."

"Marry you?"

"I know it's not legal in Ohio! I was just talking about having a commitment ceremony or Holy Union as your Grandmother prefers to call it."

"Grandmother knows about this? So that's what you were talking about that morning—you asked my grandmother for my hand?" Kyle grinned at the thought.

Moses felt Kyle's playfulness and responded, "Look, I had to ask someone for your hand who I felt sure would give me their blessing, and I had to find someone who would perform the ceremony. Helena fits the bill on both accounts since she's the matriarch of your family and an ordained minister."

"I see."

"Seriously, Ki, I don't want an answer today. I want you to think about it for a while. Wait until after you get through the next few days with the funeral. I really don't want to add to your stress. I want to help alleviate it." Moses paused and took Kyle's hands in his own. "I love you, Ki. I want to spend the rest of my life with you. But I want you to feel the same way about me. So, think it over. I'm here for you, whatever you decide."

Kyle looked silently at Moses and felt the warmth of his love surrounding him. He hadn't expected this today. But, then again, he hadn't expected anything that had happened today.

Chapter 19

Kyle, Moses, and Helena stood together in the expansive vestibule of Earth Reaping Church, waiting for the rest of the family to arrive for the private family viewing before the public funeral began. Kyle looked at his grandmother and smiled. Helena wore a traditional, purple prairie dress with long sleeves that buttoned up the front. A white scarf was tied at the neck and the V hung down her back. Her long white hair was pulled into a tight bun at the back of her head. As she leaned on her staff, her aura exuded confidence and dignity.

Sensing Kyle's question, Helena spoke. "Purple is powerful medicine for all negative feelings and thoughts, Ki. It's the most spiritual color and bonds the physical realm with the spiritual realm. Problems can't touch the energy of purple. It is my *favorite* color." She paused and looked at her grandson with deep intention. "Your choice of the brown suit is perfect for today. Brown is the color of endurance. It neutralizes negative energy and encourages stability. It represents hearth and home, both of which, you have found."

Kyle's eyes watered slightly and his mouth turned up in slight grin. "I think you're right."

Moses, noticing Kyle's tears, asked in a whispered tone, "Are you okay?"

"I'm fine, Moses. A little nervous about speaking, but I'm fine."

Just then Naomi entered the front door with Ruth and Mark following close behind. When Naomi saw the others, she skipped through the entrance and waved. "Hi, Uncle Kyle!"

Ruth reached for her daughter and gently said, "Naomi, settle down. You have to be respectful." Naomi tossed her hair in an indignant shake of her head, but quickly lowered her energy. The five adults greeted one another with handshakes and hugs.

"How was the trip up, Sis?" Kyle asked.

"Just fine," Ruth answered absent-mindedly. "Have you seen Mom?"

No sooner had Ruth asked the question when Deborah rounded the corner from the office area of the church. She looked regal in her conservative outfit. Escorted by the head usher, Charlie, on one side and the minister of music, Dan, on the other, her pumps echoed in a staccato beat on the tiled floor as she made her way towards the rest of the family. Deborah approached her family with a forced smile that quickly faded when she saw Moses.

"Thank you for coming, children," Deborah said in rehearsed tones before quickly adding, "and Mother." She looked at Moses condescendingly and then at Kyle. "I don't think we've been introduced."

Kyle faltered. Moses quickly stepped towards Deborah with outstretched hand. "I'm Moses—a friend of Kyle's. It's a pleasure to meet you Mrs. Basil."

Deborah grudgingly took his hand and forced another smile. "Oh, I see." She released his hand and clasped her own. "I'm sure you won't mind waiting here then until the public is allowed into the sanctuary. This is the *family* viewing time. It will only be about thirty minutes or so before Charlie lets the wider communities enter for the service."

Kyle began to protest, but again Moses quickly responded. "Absolutely. It won't be a problem at all. I completely understand the need for privacy at this time."

Dan looked at Moses with intense interest and then turned his attention towards Kyle. He offered him his hand. "It's good to see you again, Kyle." They shook and Dan continued, "I understand you'll be giving the eulogy today. Is there any music you'd like played while you speak?"

Kyle was caught off guard by the question but answered curtly, "No. No music at all when I'm speaking. I want to stay focused. Music would only distract me."

"Sounds good, then," Dan replied and turned towards Deborah. "I'll be in my office if you need anything before the service starts." He glanced again at Kyle before retreating to his office.

"Alright kids, and Mother," Deborah began, "we'll enter the sanctuary through the side door around the corner." She turned and walked quickly down the hall. Ruth and her family followed close behind while Helena moved at her own pace, gently tapping her staff on the tile while Charlie walked with her.

Helena regarded Charlie. He frowned at her. She stopped and said, "I am invited here this time."

He rolled his eyes at her, "Against my better judgment."

Helena chuckled. "Ah, the ego! It's never satisfied whether it gets its way or not!"

Kyle turned to Moses with tears in his eyes. "I'm sorry about that. I should have stood up for you."

"Don't worry about it, Ki. You're here and that's all that matters. I'll be in there with you in just a little while. I'm okay with it." Moses faced twisted in a smile. With a mischievous expression, he asked in a low voice, "The choir director…he's family isn't he?"

Kyle nodded with a smirk. "Yeah, but don't tell him that—or his wife."

Moses beamed. "There's my smiling Ki!" He wrapped one arm around Kyle's shoulder and gave a quick squeeze. "Now, go be with your family. I'm just outside the doors if you need me."

Kyle followed the others. When he turned the corner, he saw Helena, alone outside the door leaning on her staff. "Have you gone in yet, Grandmother?"

"No, Ki. I thought I'd give your mother and sister some time alone before I pay my respects. Go ahead in. I'll be in a minute."

Kyle stood beside his grandmother nervously. "I'm not sure I understand the point of this. Why do we have to look at the corpse? It seems silly to me. Dad isn't there. He's already gone."

Helena reached for Kyle's hand and held it firmly. "I know it's difficult, Ki. You've never experienced the death of a loved-one before, but it is a part of the mourning process—a part of the maze of life where we pause, look death in the face, and find comfort through the Great Spirit. Come on. I'll go with you."

They entered the sanctuary together and made their way towards the brushed-bronze casket with elegantly rounded corners. The velvet interior was a richly tufted eggshell that made the body appear as if it were floating on a cloud. The rest of the family stood to one side of the casket. Ruth comforted her mother in soft whispers. Helena stopped at the foot of the casket while Kyle made his way to the opening to view his father. He stood silently looking at the makeup on his father's face and the perfectly tailored Joseph A. Banks suit. The funeral home had done a wonderful job of capturing Eli's essence in the posed smile.

Kyle whispered tentatively, "I'm not sure what I'm supposed to say now, Dad. But, thank you for your love during our last visit together. I'll never forget those moments. I hope you won't be too hard on me when I speak from your pulpit today—I'm no Eli Basil, but I'll do my best for you. I hope it brings honor to your memory." Kyle sniffled as he stood watch.

Helena walked towards the head of the casket and patted Kyle's back. Kyle felt he had said all he could and moved to Ruth and hugged her. Deborah watched her mother intently as she leaned towards the casket and spoke to Eli. She left her children and made her way to the casket. As she approached her mother, Deborah saw her wipe Eli's hand with a white cotton cloth. The closer she drew to the casket, the stronger the scent of lavender became. Helena spoke in hushed tones, "Do-na-da-'go-v-i." Deborah immediately recognized the Cherokee phrase from her childhood as '*until we meet again.*' Helena left the cloth in the casket and straightened. "To-hi-du."

"Good peace," Deborah said mechanically, in a voice loud enough for her mother to hear as she stared blankly at her husband's corpse. "A state of body, mind, and spirit."

Helena turned to face her daughter and smiled lovingly at her. "You still remember the native tongue! I'm proud of you, Little Bee."

"I remember a lot, Mother. I see you washed Eli with lavender. I appreciate your thoughtfulness." Helena opened her arms in to offer an embrace, but Deborah held up a hand. "I'm not quite there, Mother. Let's just leave it as it is for now."

Helena dropped her arms and nodded. "So it is."

The church couldn't hold the overflow, so a room with closed circuit television was opened for the multitudes that wanted to attend the funeral. Several other televangelists attended, including a long-time friend of Eli, Rev. James Cook, who was leading the service. The family sat in the front pew of the church with dignitaries seated behind them including a former governor and secretary of state that held Eli's conservative political views. The music was moving and many attendees wiped their eyes with tissues as Dan led the choir in Eli's favorite hymn, *I'll Fly Away.* Rev. Cook opened the service by reading the obituary. He spoke of Eli's Godly attributes. He then announced that Kyle would be saying a few words about his father.

Kyle quickly ascended the steps to the pulpit and placed his prepared notes on the lectern. He felt a flip-flop of his stomach and sweat in his palms. He thought for an instant that he wouldn't be able to read the eulogy. Then looked at Moses sitting next to Helena and felt the warm flow of encouragement pulsating from them. Kyle cleared his throat a little too loudly and the auditorium went completely silent. He started to speak.

"Today, I have been asked to speak for the family as we mourn the loss of a father, a husband, and a pastor. This is obviously a trying time for us as a family and for those of you who are a part of the church family. I, in no way, can come close to the eloquence that my father possessed, so I hope that you will forgive me for not being a chip off of the old block." Kyle's voice wavered. He swallowed the lump in his throat and continued.

"While he was 'Pastor' to thousands of people, he was a husband to one and the father of two. Dad loved to read the Bible and he loved even more to build a sermon around the ancient scriptures for application in a modern world. In honor of his pastoral skills, I hope you will indulge me as I read a short scripture found in Job 38:16-18 as translated in *The Message*: 'Have you ever gotten to the true bottom of things, explored the labyrinthine caves of deep ocean? Do you know the first thing about death? Do you have one clue regarding death's dark mysteries? And do you have any idea how large this earth is? Speak up if you have even the beginning of an answer.'

"I chose this scripture not because I know the answers, but because I like the questions. These are questions

God posed to Job and questions my father faced in his last few days. I believe, as he faced death, that he truly began to explore the labyrinth within his own spirit. I say this because during my last visit with Dad I witnessed a very different man than his usual television personality. While most people know his charismatic flair for the dramatic, our last conversation was not peppered with spicy enunciations but rather with sweet tones of unconditional love. He had a renewed sense of life despite the weight of death upon him.

"Dad will be known as an architect of spans across divides—most notably for this church where he opened the doors to all races. As a young Pentecostal evangelist, social culture limited him to white-only churches. With the help of the founding members of this church, Dad envisioned a sanctuary filled with all creeds worshiping together, without regard to what society thought of the colors of their skins or previous marital status. When other churches expelled divorced members, Dad welcomed them into the fold. He had a vision for acceptance, and as I look around this auditorium today, I see that it has, indeed, come to pass. Dad certainly saw how large the earth was and in his own way attempted to make it smaller by building bridges to unite all people.

"As most people are aware, Dad and I had our differences within the last year." Once again, Kyle felt the lump returning to his throat. He paused for a moment and then continued. "I think it would be appropriate to say that there was a chasm between us. The gulf appeared irreparable. It seemed that we would never succeed in closing the gap. Yet, Dad found a way to span the great divide after searching the labyrinthine seas of his soul. Booker T. Washington is quoted as saying, 'There are two ways of exerting one's strength; one is pushing down, the other is pulling up.' Dad did the later, by reaching towards me in his final hours.

"In our last conversation, Dad talked about coming home; not in the sense of going home to heaven, but in arriving into the state of love as home before passing. True to his nature, he quoted scripture to me. But, this time it was different. He wasn't standing victoriously behind this pulpit waving his King James Version or pointing with righteous indignation at the camera. No, there was no crowd of thousands to hear him. No camera rolled to beam his words across the globe. He spoke only to an audience of one and with the greatest passion, sincerity, and compassion I had ever experienced from him. It was as if the Holy Spirit were using Dad's voice, gently speaking words of love. Whether it was the Holy Spirit's words or Dad's own, it does not matter. He was certainly practicing what Mother Teresa had in mind when she said, "In this life we cannot always do great things. But we can do small things with great love." I would suggest that Dad's greatest sermon was the one he spoke to me during our last visit together, although, I am sure that Mom and Ruth might disagree with me since they experienced similar messages from Dad.

"Dad was not only a consummate preacher and teacher, but also a willing student—a fact that I first realized after our last visit. He told me of his angel that was with him in the last few weeks. Several times during our conversation, Dad looked into the distance, as if in another world and then returned with a message for me. He was still learning even as he was dying!

"His final scripture quote to me was from John 14:27. I would like to conclude today with John 14:25-27 as translated in *The Message*, 'I'm telling you these things while I'm still living with you. The Friend, the Holy Spirit whom the Father will send at my request, will make everything plain to you. He will remind you of all the things I have told you. I'm leaving you well and whole. That's my parting gift to you. Peace. I don't leave you the way you're used to being left—feeling abandoned, bereft. So don't be upset. Don't be distraught.'

"I find comfort in knowing that these were some of Dad's final words while he was still living with us. As you wonder why your husband, your father, or your pastor left this earthly plane too soon for you, know that everything will be made plain. Dad certainly left me well and whole, as he has with so many of you here today. This state of wholeness certainly is a wonderful parting gift. May your own grieving be soothed as you think on this scripture.

"Thank you for coming today and for your support. Our family deeply appreciates the many acts of kindness and love we have experienced throughout Dad's illness and during this time. I leave you with the final words Dad spoke to me…'you are loved!'" The auditorium erupted in applause as Kyle made his way down the steps and took his seat in the pew next to Moses.

Moses patted Kyle on the thigh and said while the applause was still going, "That was beautiful, Ki. You did great." Ruth looked at her brother with tears streaming down her face and placed her hands in prayer position while tapping her lips and mouthed, "Thank you." Deborah sat next to Ruth in a stoic posture and seemed to be somewhere else. Helena nodded and beamed with pride, rocking back and forth in her signature style.

Deborah motioned for Charlie at the bottom of the stage stairs. He moved quickly while the attendees were still clapping. Leaning towards her, she whispered in his ear. "I don't want Rev. Cook to do the altar call. Kyle's words were perfect. We don't need anything added. Tell Dan to start the final hymn now and then let Rev. Cook know that all he needs to do is give the instructions for the closing of the funeral."

Charlie nodded and spoke into his headset walkie-talkie. As the applause faded, the orchestra immediately started playing *Softly and Tenderly*. Rev. Cook was almost at the pulpit when Charlie intercepted him and relayed the message from Deborah. As the choir sang, tears ran down Kyle's face. He thought of his father and his childhood dreams. He heard his grandmother singing, and thought of where he was today.

The private graveside service was for family only. On the coffin were one red rose and five pink carnations. After Rev. Cook concluded the final prayer, Deborah stepped towards the casket and gave Ruth two carnations and the remaining three to Kyle. "These represent the children and grandchildren. Please take them with you." She turned towards the casket as a bitter

November wind blew from a cloudless grey sky. Deborah retrieved the lone rose and pressed it to her chest with both hands. She gently touched the frosty bronze tomb, whimpering as she leaned her body against it.

Kyle's hands grew warm. He moved to his mother and placed a hand on her shoulder. Deborah's head tilted gradually towards his hand and her once stalwart body faltered. She slumped under his touch. Kyle thought *"love"* and attempted to transmit it to his mother. She straightened her back with resolution and turned towards Kyle.

"Thank you for helping with the service today. I appreciate it." She looked beyond Kyle's face for a moment. "I'm glad you and your father had the opportunity to talk before he passed. I had no idea that you had visited."

"It was a good visit, Mom." Kyle responded, but felt the distance between them return

"I'd invite you to the house for some refreshments along with Ruth, but..." Deborah's voice trailed off as she looked towards Moses and her mother. "There will mostly be other evangelists and deacons there. I don't think you would feel comfortable."

Kyle wasn't sure if she was inviting him or giving him a way out. "I'll come if you want, Mom."

Deborah raised her eyebrow in frustration. "Kyle, I *am* trying. Please don't make this anymore difficult than it already is. I allowed you to bring him with you and even allowed him to sit with you during the funeral. I *even*..."

"It's okay, Mom," Kyle offered sheepishly, "Grandmother needs to get home and you do still have the church. I understand...I think."

Deborah's recovered her false smile and nodded once. "Good. Then we understand each other. I'm sure this has been a long day for your grandmother. Drive safely on your way back to Hocking Hills." She stepped away from her son to signal that the conversation was over, and he need not show any affection towards her. Kyle turned with the three carnations in his hand and said his good-byes to Ruth and her family.

"I'll call you later tonight, Little Brother," Ruth said as they hugged. "You did a phenomenal job today. Dad would have been proud—I know I was!"

"Thank you, Sis. I love you."

"I love you, too. Give Mom some time. I'm sure she'll come around eventually." With good-byes said and hugs given, the three made their way slowly towards Kyle's car as a drizzle started to fall.

"Ah, yes...the Great Spirit is already watering the seed that is being planted today!" Helena said with delight as they reached the car. "Creator never fails. Never!"

Chapter 20

The Journey Within

The journey within is a bittersweet trek

So many hidden passages

So many buried lives

Veiled and secreted

The true self hides

Each expedition requires a noble heart

Integrity will be tested

Veracity the force

Keys of understanding

As one finds Source

The excursion from tangible to intangible

So buoyant the spirit

So burdensome the soul

The Labyrinth Home

Two divergent worlds

As one becomes whole

Each passage is an implement for growth

Realities uncovered

Idealisms healed

Self authenticated

Truth revealed

The journey within enlightens the path

Vanished obscurities

Departed mysteries

One spirit

Multiple histories

—Kyle

Kyle closed his journal. He was sitting near the center of the labyrinth at Serenity. Three weeks had passed since his father had been buried. The weather was unusually warm for mid-December. He removed the denim jacket and placed it on the ground, stretched and stood. A light breeze fluffed the curls along his neck. A movement towards the center of the maze caught his attention. He walked towards it. Arriving at the center where the wooden sign read 'Love,' he looked around. There was nothing to see but the tall grasses bending with the wind. He started to retrace his steps when he heard the snap of a twig. His heart beat quickly and his eyes narrowed, searching the landscape for the cause of the noise.

"I hope I didn't startle you," a familiar voice called from behind.

Kyle spun, surprised, "Dad? Uh..Is that really you?"

"It's me, Hoss. I thought I'd stop by and see how things are going for you."

Kyle looked bewildered. "Aren't you…I mean, didn't you already cross over?" he asked hesitantly.

"Well, yes…but like I said, I wanted to see you again. You know…offer some encouragement. Don't be so surprised! The Bible talks about the cloud of witnesses around you."

Kyle smiled at his father. "Yes, Dad, I know. I've been through this before."

Eli laughed heartily. "Oh, that's right! Papaw Buck told me about that. Amazing isn't it? I just had to try it out myself when he told me."

"And you came to me? Why not Mom or Ruth?"

"Papaw Buck recommended I start with you since you've had experience talking with somcone who's already passed over. He thought it might be a bit of a shock to Ruth or your mother. Apparently, Deborah didn't handle it too well the last time he appeared to her."

"It *is* a bit startling, Dad—even for me."

"You're adjusting now. I feel your energy level rising to meet mine. You're doing just fine." Kyle raised an eyebrow and smiled. "That eyebrow reminds me of your mother. How are things going between the two of you?"

"Well, she asked me to speak at your funeral."

"Yes. I saw that. And, what a fine job you did! Your mother was impressed, too."

"Thanks, but I'm not sure that Mom was so impressed."

"She was stirred, Kyle. She was so moved that she changed the order of the service because of your words. Didn't you notice her speaking to Charlie after you finished the eulogy?"

"No. I didn't."

"So? Do you feel things are better with your mother?"

"We haven't really talked. I've tried to call several times, but I always get her voicemail. I'm sure she's busy with church now that she's the senior pastor."

"Well, hang in there. Things will get better with her. You do have Helena, though. She is a wonderful mentor to you. I'm glad you found her." Eli looked around the labyrinth with amusement and then sat down. "This is a beautiful place. You'll do well here. Come. Sit with me."

Kyle moved towards his father and sat beside him on the ground. A tingling sensation moved up his spine. He felt a tender sensation at the base of his skull. Kyle touched the back of his neck and massaged it. "I think my body has a little trouble adjusting to your presence, Dad."

Eli nodded. "I understand. It's to do with you raising your energy and me lowering mine so that we can communicate. I wish I'd been able to do what you're doing now when I was in my body."

"And how would you have explained seeing dead people?"

"You're right, son," Eli snorted with laughter. "I wouldn't have been able to rationalize it through my dogma at the time."

Kyle smiled as he imagined his father seeing dead people when he was alive. "Dad, I know we didn't have too many heart to heart conversations when you were alive, but do you think it would be possible for me to ask your advice on something?"

Eli's eyes narrowed as he looked at his son. "I think that's why I'm here. Let me set your mind at ease. I am more than happy to discuss the proposal from Moses."

"I see word gets around quickly on the other side."

"I know a lot more in this current state than you can imagine! Take the poem you wrote in your journal just before you noticed me. What truth! How do you have such spiritual insight without crossing over? You've grasped immortality while still a mortal."

"I'm just artsy, Dad…but, thank you."

"No, it's more than being artsy. It's insight that should be shared. You have a voice that people are hungry to hear. During my life, I supplemented others with temporary liquid nourishment to feed my own ego. You have meat that isn't tied to the egotistic self." Eli watched as Kyle contemplated his words, twisting a blade of grass between his fingers. "But this doesn't help you with the main thing on your mind right now—Moses."

Kyle looked pensively at Eli. "I'm not sure what to do about his question."

"He loves you."

"I know."

"Do you love him?"

"Yes, but…" Kyle began and then his voice trailed off.

"But," Eli gently prodded, "you're concerned about the family—your kids and mother."

"Exactly! I want to have a working relationship with Mom and my kids, but I think being partnered with another man might prevent those things."

"*So many hidden passages, So many buried lives, Veiled and secreted, The true self hides,*" Eli echoed Kyle's written word.

"What?"

"*Vanished obscurities, Departed mysteries, One spirit, Multiple histories.* Why do you think you wrote those words, son?"

"I don't understand what you're asking."

"Close your eyes for a moment and let go of thought." Kyle followed his father's instruction. "I'll show you." Eli placed his hand on Kyle's forehead. Kyle felt a dizzying wave engulf his spirit as he separated from his body. His inner vision was hazy. Then it cleared. He saw a scene of two Native American men. One was performing a healing rite on a young girl lying on the ground before him and the other stood over him with arms crossed, looking proud. Kyle found himself inside the Shaman's body, looking into the other man's eyes. Although the Native American didn't look like Moses, Kyle recognized his eyes as Moses'. The two natives walked together, arm in arm, into a hut where they embraced and kissed. The vision became hazy. It faded.

Eli removed his hand. Kyle opened his eyes.

"That's just one, Hoss."

"One life?" Kyle asked tentatively.

"Yes, just like you wrote in your poem. You have multiple histories with Moses. This one is just another life, another incarnation of love."

Kyle nodded. "Okay. That resonates with me, Dad. So, your advice is…?"

Eli laughed at the question. "I just gave you my advice. You don't need anything else at this point."

Kyle felt the pain in his neck ease and his father's image started to fade. "Dad! Wait! Don't go yet!"

"*Integrity will be tested, Veracity the force, Keys of understanding, As one finds Source,*" Eli's voiced trailed off. "You have found Source. You have found home."

Kyle entered the house at Serenity just as Helena placed the phone back on the hook. She seemed not to notice him as she stared at the phone. Kyle looked intently at her as she turned to face him. "Is everything okay, Grandmother?"

"That was your mother," she answered flatly.

"Really? She called *you*?"

"Yes." A smile, faint at first, spread from the edges of her lips before engulfing her face. "She called *me*."

The silence following her last statement was too long for Kyle. "And? What did she want?" he asked anxiously.

"She wanted to invite me for Christmas dinner."

"*Really?*"

Helena nodded and continued. "You're invited, too. And, she invited Moses."

Kyle felt dizzy. He sank into a chair. "You're kidding!"

"No, I am not. And," she continued, as sat at the kitchen table, "there's more."

"There's more? What?" he asked anxiously.

"Well, Ruth and her family will be there," she answered temptingly, with just enough suspense to let Kyle know there was more.

"Okay, Grandmother! You're not telling me everything. I'm in enough shock as it is that she's invited you, Moses, and me. What else could there possibly be?"

Helena waved her hand at Kyle in amusement and grinned from ear to ear. "I'm surprised, too, but she said she wanted me to meet all of my great-grandchildren."

Kyle's face went white and his mouth dropped open as tears filled his eyes.

"You mean all *three* of your great-grandchildren?"

Kyle was so hopeful that his kids would be in for Christmas that he was afraid if he mentioned their names, it would somehow jinx it.

"Yes! Caleb and Olivia will be staying with Deborah over the holidays while their mother is visiting family in Indiana for a couple of days!"

Kyle slumped in the seat and clasped his hands to his face. "Oh my god! Oh my god! I get to see my kids."

"Yes, yes!" Helena said excitedly. "They'll arrive at Deborah's on Christmas Eve and she'll have us over Christmas Day. Their mother will pick them up the day after Christmas."

Kyle stood from his seat and started pacing. "Oh my god! It's been so long since I've seen them." He stopped and looked at his grandmother. "And she invited Moses, too?"

"Well," Helena began, "I had to remind her of Moses; but, yes, she extended the offer to him, too."

"Do you think she's sick?" Kyle asked only half in jest.

Helena chuckled at the question. "Now, Ki...don't be cynical. It appears that she's trying to build her own bridge towards you *and* me. Just accept it as such."

"Okay, Grandmother," Kyle replied sheepishly. "I hear what you're saying."

"Good! That's my two-spirited grandson."

Kyle's eyes wandered towards the ceiling. "I wonder if..."

Helena folded her hands and waited for Kyle to finish the sentence. When the silence dragged on, she prodded, "You wonder if what?"

"Oh," Kyle looked her directly in the eyes, "I wonder if Dad had something to do with the invitation. He and I were just talking in the labyrinth."

Helena's eyes narrowed. "Really? How wonderful! Maybe he did have something to do with it. What did he say?"

"Um…we were talking about things." Kyle answered absent-mindedly. "But he did talk about something that—something that I needed clarification on."

"What was it? Can I help?"

"Actually, he threw my own words back at me… something I had just written in poetry." Kyle chewed on his lower lip before continuing. "I think I know what it means. I just would have liked to have asked his opinion."

Helena looked questioningly at Kyle. "What did you write?"

"*Integrity will be tested, Veracity the force, Keys of understanding, As one finds Source.* Then Dad said that I had found home. I know he didn't mean just living at Serenity. I guess my question is, is love home or Source?"

"Good question, Ki!" Helena smiled warmly. "Love is a result or an outflow of residing in Source. The key to knowing that you're home is feeling content with yourself—not just with the physical body or personality, but with your essence. It's your spirit that is truly you, and you can only be truly yourself when your residence is in Source. When you're connected to the Creator, it doesn't matter what others think or feel about you. Besides, worrying about how others view you is just a way of feeding your ego. The ego knows nothing of love unless love is serving the ego, and, then, it is only a fleeting emotion lasting a few hours, days, or months. Thus, love is the natural flow of Source emanating from your essence."

"I see that."

"Of course you do! You wrote about it with your poetry while communing with Spirit in the labyrinth." Helena said. "Unfortunately, the brain learns slower than the spirit. The spirit *knows* while the mind wants to analyze. The two rarely work well together."

"You can say that again. I just wish Dad would have been more helpful with the current tug of war between my mind and my heart."

Helena closed her eyes and gently tapped the middle of her forehead. "I see," she said after a moment of quiet. "Did you get his blessing?" Helena smiled cleverly.

Kyle's face turned red with embarrassment. "Well… um…I'm not sure."

"Would you like to talk with me about it? I might have a blessing or two to throw your way." Helena tapped the table playfully with her arthritic fingers.

Kyle sat back down and became playful himself. "I guess that depends on what you think you're blessing."

"Don't get sassy with me, Ki," Helena giggled. "I know exactly what's been eating at you since your father passed over. Not only am I an intuitive, but I happen to be a confidant of your suitor! The poor man has been wrestling for nearly a month waiting for your answer." She paused and chuckled again. "I told him he shouldn't have told you to take your time."

"Is he really worried?"

"Well, how would you feel if you asked someone to marry you and he didn't answer for a month or even speak of it again?"

"He told me to take as long as I needed," Kyle offered in his defense.

"I understand that, Ki. But, to not even mention it?"

"I probably should say something to him, huh?"

"At this point, I would only say something when you have your mind good and made up. I'll tell him you're still considering the proposal and haven't made up your mind one way or the other. Moses has been asking me every day if you've talked to me about it. At least now I can say you have."

"Am I horrible, Grandmother?"

"No, you're not. But, quit worrying about what others think of you or about the *what if's* in life. Live right now! The ego would love to be anywhere else but in the present moment, but that's the only moment in which your spirit can live. And, it's in this moment where you will find the answer—not looking behind you to the past, or in front of you to the future. Look inside your heart—right now! The spirit is where the answer lies."

Kyle nodded in agreement and stood quickly. "I have some work to do, Grandmother! I have to do some writing and then get up to the cabin for our Friday night pizza."

"I know, Ki. Shake a leg!"

Kyle put the kitchen back in order after the Friday night ritual of pizza while Moses stoked the fire in the chimney of the cabin. With the kitchen complete, Kyle turned the lights off so that the only light in the great room came from the flames dancing in the fireplace. Moses straightened from his stooped position on the stone hearth as Kyle stepped towards him. He held out his hand to Kyle and Kyle clasped it.

"Hey, Ki," Moses started as he looked directly in Kyle's eyes, "can we talk?"

Kyle squirmed uneasily as Moses pulled him closer. "Talk about what?"

Moses placed his hands gently on Kyle's waist. "I think you know what I want to talk about. It's been a month since I asked you a serious question and I haven't heard a peep out of you."

Kyle backed away from Moses' light grip. "I don't want to talk about it."

Moses dropped his head and his shoulders slumped. "Okay...I suppose that's an answer in itself."

Kyle walked over to his coat and searched the breast pocket. He withdrew a packet and returned to a forlorn Moses. "Here," Kyle said as he handed him the envelope. "I don't want to talk about it just yet. I want you to read this first."

Moses took the envelope hesitantly and stared at it for a moment. "Look, if this is a formal rejection letter, I would rather read this after you leave."

Kyle crossed his arms over his chest. "So, you want me to leave now? I thought I should stay so I could answer any questions that weren't clear in the letter."

"Are you a sadist? Do you really want to watch me read this? I'm sorry, but maybe you should go home. If I have any questions, I'll ask them tomorrow."

Kyle was dumbfounded, but turned and put on his coat. "Okay, you can call me tonight if you have any questions. Bye." He opened the door and stepped into the night.

Moses sat if front of the fireplace with his back against the stones. He turned the envelope over as if it would disappear if he flipped it enough times. He finally shook his head in ambivalent resolution and opened the envelope. His hands trembled as he pulled the paper from inside and unfolded it. Torn between reading it and just throwing the letter into the fire, Moses stared at the handwritten message in the flickering light of the flames. He wiped the tears that were forming in his eyes and found his nerve. He read:

Dear Moses,

I want to apologize for taking so long to respond to your proposal. Over the last several weeks I've been contemplating many things—life, death, relationships, and so much more. As you know, I've mourned the loss of my father while celebrating the reconnection we made in his final days. I've spent many hours in quiet solitude reviewing all that's happened over the last several months and the many changes that I've experienced. While I needed the time for myself, I realize now that it must have been painful for you as you waited for my response.

One of the themes that's come up time and again is the premise of home. I must admit to struggling with this idea since I've always felt a bit out of place in my family—that is, until arriving here at Serenity and meeting Grandmother and you. I took a few moments today to look up the word 'home' and found that one of the definitions in the American Heritage

Dictionary of the English Language says that home is "The place where something is discovered, founded, developed, or promoted; a source." When I read that, it felt as though my heart stood still.

I realize that I've discovered my source in these last few months. It's not attached to anyone's opinion or approval or, for that matter, a single person. What once seemed like a maze of confusion, has really been my path towards Creator— my foundation. I know there are still twists and turns in the future, but I'm sure each will add to my development as a realized spirit.

This afternoon I understood another aspect of home although the word "understand" is a bit misleading since my mind can't fully grasp it—as Grandmother told me, the heart and mind rarely work well together. Moses, you are a part of home! I am still <u>discovering</u> what a sweet relationship can mean. We <u>founded</u> and are <u>developing</u> a partnership that transcends time and space. Your embrace offers sweet security, a refuge. I know that my place of origin—my very essence of being—has been promoted over several shared lifetimes.

It is with this understanding in this moment that I accept your offer to build a home together and respond with the following:

The Still Labyrinth Home

Serenity calls to me

And echoes along the maze

The Labyrinth Home

Of a life once held by form

Strewn with melancholic haze.

Substance meets sheer formlessness

Causing ego to dissolve

A spark of sheer radiance

Allows spirit to evolve.

Connecting with your clear light

I Realize—not two but one—

A stunning enlightenment

Bared, yet already begun.

Synchronicities abound

As sound and form dissipate

Meandering networks merge

For Us, we no longer wait.

Hand in hand, we'll tread together

Through the winding catacombs

I say, 'Yes,' and join with you

In the still labyrinth home.

With all my love,
Kyle

The letter slipped from Moses' hand as tears ran down his cheeks. He leapt from the floor and ran for the door. A wave of euphoria coupled with the quick change in position made him a dizzy and he stumbled into the love seat. His momentum caused him to flip over the back of the chair, landing face-up on the floor behind the love seat. "Shit!" Moses yelped as he recovered himself and rose to his feet. This time he made it to the front door and pulled it open with such force that he smacked himself in the forehead. For the second time in a few short moments, he held the wall for balance as sparks of light filled his vision. Just when he thought he would pass out completely, the spinning landscape stopped turning. He searched the dark night for Kyle.

"Ki!" Moses yelled. No answer. He felt his forehead and noticed a knot forming. "Shit! Now I've chased him away and have hurt myself in the process. What an idiot!"

He leapt from the porch and stopped. "Where are you, Ki?" he whispered and then closed his eyes. After a few deep breaths, Moses smiled. "Yeah, I feel you, Ki," he said as he started towards the labyrinth. Moses made his way through the twists of the maze to the place in the center marked with the signpost 'love'. As he rounded the final turn before the center, he stopped and saw his lover's silhouette toying with something lavender, reflected the moonlight.

Kyle's said with humor. "It took you long enough. I thought I would freeze before you got here!"

Moses rushed to Kyle, wrapped his arms around him, and lifted him off the ground. He kissed him. Setting Kyle back on his feet, he cupped his face in his hands, and said, "I trusted my spirit! I hoped you were here! I was right!"

"I was just waiting for you to join me, Moses, here in the center of love."

"I'm here, Ki. I'm not going anywhere without you." The two kissed again—a long, tender embrace.

Moses shivered in the cold of the December night. They each looked deeply into the eyes of the other.

"I think we should go inside, Moses."

"I think you're right."

Clasping hands with the purple cloth between them, an envelope of love surrounded the two men as they tramped through the crisp, circular grasses of the labyrinth towards the outer world and home.

(Endnotes)

1   1 Corinthians 13:11, *The Message*

2   1 Corinthians 13:1-10, *The Message*

3   *Softly and Tenderly Jesus is Calling*, Will L. Thompson

4   Matthew 17:20, *King James Version (KJV)*

5   Colossians 3:18, *(KJV)*

6   John 15:8-9 *(KJV)*

7   John 15:18-19 *(KJV)*

8   John 15:18-19 *(KJV)*

9   *Call Him Up-Can't Stop Praising His Name*, Ron Kenoly

10   1 Corinthians 13:4-8a, *The Message*

11   1 John 4:18a, *New International Version (NIV)*

12   *I'll Fly Away*, Albert E. Brumley

13   Matthew 17:5b, *NIV*

14   John 14:27a, *New King James Version (NKJV)*

15   John 14:27b, *NKJV*

3084561

Made in the USA